FIC   Bellamy, Joe David.
        Suzi Sinzinnati

$18.95

DATE			

Suzi Sinzinnati

WINNER OF THE
SEVENTH ANNUAL
EDITORS' BOOK AWARD

SUZI
SINZINNATI

A NOVEL BY
JOE
DAVID
BELLAMY

PUSHCART

FIC

Winner of the seventh annual Editors' Book Award

Sponsoring editors for the Editors' Book Award are Simon Michael Bessie, James Charlton, Peter Davison, Jonathan Galassi, David Godine, Daniel Halpern, James Laughlin, Seymour Lawrence, Starling Lawrence, Robie Macauley, Joyce Carol Oates, Nan A. Talese, Faith Sale, Ted Solotaroff, Pat Strachan, Thomas Wallace. Nominating editor for this novel: Elizabeth Inness-Brown.

ROO674 06699

AUTHOR'S NOTE

Suzi Sinzinnati derives entirely from my imagination. Where I have occasionally used real names or what seem to be physical descriptions of real people, it is done purely in the interest of fiction and is not intended to portray the actual lives of any real people, living or dead.

My thanks to the editors of the *North American Review* and *Kansas Quarterly*, where excerpts from this novel first appeared in print, though sometimes in slightly different form.

My thanks also to the National Endowment for the Arts, a Federal agency, to the CAPS program of the New York State Council on the Arts, and to St. Lawrence University, for grants that helped me to complete some of the work presented here.

Special thanks to Robin Rue, to Elizabeth Inness-Brown, and to Bill Henderson.

For
Kitty Parks
(1942–1968)

For
Dr. Curtis F. Bellamy, M.D.
(1900–1969)

For
my father
Orin Ross Bellamy
(1908–1974)

And
For
Ann Kyrangeles
wherever you are

Suzi Sinzinnati

PUSHCART

Chapter One

Don't take your love away from me
Don't leave my heart in misery
'Cause if you go then I'll be blue
Breakin' up is hard to do

Cincinnati, Ohio
August, 1960

ALREADY, FROM SOME slanting aerial perspective, he could visualize Indian Park, soaring in across the river above Cincinnati, picking it out, then flying in low over the treetops. The streets back of the high school, quiet, covered by a warm, airy, sun-blotched, residential shade, the roof of foliage over the sidewalks. Indian Park High School, that great reference point of his existence—he could see it as he might today or as he had more than a year ago before he left it or in some almost daily extravaganza of his mind ever since, the red brick bulk of it looming up protectively in the distance, seen from the rear during a track meet in the springtime, the bell of a well-polished sousaphone flashing with sunlight in the music room window.

This was Moke Galenaille's first trip home to Cincinnati since leaving for college a year ago. His parents had taken the occasion of his graduation from high school as a signal to change their lives forever, to finally realize their dream of moving south. Moke's father accepted a new position as general manager of a radio station in South *Florida*. The new yard in Terresonna (for whatever that mattered) looked like Africa, palm trees beside the house, the field of tall yellow grass, dragonflies the size of small birds.

1

Out the plane window now he could just see the first shabby suburbs of Covington, Kentucky, to the northeast and below, a stretch of woods and small farms on either side of a big humped-back highway. His Uncle Doc would probably already be waiting at the terminal. In ten minutes, Moke was landed and making the trek across concrete to the entrance gate, moving again on his own two sea-legs. The sun was oppressive on his neck and back, the air shimmering with waves of heat above the pavement as he walked. There was no sign of Doc at the gate or in the corridor. Upstairs Moke pressed through double glass doors to the lobby and looked around.

The one person from home he had missed most was Julie Greenway, the girl he had been going with for over three years. She had attended Smith College, an all-girls' school in Massachusetts, and they had made certain promises and had written to and visited each other during the year. But her family had moved away from Indian Park also, two hundred miles away to Akron, Ohio. So neither of them was able to return "home" to see their friends or to see each other, and this separation and some recent arguments had placed a strain on their relationship.

Then last week the mailman had delivered an ominous package. It was from Julie all right and contained upon opening: (1) his high school ring (which seemed a little ridiculous at this stage), well-polished and without its tape wrappings; (2) his miniature silver track shoe, heroic memento of his days as miler and second-string high jumper on the Indian Park track team (the track shoe was a sign that she definitely meant business); and (3) her letter:

Dear Moke,

We've gone through this whole routine before, and I really don't know where it's going from here. Since you sent the ring back, I've thought and thought about it, about this whole silly year with us a thousand miles apart, about how disappointing school was and my rotten grades and about carrying on this rather childish high school romance with you by remote control after we've both outgrown the necessity for it and the social context in which it started.

I don't mean to say that we were always childish about it or that it wasn't tremendously significant or that we didn't love each other. I don't know what it would have been like last year not getting your letter every day, but maybe I really should have accepted more dates than those four I told you about, which made you so furious. Maybe we both should have tried to be more socially adaptive rather than trying to live vicariously by mail and only for the times we could be together.

I won't forget those times, but after almost a month I still have this lingering feeling of horror about this summer in Florida. We began to resent each other. If we resented each other after only a month together, how would it be over a longer time? Your parents didn't help matters, of course, but I've begun to suspect that we aren't as basically compatible as we always thought. I haven't really ever had a chance to meet many different kinds of people. If a chance presented itself, I'd always let it drop because I'd feel that I was betraying you. Ever since we've moved to Akron I've neglected getting to know anyone. I was really feeling cut off. I might as well be as far from Indian Park as you are.

Then just after I came back from Florida I met a very nice person. He's a physicist, a graduate of Stanford, and works in a tire factory here in Akron and drives a black Austin-Healey. There are lots of people to get to know if you let your inhibitions fall away and behave less like a hermit.

I don't know where this leaves us, but I do know that this will be my last letter for some time. I need time to think things over and get some perspective. Please don't write back right away.

Remember me,
Julie

Julie Greenway—that peculiar little girl in American Government who buttoned all her sweaters down the back. Or rather she would occasionally miss one or two; and he would say, "You've got a button undone," and she would say, "Well, button it, silly," and he would button it, and she would say "thanks" as if she really meant it. All week he was seeing her as that high school nymphet, his ring suspended on a chain beneath her blouse, the band wrapped with tape and hardened with red nail polish like an amulet to fit her finger, when she wore it there. It was a way of dealing with the problem, he supposed, seeing her that way, naive, suppliant, not yet blossomed, by his returning to the bare beginnings. Or even earlier—before he knew her: that story she denied that she'd taken off her bra in Lane Goodwin's basement. His mind attached itself morbidly to such vaguely remembered ironies.

Ever since Moke opened Julie's package, he'd been rehashing the history of his life, searching for some clue to help explain his condition. Except for the fact that his family moved too often—there always seemed to be a gigantic Mayflower van pulling up to their front door—he had had a fairly happy childhood, hadn't he?

His birth—shortly after the bombing of Pearl Harbor on the same day his grandfather died of an enlarged heart. A war baby: pictures of himself in family albums in enormous officer's hats, pictures of his father, proud and tight-lipped and smiling, in Marine greens. He was a *child* of world war, quickly weaned, schedule-fed, toilet-trained too early. Father absent during crucial formative years, off blasting Japs with his trusty M-1 rifle, coasting onto foggy tropical beaches at five in the morning in iron-hulled amphibious landing craft. *Magpie to Rubie-red. Magpie to Rubie-red. Over. We read you, Magpie. This is Rubie-red. Closing in at ten o'clock with seventeen one-thousand-pound able-baker-charlie-dogs as ordered. What are your coordinates? Over. We read you, Rubie-red. This is M-as-in-Magpie. Password: Yellow Marble. My coordinates are Air Support Control. Seventeen one-thousand-pound charley-dogs at eight o'clock high. Deliver at Tokyo-700, reading 37° 50' 18" by the Jap whore. Do you re-da-da da-da-da-da-dow! Magpie? Come in, Magpie. This is Rubie-red. Do you read us? Magpie? Come in, Magpie. Magpie, come in.*

Suddenly he saw Doc, advancing on him like a walrus from the cocktail lounge, walking back on his heels and using a cane. Doc raised his heavy gold-sleeved left arm and waved, but it must

4

have thrown him a bit off balance because he took seven or eight quick centipede steps and jammed his cane down, tipping up on it across his belly and rolling back on his heels. With both hands on the cane he struggled for a moment, cane bowed to the snapping-point, feet shuffling beneath him, then his backbone seemed to relax, his knees sprung straight and his feet stood still.

"Damn feet," he mumbled.

"You're not drunk, are you?" Moke said. Doc looked insulted.

"You know me better than that, Uncle Moke."

"I don't know. I thought I smelled liquor on your breath."

"It's just these damn feet all the time."

"I know it," he said, patting Doc on the shoulder. "I'm just kidding you." His Uncle Doc had Parkinson's Disease but tried to pretend otherwise—and liked everyone else to try to pretend otherwise as well.

"You may *have* smelled some liquor, though, Uncle Moke. You may have. You want to have a drink?"

"No, we'd better get the bags."

"There's a woman in that bar there has the biggest bosom you'll probably ever see. You won't believe it."

"I'll take your word for it."

"I couldn't believe my own eyes."

Moke took Doc's arm, and Doc waddled with him slowly across the lobby to the baggage area.

Outside, the Cadillac was parked in a taxi zone. Moke put his bag in the backseat and saw Doc hand a bill to one of the taxi drivers.

Squeezed behind the steering wheel, his seatbelt snug on his belly, Doc coasted on out to the main road, sweat pouring off his forehead, air conditioner gushing full blast and all the windows open. "Candy?" Doc said. He brought a handful of M and M's out of his coat pocket and held them out.

"No. No thanks."

"They're good."

"No, that's all right. Go ahead." Doc pitched back his walrus head and wolfed two or three like pills, returning his manicured hand to the wheel with a little jerk and set down the right-hand tires on shoulder-gravel.

5

"Well, Uncle Moke, your dad said you're coming up here to pay your little girlfriend a visit."

"Yep." Gravel-dust rose like smoke off the right-hand fender. The broad road-bed curved around a hill up ahead, and down toward the river, still out of sight.

"I guess you get along pretty well with the girls, huh?" Moke didn't say anything. "Well, you're a Galenaille all right, and the old Kentucky Galenailles always do well with the ladies. Yesiree."

"You're about to run off the road, Doc." Doc slowly craned his neck to the rear, and seeing the road was clear behind, bounced on the accelerator. The Cadillac roared forward, fishtailed in a cloud of gravel, then caught the blacktop with a screech and slowed again to twenty-five.

"Got to watch myself."

"You're doing fine. Just take it slow." Doc dug in his pocket and popped some more candy in his mouth, raking his coat-sleeve across his sweat-beaded·forehead in the same motion. His head was aimed straight over the hood emblem, the steering wheel firmly held in two meaty hands. Yet, fifty yards down the road the car began migrating again.

"Good-looking is she, Uncle Moke?"

"Huh?"

"Your little girlfriend. I'll bet she's good-looking, isn't she?"

"Uh-huh." They rumbled over a succession of small potholes on the road-edge and then plunged off into tossing gravel, Doc still staring straight over the hood emblem, his arms on swivels at the shoulders. Moke didn't say anything.

"You're not getting serious about her, are you?"

No comment.

"When I was your age, I had a whole flock of girls. That's the way to do it, I'd say. Play the field. Try not to get too serious at your age."

"Uh-huh."

"You haven't ever . . . jazzed around with her, have you Uncle Moke?"

"Huh?"

"You don't jazz around with the girls, do you?"

"No."

6

"That's what gets a man in trouble, Uncle Moke. Never jazz around. It says that in the Bible, you know. Always treat them like little ladies, but don't go jazzing around."

"Um-humh."

"You believe in the Bible, don't you Uncle Moke?" He popped another pill in his mouth.

"You'd better get back on the road now, Doc. I think we have to turn left up here." The gravel narrowed toward an intersection up ahead, where a traffic light showed pale green beneath street car cables. Doc slowed the car and checked the rear view mirror, popping another pill. Then he floored it and shrieked around the corner, both legs shimmying on the foot pedals. Moke's head shot back, and a phalanx of glaring bumpers passed to the right. A horn honked.

"Slow down, Doc. For God's sake!" The tires slithered a distance in streetcar ruts, then shrieked a second time, and the car rocked to a dead halt. "Jesus, take it easy, will you?"

"Damn light was about to turn."

"You better let me drive." Doc started up again, barely crawling now.

"That's all right. I can handle it."

"No kidding, Doc. Pull over."

"That's all right, Uncle Moke. We'll get there. You just stick with your good old Uncle Doc and we'll get there all right."

They wound on through the outskirts of Covington toward the river. Up ahead Moke could see a bridge sign and a large green Cincinnati sign, and before long the Cadillac was on the ramp, climbing up through girders over the water (not yet visible), the bridge rising, the Cadillac climbing; and finally riding into full view above the guardrail, the familiar old muddy Ohio, rolling beneath them down the valley, the river and beyond it, in the distance, the cluster of buildings and the seven spired and dotted hills of Cincinnati, baking in the afternoon. The long rectangle of a coal barge lay motionless by the Third Street wharves; and higher, out to the east, Moke could just make out the first few notched spirals of Columbia Parkway, stretching out from the city toward Fairfax and Indian Park. . . .

He could still vaguely remember the long parades, his nose pressed against an iron fence, his mother, young and holding him up high, while row after row of red, white, and navy-blue Marines filed past. Somewhere out there, limber and tough, was his father. They would be trying to pick him out.

His father was wounded on Okinawa by flying shrapnel and received one-hundred-eighty-eight shots of penicillin and a Purple Heart. The day he came home, he walked right past Moke, sitting on his tricycle in someone's front yard, without knowing who he was. His father didn't like to talk about the war in those days. Sometimes he would wake up in the night screaming. One night almost two years after the war was over, he leaped out of bed during some nightmare about the war and broke his toe on the chest of drawers. At the time, he didn't think it was very funny.

In the first grade, they lived in Springfield, Ohio, and he didn't know any of the kids. When his father would drive him to school every day, Moke would get out of the car with his lunch box and walk slowly across the playground toward the towering brick building and then stand next to it with his back to the wall until the bell rang. If he walked slowly enough, his father would not see him standing there by himself. Again, when the children were turned out for recess, he would make his way down the stairs within the yelling mob, which spread out on a dead run at the door, and he would go immediately to his spot by the brick wall and wait there self-consciously until the bell rang. Someone would always come up and say, "What are you standing there for?"

"I just like it here," Moke would say.

As the days passed, a number of others would ask him what he was doing there, or they would try to tease him. Some of them came back several times. "You still standing there?" They became accustomed to him after a while.

When cold weather set in, his mother bought him a new brown leather jacket. But the first day he wore it, some big rowdy kid running by bumped him hard on the nose. He was so embarrassed and ashamed at the blood pouring out of his nose, he couldn't bear to look at any of the children who stopped to gawk at him. He bowed his head and swabbed at his nose, trying to act perfectly normal, watching the river of blood gush out onto the brown leather, ruining the sleeve of his new jacket.

There was the time they moved out to California where his father was stationed during World War II, and a waitress in a San

Diego restaurant tickled him under the chin and asked him if he was a "little soldier." He was barely old enough to talk. His father, who was then a First Lieutenant, had already informed them in no uncertain terms of the differences in quality among the various branches of the armed services several times. The Marines were "the greatest fighting body the world had ever known." Then followed the Air Force, the Army, and the Navy—in that order. "I'm no soldier," Moke told the waitress. "I'm a Marine!"

The walls of the Goodwin's guest room were papered with stale-smelling tan wallpaper. Moke flattened the halves of his suitcase across the bed on a nubby white bedspread and then went to the front window and looked up and down the street as far as he could see in either direction, checking to see that Doc had gone and squinting at some length down the block at the few visible bricks and distant gutterspout and white-painted gables where he used to live. An exotic scent of sunhot grasses swept into his nostrils and floated out through the envelope of heat, out above the patchwork of mown lawns and motionless clustered leaves and shingled roofs.

He paced around the room, then said his goodbyes to Mrs. Goodwin and headed down toward Wooster and the square, vibrating with anticipation. Unconsciously, he was following the same route he used to take to I.P.H.S., across Oak, through the hedge by the buff-brick apartment building, down the alley past backyards and garages and weedy patios. The yards seemed strangely deserted, as if an air raid siren had recently sounded to clear them out and everyone had gone to a cellar. The eggshell dome of the Indian Park water tower blossomed like a surface burst above distant silver-backed leaves. A clothesline heavy with damp laundry wilted in the heat. A rusty tricycle stood poised in mid-circuit. Air conditioners hummed.

All year Moke had been waiting for this triumphant march to the village square. On rainy Sunday afternoons at Duke he would sometimes get out the Indian Park *Chieftain* and look through the pictures and autographs and old friends' dedications telling him what a great success he was going to be in life. Now that he was actually here, the same desultory trees and buildings he had strained to call forth tended to give him an oppressive sensation of stage fright. The sun fell like limelight across his shoulders. The palms of his hands even seemed to be sweating. He was suddenly worried that somebody he might know would show up, a fleeting head in a car window, an advancing figure on the sidewalk—who could tell where they would come from? Moke had his arm all ready to wave in self-defense. All the same, it did seem more and more surprising that not one familiar person seemed to be around.

He circled the square—beneath the drugstore's orange and blue Rexall sign and the marquee of the Paramount Theatre—and padded on down Homewood. The maples were so thick and gorgeous you could chew the stems of their leaves like celery. Moke pulled one off and popped it into his mouth. He knew where he was going now. He was going to turn down Park Street past Julie's old house. He could see the corner coming just ahead, the familiar lawns and bushes in the gathering mind-buzzing August heat, the charming homes and well-cultivated flower beds with their sun-dazed petunias and marigolds, the breezeways and screened-in porches and two-and-three-car garages—Park Street, Park Street.

Somebody's Buick was sitting in Julie's old driveway, and the curtains were different. Whoever lived there now didn't take very good care of the grass, that was for sure, not compared to Mr. Greenway who used to get out there with his garden hose this time of year and give it a good soaking after dinner. Moke wanted to stop there on the sidewalk and take a longer, unhurried look, but as it was, he didn't even slow down and he barely turned his head. He didn't want to appear to be staring, after all—somebody might be looking out a window. About halfway down the block he wheeled around suddenly as if he had forgotten something and trooped back past the house from the opposite direction, this time catching a more favorable angle due to a slight curve in the road as it led up to and past the house. What could you feel about a house like this where so many intimate events had taken place in your life and that was now inhabited by total strangers who didn't take proper care of the lawn?

If Julie wouldn't come to Indian Park to see him, he would probably end up driving to Akron in a borrowed car. That wasn't such a bad idea when he thought about it. It would have to be a white Triumph identical to the one she'd cut out of *The New Yorker* and sent in a letter, that symbol they'd worked out for the idealized life to come: the white Triumph, the doctor and his wife, the oceanfront bungalow in Fort Lauderdale, morning glories on the lattice, the sunken Roman bath for nude sunbathing, pineapples in the garden, and on the wind the scent of salt and night-blooming jasmine. . . .

Chapter Two

Had a little girl but she left me
Had a little girl but she left me
Had a little girl but she left me
Well, I know-oh-oh-oh-oh-oh-oh-oh-oh

THE NEXT DAY, Julie was there. Moke had seen her coming slowly up the walk towards the big plate glass window that looked out across the Schliemann's front lawn. He had caught an accidental glint of something, her hair probably, caught for a second in the last, dying rays of tree-filtered sunlight; he had glanced quickly back across the shadowy lawn, and, seeing who it was, swallowed heavily. She was obviously in no special hurry.

Moke wanted to explain to her: how he *had* been swimming all afternoon in Bonnie's pool, it was true, diving and writhing through the water, but desperately, restlessly, like a miserable half-dead turtle; and even Bonnie's two-piece and the nice way she tossed her wet hair back over her shoulder (and even the fact that she *had* a pool), and the sun and air drying him off and the portable radio—hadn't mattered. Bonnie was their mutual friend, after all, Julie's best friend.

But when Julie came in, it was clear that no explanation would be necessary; she assumed all of it; she *knew* all right. He had happened to be *there*; she had simply come to claim him. This remarkable sense of possession flattered him. Walking back with her across the yard, he drank in several heady lungfuls of summer twilight and allowed himself a pang of unreasonable gratitude. There was a natural lilt in his step. She was his steady girl; they would be getting back late. Although there *was* one frightening difference—she seemed far more glamorous than he remembered, more streamlined.

12

"Your hair is lighter," he said.

"I just lit-and-brit it," she said.

"It looks good."

The Greenway's lavender Olds was waiting like a charmed pumpkin at the foot of the walk. The smooth steel yielded like magic to his touch. Instead of permitting herself to be quickly ushered in through the opened door, Julie pressed the leather key-case into his hand, like a promise.

"You drive," she said. Then she ducked in and scooted under the wheel. She situated herself noncommitally in the near center of her side, equi-distant between Moke and the far door.

"Where do you want to go?" Moke said.

"Just follow the hood emblem."

He pulled slowly away. They both seemed to be taking an unnatural interest in the scenery.

"You look good," Moke offered.

"You do too."

"Is it a long trip?"

"No, it's not bad."

"It *took* you long enough."

"Well, you didn't look as if you were exactly pining away in expectation."

"I was losing hope as a matter of fact."

"You know me better than that."

"Huh!" Moke said.

"How are your parents?" she said.

"Okay, I guess," Moke said. "Don't talk about them."

They had reached the square and Moke swung them slowly around, stopping smoothly at each light—the new community building, the Paramount, just starting to blaze in the thickening darkness, Cooper's sporting goods, the orange and blue Rexall sign. It seemed impossible to him that she could participate in this spectacle without feeling the weight of it—the leap back through weekend after weekend of accumulated events. He felt it as a silent but incontestable argument in his favor and groped for other relics to throw up before her unsuspecting eyes. He carried her twice more around the square and then headed for Ault Park, which seemed suddenly numinous with similar convincing possibilities. The band would be playing at the pavilion in another hour.

13

"How does it feel to be back?" Moke said.

"Not especially unusual."

"I really miss this place sometimes."

"It does seem like home, I guess."

Off to their right loomed in predictable order, the Inn, the Kroger store, and finally, yes, the dark high school, looking smaller somehow now than it had in the daylight—but still, for Moke, venerable as a Roman ruin. He skirted the block slowly, his eyes squinting out over the dark pit of the football field and track, but seeing nothing distinct except the steel fence and the prickly weed-filled hedge clogged with candy wrappers.

They headed out through Fairfax past the Double-Burger, Sugar 'n Spice, Jake's Car-Wash, the Dairy-Freeze, and the Streit-man Biscuit Company. A faint odor of Zesta Crackers and Coconut-Creme Cookies lingered in the car and out over the smokestacks and lawns as far as Red Bank Road. Moke hummed:

> Hea-ven-ly shades of night are fal-ling
> *It's* twi-light time
> Out of the mist your voice's calling
> *It's* twi-light time.

It was his favorite song the spring of the Junior class play when he'd hop in his Chevy after supper and drive into I.P.H.S. for play rehearsals, tuned into the Top 40 all the way. And just at seven o'clock when he reached the square, that friendly WSAI voice would be saying, "And now NUMBER ONE—the top hit across the nation—NUMBER ONE-ONE-ONE-ONE-ONE—the One you've all been waiting for" and the Platters would start singing "Twilight Time" and Moke would turn the radio way up and go coasting into the high school parking lot, smiling, air flooding in the sidevents, blind with happiness.

"Where are you going?" Julie said abruptly. "Are you going to Ault Park?"

"No," Moke lied.

"Where *are* you going then?" she said.

"Just following the hood emblem," Moke said, grinning.

> Deepening shadows gatha splenda (he sang)
> As day is done

14

Fingers of night will soon surrenda
The setting sun
I count the mo-ments, dahling
Til you're here with me agahn
Together at last
At twilight time. . . .

Shortly he was turning up the hill to Ault Park—the park grounds angling up above the steep wall to the left, to the right, a neighborhood of peaked-roof houses with satin lampshades glowing in the windows—lovers coasting down the cobblestones (still cuddling together), having just made out for two hours in the Ault Park shrubbery.

It was vaguely light up on top, sun not quite gone—a landscape of curbs and shaggy evergreens. Moke pulled up by the curb near the front of the pavilion—a sprawling concrete structure engulfed in vegetation on the hillside—and turned the motor off. They sat.

On humid summer evenings there was always a band. Couples would be there from Loveland and Madeira and Indian Park, girls with sun-burned shoulders who had been lying beside pools that day all over the city and horny young bachelors in white blazers and madras jackets laying out dollar bills—for a handful of dance tickets at ten cents a number. Up on the roof, if you could find an empty corner in the darkness, you could look out over the city with only the stars and the big, red, disembodied ball-like lights hanging in the air above everyone's head, and methodically kiss while the throbbing of the orchestra down below reached out into the night.

Julie got out of the car, leaned invitingly, so it seemed, against the lavender fender, gazed out across the expanse of garden and walks. Moke came around, sighed, beat the edges of his shoes together. She was beautiful, it occurred to him, leaning there against the warm metal, her breasts trim, succulent, virginal in the white blouse. He wondered what she might have done to get herself under such perfect control. Her hair, in the past either lank or fluffy, was now uncannily dazzling—a gleaming mystery that seemed proof of some inner capacity for beauty she had only recently managed to cultivate or discover.

"How long are you staying?" Moke said.

"I'm going back tomorrow."

"Really."

"Uh-huh."

"Why?"

"I have to get back."

The golden strands across her eyebrows curled above her forefinger and rustled in a glittery, willowy sheath along her left cheek. Refracted in the windshield glass, their bodies hovered at precipitous diagonals.

"I'm sorry you're going back so soon," Moke said.

"Don't be."

"Why?"

"There's no reason to be."

"Just the reason that I came up to see you—that's all." Julie looked at him without emotion. "Why are you acting this way?" Moke said.

She turned her large eyes away and gazed out across the garden. She seemed to him to have reached an unshakeable conclusion about his limitations, which she had utterly resigned herself to.

"There's really nothing I can say."

"Come on," Moke said, nudging her down the walk. "You don't have to treat me like this. Just tell me what happened. Let's just talk sensibly." They strolled down the walk past several small maroon-leafed plants in a bed, rows of shrubs—all very symmetrical.

"I just think we've become too dependent upon each other."

"Do you realize what you're doing to me? How could you *change* like this? You seem to be a completely different person."

"I just really need a chance to be on my own for awhile. I'm sorry if that seems—so terrible."

"I can't believe this. You know, I really can't believe this is happening."

"We've been growing apart anyway, haven't we? Don't you think we have?"

"*You* may have. *I'm* just the same as I've always been."

"Don't be silly."

"I *am*, damn it. *You're* the one who's changed. This is *your* responsibility. You're the one who's decided to throw everything away. I just wish I knew why."

16

"You know *why*."

"No I don't. Tell me."

"I can't go with you and be a thousand miles apart all the time. It's excruciating. It's stupid."

"What're you going to do about your *physicist* when school starts again? Leave him in Akron?"

"That's my problem."

"I may be *silly*, but *you're* illogical."

"I'll figure something out."

"You're terrible." She reached over and, oddly, patted him on the shoulder. "Julie, how can you *be* this way?"

"I don't know. I just am."

"I'm really losing my bearings because of this. If it wasn't for you, I wouldn't even be pre-med. Really. I don't know *what* I'd do."

"You'll just go right on doing what you've been doing."

"No I won't. I don't think so. I won't have any incentive."

"Yes, you will. You'll be a great success—just as you have been."

"No I won't."

"I thought you said *you* hadn't changed," she said.

"I will now."

"There's no reason to—unless you want to."

"Yes there is."

"What?"

"You don't realize. *Everything* I've done this year—was for you."

"Oh, Moke."

"Everything. Everything I've done—all the work I put in, all those god-damned chem labs on Friday afternoons, breathing sulphur dioxide while the frat boys took sunbaths on the lawn—making the Dean's list."

"Oh, stop it." It *did* sound silly, but he believed it nevertheless.

"You don't believe me, do you?"

"You're acting like a little boy."

"What do you think I was *doing* it for anyway—my health?"

"Because you *wanted* to."

"Why would I want to go through all that torture?" She shrugged. "My whole life is based on you—*you* know that."

17

"You're killing me." She seemed half-serious, half-mocking. Moke felt himself getting angry. "I don't know," Julie said, "we've been *very* dependent upon each other this whole year. We *agree* really. I just think it's basically unhealthy. You shouldn't *have* to base your whole life on someone else—especially if that person is halfway across the country and you never *see* them."

"I can't believe this! How can you be saying this? What about all the things we've been saying to each other all these years— *nothing* can really keep us apart, we said—distance or time or anything. *You* said that. I *believed* you. I took you seriously. I thought you took me seriously."

"I took you seriously. But we were just being unrealistic. It obviously didn't work out the way we thought it would."

"You might as well tell the truth. I mean—be blunt. What's the *real* reason?"

"You *know* the real reasons."

"Come on—tell me—I can take it. Do you really like this guy better than me?"

"I wouldn't put it that way."

"How would you put it?"

"I like him, of course. We have a very good relationship. We're engaged now, did you know that?"

"No. Really?"

"I know it's sort of sudden."

"You sure you're not getting too dependent on each other?"

"Stop it."

"How did you meet him?"

"You really want to know?"

"No!"

"It was at a drive-in. Kathy and I were sitting there, eating, and he pulled into the slot next to us."

"God. You mean, he picked you up at a drive-in!"

"Well, maybe we picked him up—I don't know. Something like that."

"God!"

"I can see that offends your sensibilities."

"How did it happen?"

"Oh, we just started talking. You know, we're just sitting there with the top down, munching on our Big Boys, and this black Austin-Healey pulls up right next to us. The wire-wheels are staring us right in the face and so is, you know—Rob. He's obviously not a dangerous type. So, we say 'hi.' And he says 'hi.' And pretty soon he wants to take us for a spin around the block. So, we say 'okay' and we hop out and get in his Austin-Healey. It's a nice night and we have a good time, so when we get back he asks me out—just like that. I think about it very carefully for about thirty seconds, and then I say 'okay.' "

"What does he look like?"

"Oh, he's about your height—maybe a little shorter. He wears glasses. I guess he looks a little bit like my father but not really. That's what Bonnie thinks anyway. I don't think he *really does* that much though."

"Is he good-looking?"

"You think I'd go out with somebody who wasn't good-looking?"

"Silly question." Moke looked up at the pavilion; the concrete walls were splashed with familiar green and purple lights. The band sound from above wafted out across the garden. Couples were walking up to the dance floor on both stairways; lightning bugs blinked; several stars were already visible. Julie sat down on a stone bench.

"I always *wondered* what you saw in me," he heard himself saying. "Now that I'm getting old and gray-haired I get thrown over for the first good-looking father-image who comes along." Julie chuckled in the darkness.

"That's gratitude for you," Moke said.

He pulled her toward him and bent to kiss her lips but was presented instead with a hastily turned cheek. He kissed it anyway—grateful for the least sign of indulgence.

"Let's go up now," Moke said.

"I don't feel like dancing. Maybe you better take me back."

"Let's go watch then," Moke said. "Come on." He pulled her up, tucking his arm around her waist; and they headed across the street and up the pavilion steps.

The dance floor was an oval of flood-lit turquoise stone seen through a spacious archway. An expandable semi-circle of roofless concrete was chained off outside to make room for the crowd.

Moke stopped next to the ticket booth and grasped the retaining chain and watched the dancers. "Just one dance?" he said.

"No," Julie said, "I'm really not in the right mood."

"Shit," Moke said. He scanned the crowd restlessly for someone he might know but didn't see anyone. The faces seemed oddly familiar but not recognizable. Within, the orchestra was tucked against the far wall—in turquoise suits behind four turquoise oblongs that read, in dazzling letters—Keystones. A syrupy trumpet was working its way through "Moonglow and The Theme from Picnic" while the drummer ticked and tickled his drum with a pair of brushes. One sweet-faced girl, engrossed in a flat-footed wrap-around bearhug on the dancefloor, met Moke's eyes for an instant and quickly glanced away. Moke felt tears forming in the tight corners of his eyes.

"Let's go upstairs," he said and moved off before she could object. From the top of the stairs they edged out through the massive red-fogged blackness until the nearest huddled form became visible and then veered away from it toward other patches of darkness. Each promising spot seemed empty until the last second and then, shockingly, revealed another living two-headed form—breathing or glaring at them out of the blackness. Moke blundered about, embarrassed, and finally settled beneath one of the lightpoles. "God, it's crowded."

"Necking must be popular this year," Julie said.

"I don't care how light it is—would you please kiss me." Moke drew her toward him and kissed her tentatively on the lips, then harder and fuller when he felt her lips responding.

"This is unfair tactics," Julie said.

"Hah!" Moke said. She started to say something else, but he smothered the words on her lips, kissed . . . kissed, then buried his face along her shoulder and rapturously inhaled her scent, Prell and—and Red Lilac—*his* perfume, the perfume she always wore for him because of the lilac bush in her yard that bloomed for them that first spring beside her front porch—bringing Julie home after midnight, whispering to each other in darkness, bending her slowly, ecstatically backwards over the piano. He wondered if she had ever worn Red Lilac for the physicist—she probably had. Immediately he felt drunk with grief. "Julie, I love you—I don't care what happens. I love you. I love you."

"Don't, Moke. Please."

"I can't help it. I can't help it." Already he was gasping, crying into her shoulder, hair sticking to his eyelids, back heaving in and out, up and down. God, he hadn't cried since he was probably ten years old, but now that seemed like a tremendous gap. Now he was really crying, sobbing like a maniac over all those stored-up years. He just wanted to hold her like that and sob and sob. He didn't care what anybody thought or did. Then Julie was crying too, quietly and secretly, but she was crying too—he could feel her shoulders jiggling up and down beneath his chin. He pulled back to see her face, and she was definitely crying. He could see her face in the weird light from the red globes. He kissed her eyes and kissed her and squeezed their slippery cheeks together. "You," he said. She looked into his eyes for a long time and then out across the valley at the lights from the office buildings downtown, and then she pressed herself to his shoulder again and started to cry very hard herself.

Moke doused the headlights half-a-block before the Goodwin's, killed the motor, and let the big Olds coast to a stop beyond the Goodwin's driveway. The house seemed totally dark from that angle except for a dim nightlight visible inside by the stairway, and in the yard the two thick maple trees thoroughly obscured the view of anybody who might be trying to peek out of the upstairs windows. Moke scooted over and put his arm around Julie and kissed her. Her face looked troubled. Her eyes, still swollen from crying, stared back at him with what seemed like pity or fatigue or vengeance. Still, her lips melted, she offered her throat—to Moke this seemed most promising.

He planted his lips firmly in the offered location and began to caress her exposed arm, grazing her breasts gently with the heel of his hand. Fatigued as she was, she seemed to be acquiescing to this form of persuasion, falling back into the familiar ritual.

"We shouldn't be doing this," she said.

"You know," he said, "what I think I'll do."

"What?"

"I think you're probably right. I'll probably get very involved in medicine this fall."

"Hmm."

21

"I can't imagine what else I could do. How long do you think this infatuation of yours will last anyway?"

"I don't know. A long time probably. It wouldn't be fair to ask you to wait."

"*You* don't have to ask. I just will."

"I'm afraid that wouldn't be very realistic."

"I'll take my chances, okay?"

She started to object, but he stopped the words with a light peck on her nose. "Don't say anything, okay?" he said. "Listen, I've decided," he said. "I just want you to know. Remember this. I'll *always be waiting*. Whenever you need me, I'll be ready, okay? Whether it's next year or five years or whenever." She scrutinized his face with a look of wonder and some guilt.

"No, I wouldn't want to think of you doing that."

"You won't *have* to think about me. Don't worry about me at all."

"Hmm."

"Just forget me."

"I couldn't possibly *forget* you."

"Then when the time comes, if it ever does, *I'll be there*. Okay? No matter what."

"What will you do in the meantime?"

"I'll just go on living. I'll give myself to medicine. That's what I always said I'd do. I'll work hard. Medicine is something you can get very involved in."

"What about sex?"

"What about it?"

"How will you manage?"

"I'll figure something out. I'll sublimate."

"You could go to prostitutes."

"No, I probably wouldn't do that."

"Why not?"

"I might compromise my reputation. Besides I probably wouldn't be able to afford it on a regular basis."

"Hmmm."

"I'll just channel all my energies into my work. That won't be so bad. The main thing is—ten, twenty years from now—if you ever feel unloved, you'll always have me to turn to—see. That's really a pretty good deal from your point of view."

"Oh, Moke."

"Isn't it?" She gave him her neck, which he accepted, buried his nose in her mane of hair and hugged her anxiously. "God, I love you," he whispered. "I love you. I love you. I love you. I love you." Julie was suddenly sobbing again, hanging around his neck and sobbing into his chest. He patted her and rubbed her back and ran his hand soothingly over her knees, curled towards him on the white leather upholstery. "You sweet," he crooned, which only made her sob all the harder. Lovingly he slid his hand up and down along the bulge of her thighs, first stroking her through the skirt, then reaching underneath the skirt and stroking the long lovely expanse of taut skin as far as his hand could reach.

As her crying diminished, he kissed her hard and long until both of them were aroused and breathless. "No," she said, but he forced his hand high enough to touch the fringe of her panties and let his finger rest lightly against the damp cloth. "Beautiful," he was thinking, "beautiful." He probed farther, found an edge, dipped beneath it, and finally touched her—touched her, a luxurious sensation of wetness at the tip of his left hand, middle finger. That was one thing he had flown twelve-hundred miles to do, to touch her, and now it was done. Julie sat up abruptly, pulling his hand away. "No," she said.

"Why?" Moke said.

"I can't make love to you."

"Yes, you can."

"No, I can't." She pulled her legs around and sat up even straighter.

"Why not? Don't be silly."

"I can't. I just can't."

"Don't you *want* to?"

"If it makes you feel any better—yes, damn it, but I'm not going to. You'd better get going." He tried to kiss her again, but she turned her face away. "Don't."

Moke slumped down in the seat and watched a circle of moths and leafhoppers batting their brains out against a streetlight down the block.

"We can say good-bye in the morning—I'll come by for a few minutes."

"Okay. Goodnight."

23

"Goodnight."

"Goodnight."

Moke weaved across the wet grass as far as the trunk of the nearest maple, then leaned against it to watch the car. His testicles ached. The Olds came to life—a series of clean explosions; the lights came on; then she pulled away and was gone, trailing a corkscrew of exhaust down the moonlit street.

He was awake before daylight, intermittently staring and sighing. An image of his back muscles as coiled springs—jabbing and jabbing at the mattress—had worn him down and wound him up. He leapt out of bed and tried pacing for awhile, but the floor squeaked. The hollowness and aching in his lower belly had crept again somehow into his chest cavity as a physical presence. He knelt by the low open window and tried catching a breath of air, carefully holding his nose away from the screen to keep from tattooing himself with a grid of rust and powdered bug remains. By ten-thirty she still hadn't showed up, even after he had called Bonnie's house twice to see what was taking so long—and gotten involved in two impossible conversations with Bonnie's mother.

Finally he started out walking and running toward Bonnie's house. It was over a mile. As he came around the corner of Bonnie's yard, panting and sweating like a maniac, he was sure he was too late—the lavender Olds was nowhere in sight. Recriminations thundered in his head. He stood transfixed at the corner of the yard.

Just then a lavender Olds came tooling down the block towards him. What a coincidence. The top was down, and the two girls inside looked as if they were just about to wave at him. They did, in fact, wave. The blonde who was driving had terrific hair blowing and snapping in the breeze—she looked quite a lot like Julie. In fact—Moke blinked—she *was* Julie.

Julie had on a pair of red shorts and a striped boat-neck top. As she drove, she seemed stunningly glamorous and self-willed. The exact way the arch of her nose met the air—she had a new sense of herself—which did not include him. He had never known she could be so convincingly aloof. It was as if he was not even physically present—she would not defer even that much. It was

24

almost as if she was by herself in the car. The radio drummed—to serve as a form of communication.

She drove to Eden Park. The girls had brought makings for a picnic. The view from the hillside, from the blanket. Grass. Grass. They spread out the blanket and started getting lunch ready. The pickle jar, the napkins. Bonnie had brought bologna sandwiches. Julie ate hers lustily as Moke tried to avert his eyes from her bare legs and freshly painted red toe-nails. His teeth ached, embedded to the gums in sweet mayonnaise. The way she mouthed the orange pop bottle did queer things to his stomach.

Riding back afterwards, singing songs from the windy convertible, hearing the sounds evaporate in the shimmering air. After that, they walked down shady Indian Park residential streets that still echoed faintly with the morning laughter of children taking their afternoon naps; and at one of those corners on a quiet block, she reached up and kissed his rigid unshaven face and smiled a benign good-bye. He watched her walk away, framed by arched leaves, look back once and smile. He couldn't just stand there— people staring out of apartment house windows, the proximity of three empty garbage cans—so he turned away too finally and headed slowly back toward the Goodwin's, running his fingers along the slippery top of the adjacent hedge. After about twenty paces, he started whistling. I was high and mighty da-da-da-da. Da-da-da-da-da-dum. I was high and mighty. On through the wind. On through the rain. And you'll never walk alone. You'll NEVER walk alone.

Chapter Three

Oh, they don't wear pants
on the other side of France. . . .

A CYMBAL CRASHED in the pit of the Gayety Burlesque and the piano and saxophone let loose on one chorus of "There's No Business Like Show Business." Then a voice said: "For our first number, her very first time at the Gayety Theatre, let's have a big hand for the fabulous—Hazel Storm!" The band broke into a jerky "I'm in the Mood For Love" with a

> ba-ba-ba-bump
> ba-ba-ba-bump
> ba-ba-ba-bump tempo

just as a gloved arm knifed out of the curtains and began slowly caressing the velvet. Suddenly the curtain was struck an indignant blow, flipped rudely aside, and out danced a skinny black-gowned woman old enough to be his mother. She whirled around nervously, sizing up the general disappointment of the crowd, then started crudely bumping and grinding. Moke decided that coming to the Gayety to drown his sorrows might not have been such a bright idea after all.

Deftly, unexpectedly, the stripper unzipped herself and then tried to make a production out of getting her gloves off while the dress loosened from the rear. Somebody in the back yelled, "Take it off." But that only made her slow down. She held up one loose glove and toyed with the empty fingertips. The expression on her face said: "Shall I?" Perfunctory applause. The joker in the back yelled, "Put it back on." Several guffaws. Sporadic clapping. She slid the glove down a few inches and stopped. Again her face said: "Shall I?" Sluggish applause. Now she was haughty. She slid the glove two inches back up and waited. Somebody moaned. Then it came again: "Shall I?" Brighter applause. Arrogantly she threatened to pull the glove back up to the elbow. Prolonged dutiful applause. Off came the glove. Relieved applause.

With this incentive she danced gaily out along the runway, writhing, writhing, so that with each twist the gown revealed more thigh, a pair of filmy panties, the elusive wing of a gauzy brassiere. She passed above Moke, trailing a dense cloud of perfume, then edged back. The gown was suddenly scooped between her knees and dropped to the runway. Obedient applause from the well-trained clappers. Her body was suddenly horizontal above the fallen gown, skin glistening with tiny beads of perspiration, humping, humping, then up, heels tapping, whirling. She kicked the gown contemptuously into the pit and scampered back to the stage, rolling now to the drumbeat, favoring the crowd with a distracting fingerlength view beneath her waistband. Secretly, facing the curtains, she was working at the catches of her brassiere. As it fell away, she eyed the crowd longingly over her shoulder and twitched, then again, working herself into a shimmy. By the time she spun around, her breasts were flailing so fast they were nearly invisible. A crescendo was quickly attained by the band, a cymbal crashed. "Ladies and gentlemen," the voice rose exultantly, "the fabulous Hazel Storm!" Hazel smiled a hideous orgasmic smile. Her lipstick was drawn a good quarter inch shy of her upper lip.

Moke tore the wrapper off his White Owl cigar and lighted up. He stretched back and scanned the huge chamber of the ancient theatre—three tiers of tarnished rococo boxes rising toward the apex above his head. He dragged hard on the cigar and let the acrid smoke accumulate a certain pressure before huffing.

Rumbling and screeching contended on the loudspeaker. The band slid into "They Don't Wear Pants On the Other Side of France." The master of ceremonies' voice sang out: "Our second curvaceous lovely: is she a Persian beauty queen, or the girl next door? Straight from the Sands in Las Vegas, let's have a big hand for sensational Prin-cess *Suzi Sin*zinnati!"

Boom-boom-boom-pow went the drummer. Boom-pow. An Arabian belly dancer swayed through the curtain entrance and undulated slowly out across the stage. Her face was veiled up to the eyes. Her costume was pink, translucent, billowy panels front and rear, supported by a double-row of white sapphires on a tricky garter belt, a pink wrap-around cape of the same elusive opacity, jewelled arm bracelets. An anonymous "Go" was heard from the side.

As she moved towards the runway she was nailed by a dazzling red spotlight. Legs spread, thighs tense, knees locked, she lifted and slowly stretched her front pink sash, revealing a bulging silver triangle of gigantic sequins draped with pearl-strings. Down went the sash. The princess dipped, did a deep-knee bend, stroked luscious flesh from ankle to thigh as she rose. Spontaneous applause from the crowd. Again the undulation, out along the runway. Moke himself felt noticeably moved. Next to him a baldheaded man in tortoise-shell glasses made a quiet kissing noise.

The princess crossed to the stage, her back now to the audience, and began unwinding her cape, uncovering a petite sapphire halterstrap. Working, working, working to stage-center, she dropped the cape, and gathering her panels together, yanked them forward, whisked away her veil, and peeped at the audience upside-down between shivering buttocks. Appreciative applause. Zing went the panels back in place. The princess dipped, did another deep-knee bend, retrieved her cape and turned, masking her face and upper body behind the taut cape-cloth, then sailing it gracefully above her head. A wave of electricity passed through the crowd. Her face, exposed at last, was strikingly pretty. She was young, sleek through the belly. Strings of pearls dangled beneath each silver-sequined breast cup. Enthusiastic applause.

From the band: Doo

doo

doo

doo

It had to be moonglow
Way up in the blue
It had to be moonglow
That sent me straight to you.

Princess Suzi was moving now through an effulgence of blue light. She flung aside her panels and danced out along the runway.

28

She was the soul of innocence. Not three feet from Moke, she paused. Nonchalantly she bared one succulent pasty-tipped breast. Her big mascaraed eyes swung around the audience, slowly right, slowly left—Moke felt her eyes meet his and pass on. Casually she unhooked the sapphire band and let the bra swing away. Wild applause. She was instantly bathed in lavender light.

> Bum-bum-bum-bum-ba! went the trombone.
> Bumpa-pa bum-pa bum-pa
> Bum-bum ba-bumpa
> Bumpa bumpa bumpa
> Bum-bum ba-bumpa
> Bumpata bopa
> Bum-bum-bum-bum-bum-bum-bum
> Bumpata bopa! Da-li-la Jones!

Suzi shook out her mane, tossed it forward like a wild woman, finger-combed it slowly upwards towards the ceiling. Her arms swirled; her wrists inscribed intricate patterns in the air above her head. Quickly she moved along the narrow runway, toes carefully aimed, feet arched, rump swinging. Bum-bum-bum-bum-ba! Moke was suddenly aware of a minor oscillation along the armrest. Next to him, the man in tortoise-shell glasses was discreetly jacking off under his homburg.

On stage to wild applause the princess peeled off her pink silver-sequined panties and shot-putted them into the wings. Suzi bent, licked a finger, and slid it over one supple cheek. Her eyes grew round with innocence. "You kess me ess?" she pouted. The drummer hit everything in sight.

Most of the village was asleep when Moke stepped off the bus by the Paramount Theatre in the suburb of Indian Park and headed back down Wooster toward the Goodwins. The Goodwins lived only four houses down and across the street from where he used to live in a house now occupied, tragically, by strangers. He had walked by the house several times in the last few days and tried to elicit that old comfortable feeling of "home" about the place, but the door had been painted a different color . . . the house seemed alien and unforgiving. He walked slowly past the house again now, feeling nothing, listening to his heels click on the sidewalk, a dark unrecognized figure staring in at lighted windows.

The Goodwins had retired for the evening, leaving only a small lamp turned on by the stairway. Moke closed the door carefully and creaked up the dim stairs, past the Goodwins' closed bedroom door, and into his own room, where he silently swung the door to and snapped it shut before flipping on the overhead light. The room—the guest room—was as stale-smelling as ever. He stood motionless by the door for a moment, staring dumbly at his suitcase where he had left it on the bed, and then crossed the room and flopped down next to it. For several minutes his eyes rested unblinkingly on the overhead lightglobe with its embellishment of tiny vines.

One question that bothered him particularly was whether he should send her flowers or not. A dozen long-stemmed red roses please—no. It seemed too much like a cliche from some thirties movie. Besides that he only had $160 until he got back to Florida. On the other hand, a note without flowers or *something* might go unnoticed. Candy was definitely out. A mink stole was definitely out. Carnations? Tulips? Geraniums? Moke produced his Spiral notebook and started to write:

Dear Princess Suzi,

    I hope you will read this even if I don't send flowers. I can't tell you how impressed I was by one of your recent acts at the Gayety. You have that certain indefinable something

Dearest Suzi,

    I don't know how to say this but—I think I could fall in love with you. Coming from a complete stranger, such a statement might seem a little strange, but

Dear Priness Suzi,

    I need a friend.

Dear Suzi,

As a talent scout for one of the biggest agencies in Hollywood, I can forecast with some authority, I think— after seeing your recent performance at the Gayety—a bright future for you on the stage and screen. You have that certain indefinable something that men in my field are always on the lookout for.

My recommendation, young lady, would be for you to arrange an immediate screen test and talent evaluation through my offices at the Goodwin Building

Dear Princess Suzi,

You don't know me, but

Moke closed his eyes tightly and gouged hard at the lids with his thumb and forefinger.

Dear Princess Suzi,

My name is Moke Galenaille. I am a medical student at Duke University.

Although I realize this is rather unorthodox, I have become extremely interested in you and your occupation and would like very much to talk to you.

If you are curious about this letter, or bored with life, or for any reason, please get in touch with me by return mail or call me at 337-6929.

Sincerely,
Moke Galenaille

The next morning he decided on the last of the letters—the most honest. He borrowed some bluish, expensive-looking stationery from Mrs. Goodwin and wrote it out in his best handwriting in black ink. After he had the letter neatly folded and sealed, the craziness of the whole idea started to depress him. He decided the only way to save himself and make a reasonable decision about whether or not to mail the letter was to go back to the Gayety that afternoon and see Suzi Sinzinnati again, so he did. The crowd was even larger—word had spread. Suzi Sinzinnati seemed so lovely to him that he experienced an actual physical pain in his chest and wondered if this might not be the first sign of premature heart disease. After the show that day, he ran all the way to the big downtown post office on Government Square to buy a special delivery stamp before the windows slammed shut in that cavernous building at five P.M. But he was seconds too late—the last window in the line closed with deafening finality as he approached it—so he loped back to the Gayety and, still breathless and a little dizzy, convinced the over-rouged ticket lady to take the letter off his hands.

That night around ten-thirty, the phone rang downstairs, and Mrs. Goodwin called him. Who would be calling him here, he wondered, at this hour? His parents? Doc? Mrs. Goodwin gave him a curious look as he passed through the living room to the kitchen, where the phone was. He leaned against the dish drainer and picked up the receiver. "Hello?" he said.

"Hello," said a musical feminine voice. "Is this Moke?"

"Yes."

"Well, hello, Moke," said the voice. "I bet you can't guess who this is. . . . "

Chapter Four

If the Army and the Navy
ever looked on Heaven's scenes,
they would find the streets are guarded
by United States Marines. . . .

—U.S. Marine Corps Hymn

BILL GALENAILLE, Moke's father, had his first heart attack when he was forty-nine. He had gotten up and eaten a late breakfast. He was busily brushing his teeth when without warning he felt an odd pressure building up inside his chest, a minute point of intense pain radiating outward, and his left arm growing numb. His knees suddenly felt so weak he would have slipped down, banging both kneecaps against the hard tile floor, but he managed to hold himself erect by gripping fiercely at the edge of the lavatory with his strong right arm. He clung there for several minutes, eyeing himself grimly in the mirror, and then walked himself slowly and carefully to the bed.

When Moke got home at 11:30 for lunch, he found a jumbo-sized ambulance parked in the driveway, its red rotating light eerily ticking. Behind tinted, soundproof glass in the rear of the vehicle—he peeked in—a man was lying rigidly on a stretcher—it was his father! His father's eyes were closed. Just then, two men in white came out of the house, walked briskly to the ambulance, got in, and speeded away. His mother was pacing up and down the living room: "Moke, I have some bad news for you," she said. "Your father overdid himself yesterday. They think he's had a mild heart attack." She told him what had happened.

The afternoon before, his father had tried to play basketball with them out in the backyard—maybe that was what caused it. It was a warm, pleasant afternoon, and Rockaway and Tate and Wilson and Mr. Critchell from next door, who owned the lumber company and used to play forward at Indian Park High School, were all out there on the court shooting around and feeling loose and competitive and ready for a game. Moke's father, in his old Marine shirt and khaki pants, was busy measuring and laying blocks for the new patio he was putting in around the back door. It was his one habitual form of recreation on a Saturday or Sunday afternoon, besides occasionally playing golf—just puttering around the house or yard with one of his projects. He had *built* the basketball court for Moke but never played on it much, had never been any kind of a basketball player. Yesterday, however, Mr. Critchell and Rockaway talked him into playing—they needed three-on-a-side—and Moke's father never did anything half-way. He took his shirt off and moved stiffly, frantically around the court, waving his arms, yelling, moving back and forth in a peculiar bent-kneed crouch, more like Sugar Ray Robinson than any basketball player Moke had ever seen before. Then he would let loose with one of his notorious bullet-balls that would careen wildly off the rim or backboard. "More arc," Critch would mumble, as if this spectacle somehow reflected poorly on adults in general.

After half-an-hour, red-faced and sweating, Bill begged off, went inside and fixed everyone a pitcher of lemonade. He sat briefly sipping in his vinyl-stripped deck chair as the boys drifted back to the game. Then he went to work on the patio again, pounding stakes, tying strings, hauling sand in a wheelbarrow around the corner of the garage, rolling it, tamping it, laying blocks. He was still working on it after dinner; and when Moke went to bed, he caught a glimpse of his father out the kitchen window, still working on it in the glow from the porch light. At breakfast that morning, his mother reported that the final block had been tamped into place at right around three A.M. and that his father was going to sleep-in this morning.

While his mother hurriedly, nervously fixed his lunch—she had to be at the hospital at two P.M.—Moke wandered out into the yard to check on the patio. Sure enough, overnight, they had become patio owners. It was almost as if the checkerboard of stone had descended from the sky. The patio was of alternate pink and plain blocks, incredibly symmetrical and level as a table, and in between blocks the sand was meticulously packed and brushed into smooth grooves.

Inside, Moke went into the bathroom and stared soberly at his brown eyes in the mirror, imagining them as his father's blue eyes, and imagining how it must have felt to know you were abruptly—blam!—having a heart attack. Casually, he began combing his hair. Glancing down, he was appalled to see that his father's toothbrush was still lying there in the bowl of the lavatory and a smear of toothpaste was still clinging to the lip of the bowl where the brush had first dropped and struck.

There was little doubt that his father's heart attack had given his father a "new lease on life." He went cold turkey from a two-pack-a-day Camel-smoker to a cheerful chewer of Dentine. He methodically trimmed the fat from his sirloins, cut out martinis, switched to Sucarol, and sat around in the evenings (when he wasn't on the road) reading a book called *Thank God for My Heart Attack* and staring at the folds of the curtains with an expression on his face that could only be described as spiritual. He upped his weekly offering at the Indian Park Community Church to $25, seldom succumbed to his weakness for lazing around Sunday mornings engrossed in the sports page and the fates of Dagwood and Jiggs; and everywhere he went, he carried his small plastic vial of digitalis like a talisman and bent the ear of anyone who cared to listen, telling them of his transformation.

It had been that way for most of the two years they were in Indian Park, his father working for the F. W. Ziv Company, selling syndicated television programs in the three-state region (shows like "Lassie" and "The Cisco Kid"), the most recent niche in twenty-five years of rampant job-hopping. It was inevitable that his new outlook on life would lead to yet another new employment bonanza, in this case WTSF, and no accident that the radio station was owned by a religious organization and was located in paradise. . . . Isn't this "beeaauudiful!" Isn't that "beeaauudiful!" his mother is chirping as Moke is ushered with some fanfare into a new stark-white L-shaped ranch house, a single lush palmetto palm growing in front—this only last fall, his first visit from Duke to Terresonna.

The previous afternoon he has hopped Eastern's flight 328 from Raleigh/Durham (home of the Duke Blue Devils) to Miami

International. He has listened to his mother's incessant travelogue on the glories of Florida. He has received a room-by-room guided tour of the dwelling, including a lecture on terrazzo flooring and the minor dangers of mildew and scorpions. The house resembles others he has lived in. The furniture, at least, is the same, exuding a comforting odor of "home."

Now his father has the first full day planned: a visit to the radio station, then the Bible Ranch, then lunch with Elijah Roark himself, who owns everything.

"This station was *fifty thousand* in the red when they hired me," his father is saying. They are tooling down the main drag of Terresonna in the family Oldsmobile. "Now with this new promotional idea of mine all the local businessmen are coming around. They really love me down here. I know everybody. Everybody says hello. I'm in the Rotary and the Lions and the Christian Businessmen's Club. I'll bet you a dollar to a doornail that I'll be in the black so quick it'll make your head swim."

"That's good to hear," Moke says.

"I know this business like the back of my hand. . . . Would you look at that sun up there! I never saw such weather. We haven't used a drop of oil yet and it's almost December!"

Bill flicks on the radio and plays with the bass-treble knob. "There we are," he says. "Listen to those violins! We play only high-type music—easy listening type music. None of that 'Rock-around-the clock'-type stuff that blows you out of your seat."

"No Elvis?"

"Elvis! Ha, ha, Moke, I wouldn't last twenty-four hours in this job if I tried to play Elvis. Elvis!"

"Fats Domino?"

"Fats Domino! No. That isn't the kind of music these people want to hear down here, Moke. We've got to go where the business is. Fats Domino would drive these people wild in five minutes down here, pal. You've got to have a feeling for who your audience is. You've got to play what they want to hear. . . . How's Duke?"

"Oh, okay. . . . "

"You know, if you ever decide that pre-med is not what you're really looking for, you might take a look at public relations—it's the coming thing. There's a lot of money to be made in public relations and advertising these days."

"I doubt if I will."

"You ought to think about it."

Moke's eyes follow the familiar line of the hood and come to rest on the Rocket 88 hood ornament. As they ride, he and his father are staring up the business end of a miniature chrome rocket ship, which is carrying the two-ton automobile by its fins alone. "I'm definitely not as oriented toward making money as you are. I don't think I would find it very satisfying."

"Don't kid yourself. You would be good at it—a big, good-looking fella like you—they'd be falling all over themselves to do business with you. You've always been a good salesman—remember those magazine subscriptions you sold in the fifth or sixth grade? Why, you sold more than anybody else in the class!"

"That was because you and Doc bought half of them."

"Don't kid yourself, pal. You've got what it takes!"

"Advertising seems so useless to me. I don't want to be a . . . parasite—just to make money."

"There's more to it than you think. A lot more. Why, advertising is the lifeblood of the American economy, pal. If it wasn't for advertising, we wouldn't have radio or television or newspapers. Who do you think pays for the mass media? Advertising! How else would people find out about things? Moke, this is the greatest country in the history of the world, and we owe a lot of it to the advertising business."

"It's fine, I guess, if you happen to be a money-grubber."

"Is that what you think I am—a money-grubber?"

"At times."

"Boy, that really takes the cake! Here I am, spending four thousand dollars a year to send *you* to college and you come home and the first thing you do is call *me* a money-grubber." All this blather of his father's is quite amiable and good-natured, though, as usual, heavy with message. "You better be glad somebody in this family's a money-grubber, buster, or you might have to go to work for a living."

They wind around a pleasant blacktop road next to a golf course that looks like pure living Kodachrome, and there in the distance, with four-foot-high letters on the roof spelling out W-T-S-F, is the station. "Nice setting, isn't it?" Bill says. They park and get out.

"Where's Sugar?" his father bellows, parading through the lobby.

"In back, boss," somebody calls through an open door.

"Go get her, will you," says his father loudly. "I want her to meet somebody." He unlocks a door, the door to his office, it turns out, and holds it open for Moke. "Have a seat, pal." It is a generous corner room with banks of jalousy windows overlooking the golf course, and his father's favorite picture, the Marines raising the flag on Iwo Jima, centrally displayed on a magnificent masonite wall. His father goes around the big, matched woodgrain executive desk and hunts for something in the top drawer, finally removing a square pack of Stimudents—orange, polished, triangulated toothpicks—peels one off and begins poking viciously between his teeth.

"Why, if I believed *that*, I wouldn't be worth a damn in this business." (Poke, poke.) "You have to *believe* that what you're doing matters and you have to *believe* in the product you're selling. When I worked for Hoover when I was just getting started," (poke, poke, poke) "I convinced myself that Hoover was the best god-damned sweeper on the market, bar none." (Poke, poke.) "And if I hadn't, I wouldn't have been able to sell it! Because if *you* don't believe in what you're selling, you can be damned sure no one else is going to believe in it either. And if you're a good enough salesman, you'll always be in demand."

"Here's Sugar," someone says.

"Oh, good." His father leaps our of his chair and motions to Moke to follow him out the door. "There's somebody I want you to meet in here. That-a-boy. Stand right here, pal." His father hooks his elbow around Moke's neck as if they are about to pose for a photographer.

For somebody twice Moke's age, Sugar seems nice at first glance, girlish in a pleated skirt and a sailor's suit top, plumply feminine and leering.

"Sugar, I'd like you to meet *my son*, Moke, who I've been telling you so much about."

"The prodigal son returns," she says, winking foolishly.

"He's going to be a soph-o-more at Duke next year—studying pre-med—and you should have seen his mid-term *grades* when they came in! The same all through high school—all A's—I don't know how he does it! This kid's got a head on his shoulders, I'll tell you that! (He must take after his mother—ha-ha.) But that's not the half of it. He was a high jumper and miler on the track squad." (Moke winces at "squad.") "He was president of the Pre-Med Club and the National Honor Society. He sang in the chorus and played in the band. He only missed *cum laude* by one one-hundredth of a percentage point! He acted in the Senior Play. He was editor of their yearbook. What d'ya think of that? This is one fella who can do it all! He's going to be an important man some day, and I'm awfully proud of him." His father squeezes his neck a little harder, causing Moke to stare at Sugar from a cock-eyed angle.

"Cut it out," Moke says.

"Well, my . . . my," Sugar says, licking her teeth, revealing a charmingly red, heart-shaped tongue. "Sounds like a chip off the old block to me. Sure does. . . . Hiya, Shoulders. Want my telephone number?"

Back in the office, Moke says: "I wish you wouldn't do that kind of stuff, introducing me like I was some kind of visiting dignitary. It's embarrassing."

"I'm *proud* of you, son."

"What am I supposed to *say*, standing there grinning like an idiot?"

"You don't have to say anything. There are some things you can't say about yourself. You just let me do the talking."

"Well, I have to say something!"

"You're just modest—that's a very likeable trait about you, pal. People like a modest, humble person. I admire you for it."

"I just wish you wouldn't do it anymore."

"Listen, these people *like* to hear about the boss's son. They're *interested* in what you do. They've heard a lot about you, and they want to meet you face-to-face. You don't have *a thing* to be embarrassed about, believe me.

"They've probably heard all those things about me twenty times already anyway. Why repeat it in my presence? It makes me feel self-conscious."

"Don't be silly. I'm *proud* of you, and they know I'm proud of you. A father has a right to be proud of his son. It may be a weakness on my part. I guess it may be a terrible weakness to be proud of one's son, but I can't help it; I can't help myself."

"Well, sometimes you carry it to excess." Moke begins to sound something like his mother, which he resents. His father has been doing this to him for as long as he can remember.

"This man you're going to meet, Moke," his father is saying, "is quite an unusual person." They are rolling soundlessly now across the fairways toward the distant central headquarters of the Bible Ranch in the special WTSF electrical golfcart.

"Do they own the golfcourse, too?" Moke says.

"They own the golfcourse, the radio station, an Olympic-size swimming pool on the grounds, a big Chris Craft. . . . The Bible Ranch itself is a full-scale resort facility! We even have a 1500-seat auditorium! Hell, Elijah Roark owns half of Terresonna! He's quite a promoter. But let me tell you about him: Elijah Roark—I'm not even sure that's his real name. He came down here fifteen years ago, and all he had was $1000 in his pocket and a certificate from some mail order house that said he was an ordained Baptist minister. Everybody calls him "Dr. Roark" now, but I don't think he's any kind of doctor in the usual sense. Anyway, he was looking for a place to set up a church, roaming around the countryside until one day he stumbled onto this Air Force base near Terresonna, complete with a depot and a deserted barracks. The Air Force had it up for sale and nobody wanted it. The minute he saw it, the wheels started turning. The way he tells it in his sermons, he took a lonely walk down beside the Atlantic Ocean and an angel of God appeared out of a cloud and told him this was it, to go ahead with the deal. I don't know—maybe that's the way it happened. But, anyway, he went down to the First National Bank and talked them into making one whopper of a loan, and he bought the Air Base dirt cheap and set up the beginnings of the Bible Ranch right here.

"The idea, see, was to attract Northern church groups to come down here to spend a week or two in the Florida sunshine. The idea was that a vacation doesn't have to be sinful, carousing around in nightclubs and going to floor-shows and getting soused every night. You could make it a time for spiritual renewal and meet a lot of nice Christian people and enjoy special rates and maybe even take the whole thing off your income tax.

"Well, as you might imagine, it worked all right and *then some.* He got a lot of free labor out of his guests. A lot of local people got hooked on the Gospel—he's a damned good preacher. They started doing favors for him. He started plowing all of his money into local real estate—he got in on the ground floor. A lot of old ladies started willing their estates to the Bible Ranch, which he encourages. Elijah has what he calls the "Eternal Life" plan, where you will all of your property over to the Ranch. To make a long story short, he's made a bloody fortune down here. He got in just before the big boom in Florida real estate. Prices shot up overnight. Now Elijah Roark is a millionaire several times over, a *multi*-millionaire, and he owns half the county and two or three shopping centers and an island in the Bahamas and WTSF and so on. It's one hellava American success story if there ever was one!"

The cart rolls across a sandy unpaved road that marks the fringe of the golfcourse, and Bill navigates among several clumps of coconut palms and decorative bushes and brings them out in view of Bible Ranch headquarters, an immense flat building with a lot of aluminum jalousy windows, gaudy flower beds, and well-clipped shrubbery. On a marquee over the main entrance is a sign: "Terresonna Bible Ranch, Inc.—In the Heart of the Florida Gold Coast—A Winter Paradise for All God's People."

They park the golfcart next to "Elijah's car," a Chrysler Imperial (Mark IV) with fender-mounted taillights, and stroll across the thick grass, pass under the marquee, and enter the holy building. Moke waits in the outer hall, gawking at some bulletin boards, while his father joshes with the secretary and they wait for Elijah Roark to emerge.

TEENAGERS WITH A PURPOSE, reads a caption on one bulletin board: "These are only some of the teenagers from the Terresonna Youth Ranch who, through the ministry of TRUTH FOR YOUTH, are going ON IN THE LORD, and attending Bible School THIS YEAR!

"How we praise the Lord for the lasting results from the teenage conference this past month! August 5 we had a pool party and 12–15 trusted Christ as their Savior out of 35 in attendance!

These teenagers are determined to "GO" for the Lord in making this coming year really COUNT FOR CHRIST in THEIR high schools.

"MANY of these young people have come back from the Bible Ranch with changed lives! For instance, Shelly, the new teenage convert mentioned in last month's newsletter, dedicated her life to Christ in August. She is now deeply burdened for her family and unsaved friends. . . . "

Another offering reads:

Going All the Way with the Eternal Life Plan: "We talk about tithing during our lifetime yet forget about tithing our after-death assets!" an Indiana pastor remarked recently. It is an arresting thought. Tithing is usually interpreted as a gift of one-tenth of all we own. Usually, we relate the tithe to life-time gifts and exclude any mention of it from the language of our wills.

But doesn't God have as much claim upon our estates as do our heirs? If we acknowledge that God is the title-holder of all we possess, and thank Him that we retain nine-tenths of this property for use during our lives, it shouldn't be too hard to draft our wills properly. A part of the wording of our wills should rightly include the leaving of AT LEAST the tithe for the Lord and His continuous works.

Surely one of the great areas of the Lord's work is the Terresonna Bible Ranch, Inc. You are invited to write for further information and counsel concerning the planning of your estate, keeping the Lord inmind.
—Dr. Elijah Roark

FAMOUS ATHLETE APPEARS

A student-initiated convocation at the Terresonna Youth Ranch, featuring the appearance of big Bill Brenkowski, defensive end of the Green Bay Packers, was thrown open to all members of the community, as well as team members from nearby high schools. Bill, an articulate and intelligent young man, as well as a star of professional and college football, spoke on the theme,

"Athletics and Christianity." His very clever analogy of relating the game of football to the game of life was well-received. He indicated that just as a game must have a goal, life must have a goal, and we cannot exist unmotivated. We receive our motivation and our courage from the Almighty to face life's wedge plays and to be part of the solution of the problems which surround us and not be problems ourselves.

He reminded the young people present that when a player loses his poise, he cannot carry out the details of the assignment, so we must, like the athlete, make one play at a time.

On the subject of opposition, Big Bill commented that it is not always from your opponents—sometimes it is from your own teammates. Therefore, we must relate not only to our Maker but to each other. Brenkowski concluded by saying, "We live in a frightening world, and I say this not to discourage you but to challenge you to be part of the solution!"

Dear Dr. Roark,

We returned to Little Rock from our first visit to the Terresonna Bible Ranch almost a month ago, and I just want you to know I have never felt so much love, so alive, so tremendous, in my entire life!

My dad wrote you last month. I'm his almost-17-year-old daughter! We're talking about coming back to Terresonna again next year!

I've been reading the Bible every day, and some of these passages really excite me! I just get so emotional when I think about how beautiful "God's Word" is and the people who are into it because of the love that fills and overflows inside my heart. Wow, God really knows what he's talking about!

So far I've read all of *Genesis* and *Exodus*. *Genesis* is just fantastic! God is such a wonderful Father and, oh, how He takes care of His children! I'm so glad I'm His child! And *Exodus*! This really is a tremendous book of the Bible. God is so real! and so concerned about His children. It's so cool to see the spirit of God move as He does it in *Exodus*! Isn't He wonderful!

I want to get out and tell the whole world about it!
I'm so glad I'm not of this world! I'm just going to explode I'm so happy!

Love ya,
Billie Jeanne Prichert

"Biiilll, so glad you could make it! Sorry to keep you waiting
out here like some errand boy, har-har-har. I was on the phone
with Ted Asher down at the First Federal. . . . " The voice comes
booming out of the inner office, an unctuous baritone with the
practiced, self-conscious intonations of the radio announcers Moke
has listened to all his life, at dinner, at the office, or over the
telephone, asking for his father. Moke backs up a step and peers
noncommittally through the open doorway. His father is grinning
ear-to-ear and shaking the hand of an enormous pot-bellied,
bullet-headed gentleman in an Hawaiian shirt. "And you brought
the *boy* and here *he* is!" Roark bellows, and the two of them are on
him like lightning, Roark pumping his hand in his warm, soft
mitt. "And I'm so glad to finally meet you, Moke Galenaille. Your
father doesn't talk about anything else."

"Glad to meet you, too, sir." Roark's sheer bulk makes Moke
feel diminutive—six-six and two-eighty at least, Moke guesses, a
gigantic, affable, paternalistic Buddha-figure with shifty turquoise
eyes, tanned as a berry, and stuffed with expensive beefsteak, a
father for his flock.

"Yep, he's quite a kid," his father is saying. "You know, Elijah, Moke is quite a modest fellow, too."

"You don't say!"

"You'd think that a young man who had accomplished as
much as he has at the age of eighteen might be a little on the
conceited side, but, believe me, you won't find a more humble,
considerate person than this fellow right here." He pats Moke on
the back. "Why, I was just telling little Sugar about all the things
he's done—about his A's and being elected to the National Honor
Society and so on, and his athletic accomplishments—this man
right here is a *gifted* natural athlete, Elijah—and afterwards he said
to me, he said, 'I wish you wouldn't talk about me like that, Dad.
It isn't very modest, is it?' That's exactly what he said. Now that's
what I call humility." Roark nods approvingly.

"Yes it is, Bill. And it's an example I wish more of our young people could follow. It certainly is. . . . Shall we go on down to the car?" They head out under the marquee toward the waiting Imperial.

"Another thing he told me this morning, Elijah—now listen to this if you don't think I have a hard row to hoe—he said his old man is a money-grubber!"

"A money-grubber, eh?"

"Yep, he thinks I place too much emphasis on making money. That's a fact."

"Well, this could be the beginning of an insight, Bill."

"You think so?"

"Yes it could. 'O ye of little faith,' said the apostle Paul, 'the love of money is the root of all evil. . . . For we brought nothing into this world, and it is certain we can carry nothing out of it. . . . Getting and spending, we lay waste our powers . . . and as ye sow, so shall ye reap.' " Bill's face grows sober at the timbre of these holy words. They get into the car, sandwiching Moke in the middle as Elijah guns the big engine into life. Roark pauses thoughtfully, gazing at a spot of blue cloud above the waving palm fronds and the flat roof of the Bible Ranch headquarters. "It is important to bear in mind, Moke, that Our Lord Gawd is very much in charge of these matters. Notice that Paul does not say 'money is eevill.' He says 'the *love* of money' is the dangerous tendency. It is when we love money more than we love Gawd that we get into trouble. Now, the power to make money is a gift from the Lord. Yes it is. Gawd did not intend for us to suffer in poverty all the days of our lives. And money made and spent in furthering His Holy Works is certainly in accordance with Gawd's wishes. And, don't forget that capitalism is in the spirit of American life, and we are a favored land in the eyes of the Lord. Yes we are.

"We're so glad to have a man of your father's experience, Moke, to aid us in our mission. It is a minor miracle that we found him. He is an earnest man, a good man, and, of course, he works to make money. But what he does is nothing to be ashamed of. We all have to earn our daily bread. Your father is doing the Lord's work. He is doing it and he is doing it very successfully, I might add." Elijah winks, extending his mammoth arm along the luxurious seatback to cuff Bill affectionately on the shoulder. Then he

cranks the car into reverse, brakes, turns, and whizzes them towards the exit sign, which, on its reverse side, reads, "All One in
Christ Jesus."

If this car is an example of a Heavenly recompense, Moke is
thinking, Our Lord Gawd must surely like what Elijah Roark is
doing: power-steering, power windows, power everything.

"I don't know what it is, Moke, maturity, old age or what, but
I've been bitten by the religious bug lately myself," his father is
saying. They have finished lunch, dropped Elijah back at headquarters, golf-carted across to the station, and are now on the way
back "home." "I think it was probably the best thing I ever did to
come down here."

"Well, they certainly seem to think highly of you."

"Well, they're good people—all of them—devout, pure-
minded people. You won't see them drinking a drop, smoking, or
playing around with the women. It's none of that hard-driving sort
of life where you're always under pressure to perform, perform,
perform. I'll tell you, it's a relief. All that pressure just puts you in
the cardiac ward—that's what it did to me. That was it in a nut-
shell. And *I'll tell you*, once you've been that route, your thinking
changes a little bit. You begin to wonder what your life adds up to.
When these people go home at night, they're able to look themselves straight in the eye and say: 'Lord, I'm a little bit bigger
man today than I was yesterday,' and, believe me, that's one of the
best feelings there is in the world."

"Yep," Moke says, "I guess you're right."

"You bet I'm right, pal."

That evening after dinner Moke is sitting out on the patio,
watching the pink sky across the field of yellow grass and thinking
and composing his daily letter to Julie:

Dearest Julie,

You wouldn't *believe* what is happening down here. I
think my father is turning into a holy roller. Today I met
the head of this organization, the Bible Ranch Corp. that
owns the radio station, and he is the most incredible sort
of crackpot fundamentalist nitwit you could ever imag-

ine. I couldn't believe it. For obvious reasons I kept all philosophical conversations to a minimum, but one thing I did find out at lunch was that these people don't even believe in Darwin! They don't even believe that dinosaurs existed! They are *that* primitive. . . .

Through the screen to the living room Moke can hear the Huntley-Brinkley Report and then his father's rising and falling voice superimposed over a commercial for denture adhesive: "Guess what your son called me today," he is saying to Moke's mom, "A money-grubber! Did you know your husband was a money-grubber? I bet you didn't know you had a money-grubber for a husband, did you!"

"Let me tell you about a funny thing that happened today," Bill had said at dinner. "Funny things" were always happening to Moke's father—his life was full of adventures.

His father had paid a call that afternoon on a man named Ralph Peterson, owner of the Flamingo Furniture Mart, Inc., to tell him about the special deal WTSF was offering on thirty-second spots preceding the Six O'Clock News. There were no customers in the store and the two men sat in the office talking at a leisurely pace, sipping coffee, getting to know one another. Bill was bothered almost immediately, he said, by an odd sense of familiarity about Peterson. He *reminded* him of somebody, but he couldn't say who. He thought for a minute that maybe Peterson was somebody he might have known in Pittsburgh, but Peterson said he was originally from Minneapolis. Then they started talking about the War, for some reason, and it turned out that Peterson had been a Navy pilot in the Pacific; and Bill told him he had been in the Pacific too—with the Leathernecks. "What a coincidence!" Bill said, always ready to capitalize on anything he might have in common with a potential client.

"Yeah, I was with the First Air Squadron at Okinawa," Peterson said.

"I'll be damned!" Bill said. "I was with Air Support Control on Okinawa! I had a bad shrapnel wound in the hip and eventually got shipped back stateside, but I talked to an awful lot of flyers in those days."

"What was your code name, Galenaille?"

"I was Magpie," Bill said.

"Magpie!" Peterson said. "*You* were Magpie!" Peterson reached out and grabbed Bill's arm in both hands. "I thought there was something familiar about you. Why, I talked to you twenty times every mission we flew. I swear! I was Rubie-red!"

"*You* were Rubie-red! I'll be damned!" He looked at Peterson in an entirely new way.

"You were the best god-damned controller out there, let me tell you that, Galenaille. God, I never thought I'd ever meet Magpie face-to-face. Isn't that a bitch! You *saved my life* a couple of times a day out there, you bastard."

"Yep, I was Magpie all right. Put 'er there, Buddy."

"And you're still doing radio work—doesn't that take the cake!"

Bill stayed at the Flamingo Furniture Mart shooting the bull with Rubie-red until well past closing time, and when he came home he had a new sponsor for the Eight O'Clock-, the Noon-, and the Six O'Clock News, plus a whole series of afternoon commercials; a new member of the Keyboard Quiz promotion; a candidate for the Christian Businessmen's Association; and a new golf partner.

When Julie had been down for her visit, there had been a number of religious arguments. Like obedient children, they had gone to church together that first Sunday. Julie had gotten one look at Elijah Roark's unctuous charm and decided he was patronizing, covert, malicious, deceitful, unholy, and probably a criminal. Moke knew it was bad, but he wasn't certain it was *that* bad.

One night the last week in the middle of this dinner they were enjoying at a Polynesian restaurant, Julie informed his parents that she didn't want to hear any more sanctimonious crap about the Bible Ranch. She happened to be an atheist, she said, and Moke—in case they didn't know it—was an agnostic, and she thought the Bible Ranch personnel were a bunch of neurotic, lower-class riffraff. Moke just about gagged on his Succulent Pineapple and Fluffy Rice Delight.

Bill said he was sorry she felt that way, but that, whatever *she* thought, it was good Christian men and women just like them who had made America the great country it was today.

Julie said the country was going down the drain, as a matter of fact, but she would have to agree that the muddle-headed fundamentalist Christians were partly responsible for it.

Moke's mother asked Moke just what Julie meant by "an agnostic" and wanted to know if he thought Julie was right about his being one.

Moke said an agnostic was a person who felt there was no empirical proof one way or the other about whether God exists or not and he hated to say it because he knew it might upset them but that really *was* what he happened to believe right then—after giving it considerable thought first semester.

Bill said you spend $4000/year to send them to the best colleges in the country and they come back a year later and think they know everything about everything. "Eighteen years old and they know it *all*!"

Julie said that as a matter of fact she thought it was the older generation who pretended to know everything about everything—without any proof at all—not the young, who, she thought, on the whole possessed a general and much more healthy brand of skepticism.

Moke's mother wanted to know whether it was possible to be an agnostic and a Christian at the same time.

Bill said as far as Moke was concerned he was pretty damned sure it was just a stage he was going through—nothing to get excited about. When he was eighteen, he said, he thought his own father was pretty god-damned stupid too, as a matter of fact. Then when he got to be twenty-one he couldn't figure out how the old man had learned so much in such a short time.

Moke said he *never* said he thought anybody was stupid in the first place and the whole discussion was pointless and needlessly upsetting for everyone and he thought they would all be better off if they changed the subject.

Julie said that was just fine with her as long as the Galenailles could kindly refrain from bringing up any more half-baked religious claptrap in her presence, or for that matter, any more fascist slogans about America the Beautiful.

Moke's mother said Julie was a very sweet girl but that she did have one or two things to learn on the subject of tact.

Bill said Julie was a very smart girl—as smart as they come—and he wasn't a bit worried about the way she would turn out in

49

the end. One of these days, he said, he knew she would see the light—he would bet on it—and until that time he for one would defend her against anyone in the world just as if she was a member of his own family.

His crazy father, always a peacemaker, always generous to a fault, in spite of his dogmatic patriotic and religious simplicities— willing, for instance, to sponsor this whole unpremeditated excursion to Cincinnati and Indian Park merely because Moke has decided it is necessary. While dropping him at the airport, for instance, launching again into his impossible pecuniary ritual: "Hey, hold on a minute, pal. How's the money situation? Could you use a little extra?" His father reaches automatically for his wallet.

"No, I don't think I need any."

His father opens the wallet anyway, revealing the array of cards—Carte Blanche, American Express, Diner's Club, a half-dozen oil companies. He thumbs through the thick wad of bills. "You better take some, just in case." He rolls out two bills and places them in Moke's inside shirt pocket. Moke pulls out the bills and looks at them—two hundreds.

"I don't need this much! The ticket is already paid for." He tries to give back one of the bills.

"No, that's all right. You never know when you might need it."

"I doubt if I'll need this much," Moke says. "Money doesn't grow on trees, you know," he says, grinning at this use of one of this father's favorite metaphysical observations.

"No, I know it doesn't. But you take it. You can give it back later if you don't need it. Don't worry about it. I don't want you going broke up there—that's all. I can afford it, believe me. I can afford it."

Moke puts the bills in his wallet. "All right."

"Listen, why don't you take my American Express card too." He reaches for his wallet again. "That way if you need anything. . . . " Moke puts his hands up in a defensive position.

"I wouldn't even consider it," Moke says.

"You should. It might come in handy!"

"No. Put it back."

"There aren't many people I would trust with this, son, believe me. But I know you would never misuse it, Moke. You'll be responsible about it. That's why I'm offering it."

"Put it back. I don't want it."

"You better take it. You might need it."

"I have plenty already, really. More than enough!"

"Well, if you change your mind, just drop me a line and I'll mail it to you."

"Okay, fine. If I need it, I'll say so."

"So long, buddy."

"So long, Dad." They shake hands.

"And don't forget to give my best to little Julie."

Chapter Five

You are my special an-gell
Right from par-a-dise
I know that you're an an-gell
Hea-venn is in your eyes

SUZI WAS IN A ROSEBUD COSTUME this time—petite rosebuds on the
nipple-tips of her bra and a big one over the satin triangle of her
G-string—absolutely stunning, Moke thought. At the end of her
act, Suzi peeled off a rosebud—the bra was a cut-out with rosebud
pasties—and held it up. Several hands waved around him, but
Suzi came straight to him and handed him the pasty. He felt the
warmth of her hand for a moment and then she danced away.

Past midnight, and Moke stood out under the marquee in the
appointed spot, the wind in his eyes, fingering the sequins on the
pasty inside his coat pocket. He could just make out the flanks
and tail of the equestrian statue at the end of Garfield Place half-
a-block up. The headlights from the thin stream of cars turning
off Garfield up Vine Street slid across the horse's tail and made
fiery balls of light in the gigantic plate glass windows of the City
Library, long since closed for the night. He checked his watch—it
was now a good half-hour since the furtive crowd of men had staggered off in all directions, the Gayety bulbs had gone out, and the
candy butcher—300 pounds and sporting an Elvis haircut—had
looked him over and locked up. Moke started playing a game of
which pair of lights would be the police cruiser and *what* he would
say when they pulled over: *"It's all right, Officer, I'm not trying to
break into the Gayety or anything—heh-heh. I'm just waiting for one of
the strippers to get her clothes on"*—something like that.

One of the Gayety doors opened and Hazel Storm and another girl came out. Neither of them looked at him. They stood

off to Moke's left, talking. Hazel edged down to the curb as if she
was about to hail a taxi. The other girl didn't seem to know what
she was going to do, and then Moke realized with a start that it
was Suzi. "Oh, I didn't recognize you," he said, going over. She
looked at him intently; her face seemed recently scrubbed clean.
Close up, she had big, impressive eyes.

"Well," she said, "It's pretty hard without my fake eyelashes." She smiled up to him out of the corners of her eyes. She
was shorter than he expected, maybe 5'7".

"Are you Moke?"

"Yeah."

"I was hoping it would be you."

"How could you guess?"

"Oh, when the runway lights turn on, you can see everybody
pretty easily. You fit the description."

"Hey, where shall we go?" Moke said.

"I want you to meet someone first," Suzi said. "Moke, this is
Hazel Storm. Hazel, this is Moke . . . *how* do you pronounce your
last name?"

"Gail-nail."

"Nice to make your acquaintance," Hazel said, staring at the
sidewalk. She was at least forty.

"Actually, I'm starved," Suzi said. They agreed to look for a
place to eat.

"You want to come too?" Moke said to Hazel.

"We stick together pretty much," Hazel said, pointing awkwardly at Suzi.

"Terrific," Moke said, almost cheerfully enough. What he
thought was: "Terrific!"

Still, he was elated. He thought of himself back at the Goodwins, leaning against the dish drainer and talking to Suzi on the
phone. And now *here*—it was hard to believe. He wasn't going
back there tonight for anything. He felt reckless, desperate. Let
the Goodwins think he was staying with his uncle. Maybe the
women would lead him into a trap; maybe he would get mugged
in an alley, stabbed to death, his undiscovered body mouldering
for weeks in a thin puddle of oily lettuce leaves, potato peelings,
tea bags and coffee grounds next to some garbage cans with rats

53

scrabbling over his shoelaces and sucking out his eyesockets at three A.M. Maybe they would take him back to their hotel and Suzi would casually take her clothes off and ask him for money. He only had $150 left, but he didn't want to think about that. He was going to play it by ear all the way and find out what was going to happen. Suzi was the most attractive girl who had ever paid any attention to him. Maybe she was the most beautiful girl he had ever seen; his throat was thick with lust; he felt he might go into a swoon just talking to her. She was priceless—even with her hair pulled back in a knot as it was now and this nondescript sack dress with small green polkadots. They walked on up Vine Street, bright and deserted and dreamlike.

"What kind of doctor are you studying to be?" Suzi said.

"Maybe a psychiatrist," Moke said, "or a brain surgeon. I don't know yet for sure."

"Oh, I *thought* maybe that was it. Is that why you wanted to talk to me?"

"Yeah, *that* was the reason," Moke said, teasingly.

"Oh, you," Suzi said.

"He's kind of cute," Hazel said. Suzi looked slightly embarrassed.

Hazel hobbled along in highheels as if she had never learned to walk in them properly, her neck tilted back and her nose held high in a ludicrous imitation of hauteur. She was asked along as a chaperone, Moke figured, in case he turned out to be a rapist or a purse snatcher. These women probably had passes made at them all the time.

"Here's a place," Suzi said. They went in. It was a brightly lit cafeteria-diner smelling of mustard and burned grease, with a long stainless steel lunch counter and several burly truckdriver types sitting on barstools and at some smoky tables in the rear. It was packed, considering the hour—quarter-to-one on the Coke-clock over the grill. Heads rubbered around as they entered, and Moke noticed worriedly that Suzi and Hazel were the only women in the place. They avoided the fixed stares and proceeded to take trays and gawk at the wrapped sandwiches, sweating juice glasses, and an array of pies. The room had grown noticeably quieter. Suzi, and then Moke, chose big 60¢ glasses of orange juice and then stood waiting for Hazel to make up her mind. "Hey, mister," she yelled to the grill chef who was ignoring her, "you got any foot-long hot dogs?"

Hazel sat munching her hot dog and dabbing mustard from the corners of her mouth with a balled-up Kleenex.

"You're younger than I thought you would be," Suzi said.

"So are you," Moke said. "How old are you?"

"That's for me to know and you to find out," Suzi said.

"Is Suzi your real name?" She sipped her straw thoughtfully.

"Uh-huh."

"You don't lie very well." She gave him a guilty but endearing look, like a child confident of the sympathy of an irritated parent.

"How do you like me without my make-up?" she said, testing him, changing the subject.

"Sensational—you're a knock-out either way. You were by far the favorite dancer up there, you know. I mean—I mean—with all due respect to Hazel, who dances a mean number. But I was wondering why they didn't feature you, like—what's her-name?"

"Well, aside from the fact that she jerks off the manager before *and* after every show, I can't think of any reason either," Suzi said.

"You shouldn't say that," Hazel said, her mouth full of half-chewed bun.

"Well, it's true," Suzi said.

"It sounds vulgar," Hazel said.

"The real reason is I haven't been dancing very long," Suzi said. "I'm just a novice. And nobody knew what I was going to look like when they booked us. So—you know. That's the way the mop flops, to coin a phrase. . . . "

"It doesn't seem fair," Moke said. "They should consider themselves lucky even to have you." He wished he could get the stupid, sheepish smile off his face as he said it. "I hope that doesn't sound ingratiating," he said. "*I mean it.*"

"That's nice of you," Suzi said.

"He really is very sweet," Hazel said. "Don't you think?"

The jukebox whirred and a platter skittered onto the turntable.

Once there were greenfields
warmed by the sun
Once there were valleys
where rivers used to run
Once there were blue skies
with white clouds high above
Once they were part of
our everlasting love. . . .

"God, that's a sad song," Suzi said.

What was he going to do now? He started to feel desperate
again. He thought of the blue and red airline ticket tucked away
in the breast pocket of his madras jacket hanging in the Goodwins' guest room closet. What *could* he do? Fly back to the Florida
wasteland with its hayfever and palmetto bugs and Bible Ranch
fanatics? While away three lonely weeks, suffocating in the salt-
sea breezes and humoring his parents? Then drive the nineteen
hours back to Duke for three more years of anxiety and humilia-
tion? His empty mailbox. His palms sweating in chemistry class or
so icy cold he would press them between his thighs and the curved
wooden seat until the circulation was cut off and he would have to
shake them in order to write again, watching his white knuckles
furiously inscribing formulas for page after page.

It's now or never, Elvis said.
Come hold me tight
Kiss me, my darling
Be mine tonight
To-mor-row
will be too late
It's now or never
My love won't wait.

"How long will you be here?" Moke said to Suzi.
"Our show ends in just two more days," she said.
"Then another group comes?" She nodded.
"Where will you go?" She looked at Hazel.

"No place," Suzi said.

"No place! Don't you have a circuit? I mean, I thought you would move on to some other city like Baltimore or St. Louis."

"No. We're quitting for a while."

"You must be sick of cities."

"Oh, wow," Suzi said. "Sick and bored."

"You should go south for a while," Moke said. "The sun would do you good."

"Where to?" she said.

"Oh,"—he moved his arm in a vague, sweeping gesture—"almost anywhere, just so it's south. You could easily come south with me," Moke said. "I've got a place in Florida."

"Florrrida!" Suzi said. "Oh, wow."

"Oh, we couldn't possibly do that!" Hazel said. Moke looked at Suzi for some clue to explain Hazel's presumption of authority.

"Maybe Suzi *could*," he said. "You wouldn't have to come."

"Well, honey, we can't afford it, for one thing," Hazel said to Suzi, who had immediately warmed to the idea.

"Think about it," Moke said. "Three days from now we could be on the beach! Just think of it!"

"Oh, wow," Suzi said. "Would *that* be beautiful!"

They left the restaurant and walked some more. The moon was out over Garfield Place, the city streets almost empty and peaceful. When they passed the Cincinnati Club, Moke told them about his Uncle Doc who lived in there and had been the first Eagle Scout in the state of Ohio. But now he had Parkinson's Disease and he couldn't practice surgery anymore, and so on. They wanted to know what his father did for a living, and he told them how his father managed WTSF in Terresonna, Florida, and liked to play golf a lot and was pretty religious, and so on. And he told them about the Terresonna Bible Ranch and how Elijah Roark came to Florida in 1949 with a thousand dollars and a vision and bought an abandoned air base, and so on. Then he told them about Indian Park and Hazel said she wasn't sure but wasn't that quite a wealthy suburb here and Moke said well it was a pretty damned nice place as far as he was concerned—no doubt about that. Suzi wanted to know was Terresonna on the ocean and everything and Moke told them about how Terresonna was in the exact

57

heart of the Florida Gold Coast and had great beaches and sea-shells and terrific royal-palm-lined avenues and exotic places to eat and indoor and outdoor swimming pools in practically every house and yacht harbors and Chris Crafts parading up and down the Intercoastal waterway and nightblooming jasmine and tropical vegetation of every sort and even banana trees not to mention the fact that it was a secret watering spot for the very rich and had unbelievable sunshine that gave you a special golden-brown tan that made your body feel like silk or something and was one of the neatest places he had ever visited let *alone* lived in. Moke mentioned how he had this "in" with the Terresonna Bible Ranch and they owned a lot of real estate in Terresonna and he could probably get them these fantastic oceanfront suites for a couple of weeks at a ridiculously cheap rate and Hazel started acting very suspicious and said she'd heard *that* one before about how some people's ridiculously cheap rate was the next person's excuse for murder let alone shady deals, unethical rackets, crossing interstate lines with stolen property, illegal prostitution, the Mann Act, off-track betting, bookies getting their brains kicked out, and the Mafia.

"Stop it," Suzi said, and Moke, who was about to say, "Oh for crying out loud," didn't say anything. The three of them stopped dead in their tracks. "I think we ought to go back to our room now," Hazel said, as Moke sank back against the nearest building and was suddenly very tired.

"I really wish you would come," Moke said to Suzi. "I'd even pay your airfare down. Don't worry about the money—that's the last thing to worry about."

"That's very nice of you," Suzi said.

"Thanks but no thanks," Hazel said. "How does that grab you?"

"Oh, stop being so rude, would you!" Suzi said. "My God, you're a case!" and she took Hazel off to the side. The two stood ten feet away from him, yakking for quite some while—Moke thought he could distinguish bitchy, paranoid tones coming from the old woman, supplicating inflections from Suzi, but he wasn't certain. This is the way the world ends, Moke thought, surrounded by twenty-story office buildings in the middle of the night—and then chuckled at his own sentimentality. He was getting almost too tired to care. A wizened drunk wandered by and gave Moke a distant Howarya ol' buddy. Same to you, ol' buddy, Moke waved back. Then Suzi was coming toward him as if in a dream and she had a very serious expression on her face and he could smell her perfume and God was she beautiful—and he realized for the first time how much she resembled . . . Julie, just a miraculous physical resemblance, no doubt about it—and he realized how stupid it was to care about what happened now as much as he actually did care and then she said: "We've talked this over and we're going to give your offer serious consideration." Moke held his breath. "I really want to come," she said. "I just have to talk her into it."

"Can't *you* come then? Why worry about her?" Moke said.

"I have to," Suzi said. "She's a wreck. I really ought to get her back." They both looked over at Hazel who was positioned by the curb in her waiting-for-a-taxi pose. In the baggy purple dress, she looked indescribably slutty. Suzi sighed.

"There's something you should understand, Moke," Suzi said, bringing her face very close to his. A startling amount of pain was visible in her lovely eyes. "I wouldn't tell you this except that I think you're probably very sweet and will understand. You see . . . ," she said, "Hazel is my mother."

They arranged it. Every day Suzi came to meet him at the Library at two, four, and six—between acts—smelling of lilacs and smiling in her plain polkadot dress, hair pulled back, and her white-rimmed sunglasses to cover up the heavy mascaraed eyejob. At two and four, she had ten minutes. At six, they had time for dinner and a stroll along Garfield Place before the evening show. Always she had her hair pulled back "like a school teacher" and the white-rimmed sunglasses and usually she had nothing on under the drab dress she had thrown over her head in order to run out the alley door and up the street to the Library and Moke. It was hot during the day but pleasant in the evenings and the pigeons cooed and waddled around the park benches, and Moke and Suzi would sometimes sit and he would stare up through the blue air above Suzi's head, above the buildings and the Hudepohl Beer sign and the faintly waving branches of the young sycamore trees along Garfield Place and marvel at his incredible luck and wish this would never end.

Her real name was Sonya, it turned out, Sonya Velonis. That she was willing to tell him her real name seemed promising—if it *was* her name. (Obviously her real name couldn't be Suzi Sinzinnati! though he *had* gotten used to thinking of her as Suzi.)

They had *not* given him a definite answer the first day about Florida—just that Hazel was thinking it over, and Suzi (Sonya) said *she* "really wanted to." Then Thursday in the park, Sonya said: "This is going to go over like a pregnant pole-vaulter, but . . . " and she told him they had decided to sign up for another week at the Gayety—the new road show came in on Fridays but they were short some dancers and the manager put the pressure on for them to stay on—but *the good thing* about this, she said, was it would give them time to get to know each other better and give the women time to save up some extra money for the Florida trip and for Hazel to get used to the idea. This was a *very positive sign*, Sonya said, that Hazel was serious about the trip because they were both *fed up* with Cincinnati and wanted to get back home—Montreal, of all places: they were Canadians. But winter wasn't *that* far away, and Hazel wasn't *that* hot to get back to freezing weather so soon, and Hazel figured they deserved a vacation after "grinding their asses off all summer long with a bunch of filthy people in every filthy slum in every filthy city in the United States." Moke wrote to his parents and said he had run into an old college friend—what a coincidence!—a very nice girl who was visiting relatives in Cincinnati and he had asked this girl, and of course her mother, who was in Cincinnati (visiting relatives with her daughter) to come back to Florida with him and they just might do it!

"That pre-marital coitus is often unsatisfactory is commonly believed by most persons and asserted with considerable positiveness by many who consider such activity morally wrong. Many of those who have written on the subject . . . assert that pre-marital activity always brings psychologic disturbance and lasting regrets. The positiveness of these assertions might lead one to believe that they were based on sufficient investigations of the fact, but data which might sufficiently support such statements have never

been accumulated by these writers or by other students in this field. . . .
As a matter of fact, some 69 per cent of the still unmarried females in the
sample who had coitus insisted that they did not regret their experience
(Table 92)."

Way to go Kinsey! This is what the empirical method is all about! You want to know the number of teeth in a horse's mouth, you *count* them! Zoology 102.

Moke rubs the back of his neck and scans the aisle with a shrewd, thoughtful glint in his eye. He is seated in an enormous, airy room on the second floor of the Cincinnati Public Library, chrome and imitation walnut tables, green naugahyde seats, this way a battery of cardfiles, that way distant plateglass overlooking Garfield Place, acres of chest-high shelves from anthropology to spectoscropy, bulletin boards cleverly arranged by experts, elevators, men's room, check out desk-in-the-round with the crisp 29-year-old librarian who doesn't seem to mind at all giving him Kinsey's report on *Sexual Behavior in the Human Female*—a red-hot, under-the-counter item.

His watch reveals: it is almost time for Suzi. He folds his thumb into Kinsey and places the spine up against his shirt where no one will see it: no need to cause a sensation. He glides around the tables and racks towards the men's room like a smooth-running fullback in slow-motion. You have to look confident: as if you know *where* you're going, as if you know *what* you're going to do there. Good advice. He straightarms the door, dodges through, confronts himself in a solid band of mirrors above limpid white-throated lavatories and a marble shelf. Such luxury in this castle of his, he thinks, looking around for the urinals. Instead his eyes alight upon a Kotex dispenser on the wall and his blood jumps! Oh my God! He's in the ladies head! He does an abrupt about face just as a toilet begins flushing loudly and an approaching tap-tap-tap-tap-tap-tapping of high heels is heard through the door in the outer aisle. Oh my God! Quick, he tries to enter one of the stalls: they are pay toilets. His thumb is still stuck in the *Kinsey Report*. He drops the book with a bang. He fumbles wildly with the dime. Slips it in the slot, kicks the book with his toe, whips the handle loose and open, rides the door closed with his speeding body. Click! Whew! He picks up the book to dust it off and hears the tap-tap-tap-tap-tap-tapping getting closer. Frantically, he realizes his pantlegs and feet are visible from underneath. He raises one leg and looks around for some place to put the other. The only fulcrum available is the toilet seat itself. He is in a sweat. He places one foot on the toilet seat and raises the other up in position on the opposite side of the open lid and squats there, gripping the *Kinsey Report* in a deathlock against his bent thigh, thinking "Oh, no!" A part of his mind is working over the geometry of this horrid faux pas. His mind hypothesizes: Isn't it true that the 1st floor men's room is exactly in this location? The outer door swings and the tap-tap-tap-tap-tap-tapping enters stage center, comes closer, closer; there is a pause, the snap of a pocketbook. Moke holds his breath. Oh my God! She enters the stall next to his. He hears a sliding of cloth, and then a stream of urine thunders into the commode. He fights an impulse to cover his ears and begins to giggle quietly instead. He tries to squelch this immediately but only giggles harder. He punches himself in the stomach and clears his throat as sedately as possible. This only starts him giggling again. What has he *ever* done to deserve this? What untoward series of events brought him to this juncture? English 101. He cackles hysterically into his kneecap. The woman is taking forever. He leans forward to get a glimpse of the shoes, but they are too far under. He tips too far forward and almost falls from his perch. Some scribbling on the wall: "What is the cure for the rare Hawaiian disease lackanookie?"

"Slipadictomy." Oh, no.

Moke realizes he has to get ahold of himself. Already he can see the headlines: TEEN PUNK NABBED IN MORALS ARREST. His father opens the crackling newspaper, fresh from his doorstep, leans back in his white wrought-iron breakfast chair, and reads incredulously: STRIPPER'S BOYFRIEND IS LOCAL RESIDENT, MOKE GALENAILLE HELD ON LEWD AND LASCIVIOUS CHARGE, BOND SET AT 100 M.

Suddenly, the tap-tap-tap-girl is stirring and clicking. The toilet flushes loudly; the door latch pings. She taps to the mirror. Water gurgles. Tap-tap-tap, she prances around. The towel roller creaks and vibrates. Rip, the towel flies off. Again! Creak-rumble, rip! Moke strains to hear the taps leaving; he doesn't hear anything! Could he have lost it in the noise of the towel roller?! He waits, waits, holding his breath; finally he is rewarded by the squeak of a heel, and the tap-tap-tap-tap-tapping recedes steadily. A rush of air signals the door has been thrown open. The pneumatic hinge exhales slowly and mightily, then all is quiet. Stealthily, his hand moves the doorlatch aside, and he peeks out. All clear. He zips around the stall-door. Three giant steps and he skirts the outer panel, seizes the chromium doorhandle, flings it, and is out, walking steadily down the aisle next to spectroscopy, his nose straight ahead, arms pumping fluidly at his sides, a man with a purpose and with no time to waste. He takes the stairway door and dives the three landings to the ground floor in two hops each, his soles stinging all the way. He turns the corner by the elevators, crosses behind the groundfloor circulation desk to the card catalog, opens a drawer, any drawer, and begins to take notes at a furious pace: LC number, author, title, date of publication. Crouched over, writing so briskly, he is obviously a man who has been hard at work for a good two hours. *"I don't have any idea what you're talking about, Officer. . . . "* A hand touches his shoulder and he jumps. He turns around. It's Suzi! Smelling of lilacs and smiling between acts and in her plain polkadot dress, hair pulled back, and her white-rimmed sunglasses to cover up the heavy mascaraed eye-job she wears on stage. Moke rests his head against her shoulder and says "Whew!"

"What's the matter?" Suzi says, laughing at him.

"You won't *believe* what just happened to me!" Moke says.

When the "new road show" came in on Friday, Sonya got Moke in through the alley door. He could watch the show whenever he got tired of reading or walking around. The "new star" was a red-haired vixen with cat-eyes and a sleek, sensuous body. Moke had to admit she wasn't that bad. She would come in wearing a leopard skin under a thick velvet dress and walk back and forth like a debutante and when the faster music started she would peel to the leopard skin and dash around the stage, snarling and hissing and making clawing motions with her fingernails. After that, she would go into her bump-and-grind routine; she would untie her hair, a gorgeous full-bodied cascade of curling orange mane, and cup her breasts and then slide her fingers slowly down across her belly and under the G-string and touch herself and then she would lick her fingers and wink. And she liked to talk to the audience: she would say, "It's the *only* thing there is, Baby," rubbing herself. "It's the only thing that really matters. Oh, do it to me!" And the fast music and loud drumming would pick up and she would start her pelvis bumping and humping and climax with three or four high-pitched screams of parodied ecstasy. Moke asked Sonya what she thought of the new "star," and Sonya said she was okay except that she was a lesbian and was always trying to feel her up. Moke said does that happen very often backstage and Sonya said are you kidding, it's an occupational liability. Moke said, "Really! Who does it?" Sonya said: "Everybody except me and my mother."

One afternoon before dinner they were walking along Garfield Place. Sonya liked to hold hands as they walked and talked. The pigeons cooed. The rush hour traffic poured out of Shillitoes Parking and off Vine Street and gathered in slow-moving lines on either side of the park, gleaming pastel masterpieces from Detroit's keenest-eyed designers, Oldsmobiles and Buicks with brand new tires heading home to Madeira and Amberly Village and Indian Park with seats and trunks full of spice-racks and ironing boards and vacuum cleaners and fall fashions and back-to-school supplies and end-of-the-season-sale bikinis at half-off and Ricky Nelson's new 45 "Young Emotions" and Camay beauty soap and Lavoris and plastic garbage bags and spot remover.

It made Moke depressed for some reason. Sonya wanted to know what was wrong.

"Oh, I'm thinking about Julie Greenway," he said.

"Is she the girl you just broke up with?" Sonya said.

"She's the one," Moke said.

He had already told Sonya—the first night—that there was "this girl" he had broken up with, and Sonya had seemed, you know, really understanding about it and everything. But he hadn't wanted to talk about it in front of Hazel. Sonya had said: "Do you make a habit of picking up burlesque girls," and Moke said "No—this is the first time. Up until yesterday, I was going steady with the same girl for the last three years!" and even Hazel seemed to understand that, and to soften up and look at him a little wistfully. It made sense to them; maybe it made him seem less threatening.

Now that he was alone with Sonya and she looked so much like Julie (and here he was in Cincinnati, his old lost home) and everything seemed almost perfect—he was suddenly impressed by how crazy it all was, what a nutty fantasy he was trying to act out, what a blow he was setting himself up for. Jesus, it was incredible. Within two weeks, at the best, he would pack Sonya off to Montreal and probably never see her again. What a totally screwed-up world.

"Did she break up with you," Sonya said, "or did you break up with her?"

"I—she . . . *I* don't know. I can't figure out *what* happened. A little bit of both. . . . "

"Go ahead," Sonya said. "Tell me everything."

He did. He told her everything, almost everything. He told her about last year, about leaving Indian Park, about medicine, about Duke. He told her about how sometimes he just wanted to say "Fuck it all" and to take off across country on a Honda 350 and work in the fields and pick grapes and "be physical." "I mean, maybe that's my true destiny," he said. He told her about how *he* never really wanted to be a doctor anyway—it was really Julie's idea. Now that this fantasy of theirs was exploded, why should he go on living as if it still existed?

"You're really very sweet, you know that?" Sonya said. "I really like you."

"I like you too," Moke said . . . "You know something?"
"What?"

"The craziest part is that you remind me of her—Julie. You remind me of Julie. I hope that doesn't make you upset." She thought about it.

"No, how could it? It's very flattering."

"I do want to get to know *you*."

"I want to get to know you too. I think you're basically a very nice person."

"You're the nicest person I've ever met," Moke said.

She leaned over and kissed him on the cheek. Moke brushed his lips across her cheek and kissed her mouth. It was a beautiful mouth—a hot, stinging, luscious kiss.

"I'll give you thirty minutes," Sonya said, breathlessly, "to cut that out."

Bill Galenaille
General Manager
c/o WTSF Radio
Terresonna, Florida

DEAR DAD STOP SOMETHING HAS COME UP
STOP BETTER SEND AMERICAN EXPRESS
CARD AFTER ALL STOP SEND TO DOC AT
CINCINNATI CLUB ADDRESS ASAP STOP
WILL EXPLAIN EVERYTHING UPON RETURN
STOP WILL ABSOLUTELY PAY YOU BACK I
PROMISE STOP LOVE MOKE

Chapter Six

Oh—Malinda, she's a solid senda
You know you better surrenda
Oh—Malinda, she's a solid senda
You know you better surrenda
Slippin' and slidin', peepin' and hidin'
Won't be your fool no more

MOKE GOT OFF THE BUS at Eighth and Vine and looked around. Downtown Cincinnati. Up Vine Street, the Netherland Hilton. Across the street, the library's mosaic pillars and the seductive red Gayety beyond: Burlesque—CONTINUOUS spelled out in frosted light bulbs; an old, dilapidated, tawdry building with an orange and red marquee and streetside blowups of semi-nude beauties in rhinestone-studded G-strings. "Get the Gayety Habit" a big joke at I.P.H.S.

The Cincinnati Club on Garfield Place was a heavy stone milk carton of a building with a doorman and a white-fringed blue awning out to the curb like some kind of hotel. Moke mounted a short flight of marble stairs to the lobby. Off to his left he could see another large room with leather chairs and couches inside, a huge fireplace, the glittering tips of chandeliers dangling just beneath the oak-trimmed doorway.

He found out Doc's room number from the desk clerk and went up ten floors and down a long hall to room 1012 and knocked. No sound from within. Another knock on silence. Doc was slow. He tried the knob. The door was not locked. He went inside and closed the door behind. All the lights were on. A rumpled bed. A cluttered dresser bearing the familiar gold-framed 8 x 10 glossy of Lt. Commander C. F. Galenaille, U.S. Navy—Doc in middle age—a memento he must have salvaged before Bee locked him out. No sign of the occupant, however. Smashed M & M bags in the waste basket—huge bags. The bathroom equally vacant. The half-opened medicine cabinet unbelievably crammed with small bottles, squeezed out tubes, pill samples, spilled (orange and purple) tinctures, syringes, tweezers, a hypodermic needle. Three damp M & M's adhered in the throat of the lavatory.

He thought about the crazy game his father and Doc always played in restaurants, never tiring of it; and Moke always got rooked into it when he was with them. They would have lunch at Frisches or some other restaurant, and when it was time to pay the bill Moke's father would say, "Moke, you take this bill over to the waitress and tell her that your *grandfather*, the doctor, would like to pay for everything. And you point to him over here so she is sure to know which one he is." Doc would wheeze in delight at this, and when the waitress finally showed up, Doc would point to his younger brother, Moke's father, and say "Give the bill to my *father* over there. He likes to pay all the bills," or alternately, "Give the bill to my *uncle* over there," pointing to Moke. Then he would go into a wheezing fit as Moke's chuckling father would say to the waitress, "My father over there is quite a joker, isn't he?" At this point the waitress would drop the check and remember some pressing business she had to do in the kitchen, anything to get away from these two chortling maniacs, who were now both reaching for their wallets and about to start arguing, "I'll get it. *You* got it the last time." "No, *you* got it the last time. Let me get this one."

Moke peed and went back to the bedroom and sat down on the bed. After that he paced for a while and looked out the window at an array of sooty rooftops. It was pretty depressing to see Doc's room like this. Since his second wife, Bee, had divorced him, Doc was more or less destitute and helpless. Did he receive some kind of a pension? Moke wondered. How did he live? His hands were too shaky for surgery anymore, even if the City of Cincinnati hadn't condemned his building and the neighborhood it was in in a fit of urban renewal and destroyed his practice. For thirty-five years Doc had run the only small private emergency "hospital" in Cincinnati's West End, the black ghetto. The Galenaille Hospital contained one doctor, Doc, one nurse, Gertrude, and Ruby, the black receptionist and records clerk. Every time Moke visited at the hospital every seat in the waiting room was filled and people were leaning against the walls up and down the hallway and sitting on the endtables. When Doc emerged from his office—he always came to get his patients in person—he carried his left arm as if in a sling with the forefinger pointing outward as in a perpetual frozen gesture of "next." Even then, before his Parkinson's disease, his relatives habitually referred to him as "poor Doc." Maybe they thought he worked too hard for too little in return or didn't have the sense to look out for himself. In fact, he seemed a man almost entirely without self-pity or self-concern, generous and gullible to a fault, a big avuncular bear of a man with a clipped white chevron of mustache like some VIP rear admiral in the RAF.

Doc's first wife, Edith, also a physician, was an extraordinary Chinese woman he had met in medical school. She died young—Moke barely remembered her—but her influence permeated Doc's tastes, his lifestyle, every aspect of his existence. Doc's large Tudor-style house on Springfield Pike was full of Oriental rugs and expensive Chinese antiques, elaborate carved ivory figurines and enameled boxes and hulking inlaid cabinets with sliding panels and intricate drawers that Moke snooped through as a small boy. In the fall the backyard was full of rotting apples because Doc never had the time to worry about them, and two denuded cherry trees hung with tiny mirrors that tinkled in a breeze and were supposed to frighten birds away, though Moke personally sat in the trees most of one summer Sunday afternoon and the birds gobbled cherries all around him.

Doc's second wife, Bee, was a fortyish beautician from down the block who went into early retirement soon after she married the doctor. She slept late, wore fuzzy house slippers and gap-opus bathrobes in the middle of the day, and wasn't much of a housekeeper. When word leaked out that she was "too god-damned lazy" to get up and make Doc's breakfast for him in the morning, some of the Galenaille relatives decided she was uppity, slovenly, and had only married Doc for his money. When Moke's family visited evenings, Doc would be lying around in his baggy underwear watching "I Love Lucy" on his old black and white TV set and wheezing and snorting with grateful laughter and Bee would be sitting in the other room, her plumpish legs crossed at the thigh, filing and manicuring her nails in one of her severe pulled-back hairdos, waiting for Doc to die—or so it was ventured. In spite of everyone else's opinion of her, Doc was utterly devoted to Bee throughout their marriage, which lasted longer than anyone but Doc suspected. He doted on her and idolized her and was so wounded when she sought to divorce him (older and sicker and getting a little foolish) that he let her have everything she wanted—which was nearly everything he owned, his house and everything in it, a fortune in antiques, everything but his Cadillac and the clothes on his back—probably even the old stiff merit badge jacket that Doc would get out of a trunk in an upstairs closet about once-a-year at Bill's insistence and display for Moke.

Doc actually had been, in his long past youth, an Eagle scout and one of the earliest serious scouts since scouting had been organized in the state. Doc had been, technically and officially, *the* first Eagle scout in the state of Ohio, and he still had a yellowed news clipping to prove it and thirty-eight merit badges sewn all over the front, shoulders, and up and down the sleeves of what looked like a WW I moth-eaten army infantry jacket. The jacket in all its glory was too small and tight in the armpits for even slender Moke. It was difficult for Moke to imagine how it might ever have fit such a huge-limbed, corpulent, walrus-faced fellow as his Uncle Doc; but of course, it had, it had. Bill impressed this upon him. Moke was *related* to the first Eagle scout in the state of Ohio. Thus, he was given to understand, his own horizons were similarly unlimited.

The door opened and the venerable scout himself shuffled into the room. He was clutching a box of Kentucky Fried chicken and showed no surprise at seeing Moke perched on the bed.

"Why, hello there, Uncle Moke! Looks like you beat me home."

"Yep."

"I'm not as fast as I used to be, that's for sure."

"You look pretty chipper to me."

"I thought we could eat this good chicken right here in the room, if it's okay with you, Uncle Moke. It's Kentucky Fried—they don't make it any better than that."

"Sure thing."

"The last time I went to the dining room downstairs I fell down twice, once going in and once coming out. I ran into a table and spilled silver platters all over the floor."

"That's okay. I'd rather eat here anyway, Doc."

"I got us some dandy sauerkraut. I bet it's the best you've ever tasted."

"Terrific, let me at it." Moke jumped up and began clearing off the edge of the dresser, then pulled up two of the heavy mahogany chairs and arranged them catty-cornered to the feast in the box.

"I've got a nice bottle of Seagram's here somewhere," Doc said, rooting in a drawer.

"That's okay. Water's okay for me." Moke went in to the lavatory and ran himself a glass of water.

"You sure?"

"Yep."

"Then we can have M & M's for dessert." Doc threw back his head and wolfed a handful of M & M's, which he began chewing like a dog with taffy in its teeth.

"Want some?"

"No thanks. I'll wait until afterwards, I guess."

"Well, how's your little girlfriend, Uncle Moke? I'll bet she was glad to see you, wasn't she?"

"Yeah, she sure was."

"Why don't you bring her down for a visit some time, Uncle Moke? We could have a night on the town. I'd like to meet her . . . I sure would. You know me, Uncle Moke. I always had a way with the ladies, yesiree. We could live it up, just the three of us."

"I can't make any promises, Doc, but I'll see what she has to say on the subject."

"Don't worry, Uncle Moke. I won't try to take her away from you. I'll behave myself. I'll be a paragon of virtue."

"I know you will."

"The old Kentucky Galenailles always had a way with the opposite sex, you know. They knew what to do and when to do it, but they always behaved like gentlemen."

"I know it."

"They caused a lot of heartbreak in their day, of course, but they never did it on purpose. They were faithful and true."

"You've told me all about it before."

"Somebody should write it all down before it's forgotten—you know that—the history of the old Kentucky Galenailles. It would be a bestseller I bet."

"Yep."

"I bet it would sell a million copies with no trouble at all."

Out on the street Moke felt relieved to have the dinner over but a little bit out of his head. He needed something. He felt almost faint. He zipped away from the blue awning of the Cincinnati Club at lightning speed. Cincinnati. His city. He rounded the corner at Vine and zig-zagged a block toward the Gayety. Once, when Doc was still practicing, Moke had gone down to his office for a shot and while preparing the needle and syringe Doc had told him how one patient in every ten thousand dies instantly upon receiving a simple shot in the arm. Doc wasn't trying to scare him or anything. Rather he was imparting essential medical information that might come in handy for a future medical student. Not every medical student, after all, had the benefit of counsel and experience of a close relative who was already a member of the profession. Doc had even taken him to Good Samaritan Hospital the week before, where Moke had donned a greenish surgical costume and stood without fainting for two hours in the corner of an operating room (proving he could do it) watching blood drip into a washtub-sized basin from the uterus of a completely swathed, anonymous, and invisible woman undergoing a hysterectomy. Still, on the day of the shot, one-in-ten-thousand odds seemed to Moke a slim, shaky margin in his favor, a completely unacceptable risk. What if you just happened to be *the one?* Was any shot worth taking the chance that you might be *the one?* The needle burned like fiery death in his arm muscle and when he stood up and began to walk down the narrow hall, hundreds of blue and yellow spots appeared before his eyes and passing clouds swept in from both sides, and the next thing he knew he was face down on a cot in a room he had never seen before thinking "so this is how it feels to die instantly" and Doc was applying a cold cloth to the side of his head and patting him on the shoulder and clucking to his mother somewhere in the distance.

If the blue and yellow spots started to appear while he was here in downtown Cincinnati, he would probably get smashed to a pulp by a hot-footed yellow cab or slump to the sidewalk battering both elbows and scraping his cheek until it was unrecognizable, like a gob of Kennel Ration. His wallet would slip down a gutter and no one would know who to telephone from the morgue. His remains would go on file as "unidentified white male, app. 18 years of age, with a small birthmark on his penis signifying that he died for love," as in an old folk ballad.

Hazel would never allow Sonya to be alone with him after show hours. "You have to try to understand about my mother," Sonya said. "She's had a rotten life; she doesn't trust people. She was involved in Chicago way back when; she's seen people murdered."

"Okay," Moke said.

Moke had been sleeping in a $3/night room on the tenth floor of the same hotel Sonya and Hazel were staying in—and every night before going to bed carefully checking the lumpy mattress for bedbugs. The women were sleeping until almost noon, rushing to the Gayety, working (except for breaks) until almost midnight, and then wandering about with him until three A.M.

Wednesday that week Sonya has surprised Moke at eleven in the morning in his shabby tenth-floor room and told him excitedly that Hazel had finally agreed to go! She is totally fed up with decadent Northern cities: filthy-minded perverts on every street corner, grime on every railing, trash in every trashcan, sweltering overcast skies without a drop of sun, and "foul-mouthed bitchy faggoty managers who aren't satisfied with a free feel now and then, but have to insult you viciously as often as possible—not to mention the art of the dance—just to get their rocks off."

Sonya has dragged Moke down to Shillitoes, that excellent store, where they are working their way through the women's swimsuit section—right next to slips and lingerie. Several decapitated mannikins, in various states of undress, hover atop garment racks—and are artfully arranged around the walls—causing Moke to continually avert his eyes. In a place like this it is pretty difficult to avoid looking suspicious, Moke thinks. How do you walk past a brassiere, for instance? It isn't easy. The eyes mustn't linger on these filmy creations or the vice cops will be on you in a minute.

Sonya has accumulated an armful of bathing suits. "Sit in this seat," she says, pointing, "and I'll try these on for you, love." He walks over, sits obediently in a corner between a mirrored pillar and a wall of blouses, grateful for a respite from the flying undergarments. Sonya disappears in the direction of the dressing rooms.

In two minutes she is back and barefoot, wearing a bright yellow Jantzan one-piece with meshed scoops at the sides—which shows off her sleek belly flesh. She parades back and forth before the mirrored pillar, giving him a bewitching kittenish smirk, spins and narrows her eyes critically at the mirror-image of her back and the line of the suit across her bottom, suddenly snaps elastic, giving him an instantaneous heart-stopping view, and flits back to the dressing room. The next suit is a turquoise bikini, alarmingly spare. The ritual is repeated seven or eight times—he loses track. A saleswoman appears and tries to involve herself, but Sonya ignores her.

Sonya marches out in yet another stunning creation, eyes herself in the mirror, rocks up on her toes, back on her heels, flexes her thigh muscles, does a deep knee-bend, takes a deep breath, slowly exhales and smiles—idiotically. "What is this?" he wonders. "Her daily work-out?"

She comes out finally, ready to go. Moke stands up, jiggling change. She snags his wrist. "I could only get three on under my dress," she whispers, slipping a tiny folded flag of cloth into his hand. "Can you get this into your pants? Oh, please." Without thinking, he gingerly pockets the thing, figuring it to be a handkerchief, and only after it is pressed snugly against his leg and they are heading airily for the doors, does the implication of what she has said register.

Oh-my-God, they are *shoplifting*—sirens start to go off in his brain. He has never stolen *anything* in his life except a box of caps from a dimestore once when he was five years old and he is still guilty about *that*. They could be busted any minute and so long to Medical School if that ever happens. He brushes his hair back nervously and realizes his forehead is beaded with sweat. Sonya is

74

dawdling over a glass case full of jewelry. Ye gods! Every house dick in the place probably has them under surveillance. He mustn't look too fidgety or scan the aisles for the law. Just stay cool and act very interested in tiny pearl earrings and sixteen kinds of ugly floral sunbursts. Then when Sonya smiles, all nonchalance and regal aplomb, what else is there to do but follow her smoothly out the revolving doors and into the wave of sultry August air and out along the grainy sidewalks of the Queen City, gawking at the crossfire of happy shoppers, the chaos of utility poles and elegant black asphalt, and pray to high Heaven that the house dick is not there now in that vacuum you feel near your spine, getting ready to pinch your arm between his bulbous nicotine-stained fingers, flash the badge, and haul you off to the clink in his conspicuously unmarked car with the gun-metal blue Smith & Weston automatic in its carefully oiled dash-mounted holster.

Safe on a bench at Garfield Place there are a few things to hash out.

"Oh, wow," Sonya says. "Now we have to go. There's no stopping us—no matter what Hazel says or does."

"Jesus, Sonya, you had me scared shitless. What are you trying to do?"

"Did you see me come? I hoped you wouldn't mind. I do have some little turn-ons that take a while to get used to."

"You mean in the store?"

"Right in front of the mirror, silly! Didn't you see me? I was absolutely beautiful."

"I don't think so," Moke says, puzzled. "You mean you did it right in the middle of the store?"

"Well, I got it started in the dressing room. You know. But I had the orgasm in front of the mirror."

"Jesus, Sonya. You are too much."

"I hope you don't mind," she says, looking suddenly worried. "Sometimes I get so incredibly pent up after dancing. . . . I started to get so excited thinking how gorgeous I would look in these new things! I used to masturbate a lot," Sonya says, "sometimes six times a day."

"God, that must be some kind of record," Moke says.

"I doubt it," Sonya says. "You don't *know* how many over-sexed people there are in this world. . . . Of course, at first I was very, very private about it; but when I was about thirteen I branched out into doing it in public or in boring classes or during the horrible, interminable sermons when I was a member of the choir. I always had a fantasy of doing it with the collection plate, but I could never figure out *how* exactly. Must have been pretty horny all right."

"*How* could you do it?"

"All I did then was cross my legs and squeeze the thigh muscles together over and over. It's easy for girls. God, I have a hard time sometimes keeping from coming just walking to the drugstore in a pair of tight Levi's!"

"But didn't you make noise or anything?"

"I would just disguise it by having a coughing fit or clearing my throat or pretending to lean over and scratch my leg or something. No one ever had any idea what I was doing, of course. I barely did myself. They just thought I coughed and itched a lot—a nervous adolescent, you know. . . .

"Then when I was sixteen or so, I was going out with this older man who kept taking me to restaurants where there were, like, tablecloths that hung down all around and the lighting was low and 'romantic.' He kept feeding me spicy foods and luscious liquor and the usual lines, and he never suspected that while I was demurely eating with one hand. . . . "

"No!"

"Yes! It was all I could do to keep a straight face. Some of the time I wanted to tip over the table and pull my skirt up to my belly button, no matter who was watching. But, luckily, I resisted that impulse, which was a good thing. I mean, besides the possibility of getting busted and everything, I found out I really dig doing it close to people sometimes, without them knowing it . . . like with you in that store we were in."

"That's pretty weird all right, but there's no point in being guilty about it, I guess."

"Right. I decided I don't care how weird it is. It doesn't hurt anybody, right? . . . The reason I'm telling you this, Moke. . . . You see, well. . . . I know we're going to be seeing a lot of each other in Florida if we go, and I want you to know that I like you a lot. I really do. But I do have some quirks that you should know about. You might have the idea that because of my job at the Gayety and everything that I'm a certain kind of girl."

"No, not at all. What do you mean by that?"

"Well, this may come as a surprise to you, Moke. But, in spite of my strange life and oversexed habits, I'm still what is known as . . . 'a virgin.' Pretty astonishing, isn't it?"

"Too much," Moke says.

"It's just one of those things I happen to feel very strongly about, and I want you to understand that, okay?"

"Okay."

"I knew you would understand! The reason I agreed to come in the first place was because I was convinced you are such an understanding person, Moke Galenaille, and, lucky for me, you really are!" She kisses him hard on the mouth. "Uh-oh, now I bet I've gone and wetted through all three swimsuits!"

Then she rushes off to the Gayety for her second-to-last day of humping.

It was enough to mention to Doc that Moke's "little girlfriend" had decided to go back to Florida with him, since he *did* have to go back so soon, and that her mother was coming along too, to elicit an enthusiastic avuncular offer of transportation to the airport. No need to complicate the explanation with too many details such as the fact, for instance, that this particular little girlfriend was not the same little girlfriend that he had come to Cincinnati to see in the first place, or that this little girlfriend was really a Gayety stripper named Suzi Sinzinnati who just happened to be a virgin, believe it or not, but had nevertheless been setting Sin City on its ear, or at least that portion of Sin City that constituted Gayety audiences, for the last two weeks now with her incredible body and her sheer unaided lewd and lascivious imagination. Or that his girlfriend's mother was really Hazel Storm, witchy Hazel of the sagging tits and catcalls, who was probably a reformed hooker or maybe one of Al Capone's or one of his henchman's old mistreated bootlicking, hoity-toity, garter-snapping, punched-in-the-eye-and-spat-upon-and-abused flagrant hussies a long time ago in Chicago.

The gold Cadillac limousine service was supposed to meet them in Government Square, where they would be presumed to have disembarked from the Indian Park bus and, in fact, had just labored four blocks over from their fleabag hotel struggling with Hazel's ratty cardboard suitcases, overstuffed shopping bags, and a

77

two-ton hat box crammed with heavy make-up containers. Much to Moke's relief, Doc was already there, in plain sight waiting when they arrived, the Cadillac wedged between two buses next to a fire hydrant, the right front tire resting at a cockeyed angle up on the sidewalk. The women were, of course, pleased and impressed with the car and willingly humored the driver, who plied them with M & M's and a story or two about the old Kentucky Galenailles all the way to the airport and kept saying "Gesundheit" over his shoulder as Hazel's hay fever was acting up and she kept sneezing in the backseat and pressing a frayed bit of Kleenex to her nostrils. Doc wandered off in the airport lobby, luckily enough, and was absent when one of Hazel's valises broke open in the middle of the floor, revealing fake furs and feathers, a black lace garter belt, long gloves, and sequined pasties rolling like mice—which might have been a little difficult to explain on the spur of the moment. At the last instant before boarding, Doc reappeared and pressed a red box of Dristan into Hazel's palm that he had managed to find somewhere in a vending machine and earned himself a "why, you dear man!" and a spontaneous peck on the puss for his trouble.

Chapter Seven

Earth an-jel, earth an-jel
Plee-eease be mi-hine
My dahling dea-hear
Lo-ove you all-hall the ti-hime
I'm just a foo-hool
A fool in love with yooou

"THE WAY IT WAS with Julie and me . . . ," Moke says, "everything was so magnified. It was the separation—partly. Like, there we were a thousand miles apart and just dying for each other, longing, longing, writing letters every day. Like, the biggest emotional event of every day was just going to the university post office. No kidding. And some days she would write me ten or fifteen-page letters. We got to the point where she would write to me in the nude—that was a rule—she *had* to write in the nude and I would get these incredible erections even if she was just talking about how she blew her Calc exam because I knew she was in the nude when she wrote that. Then I would write back an eleven-page letter telling her about this terrible erection her last letter had given me and how I had to skip dinner because of it—and, you know, things like that. We made fun of ourselves but it was killing us. It was really killing us."

"I know what you mean," Sonya says.

Moke stares out across the perfect sweep of curving metal to the hood emblem of his 1954 orange Pontiac: it's an Indian head with a light inside, though now the light is out. They are parked on top of the circular drive at the Terresonna Municipal Beach. The crickets are singing their hearts out in the sumac and scrub palm thickets along the oceanfront.

"And then we'd have these two-or-three day visits over Christmas or Easter, and we'd spend the whole god-damned time in bed in the hotel room, just lying in bed all day making love. . . . And talking. Just. . . . We wouldn't even eat! We'd forget about eating and get absolutely starved and go out for a walk. Then when we finally did eat, everything was so delicious it practically killed you—it practically gave you another orgasm."

"It must be terrible to lose something like that."

"Oh, we were so dumb. We should have gotten married or something, but we were too young to know any better."

"I don't think marriage cures everything necessarily."

"No. Of course not. I don't think so either. But . . . "

"I'm not going to get married until I'm at least twenty-eight or twenty-nine."

"Really!"

"I want to meet a lot of different people. I want to travel. There's so much to *do*."

"Yeah," Moke says. "I know what you mean. Still, if you happen to meet someone you want to *stay* with . . . what do you do?"

"I guess if I had had a better example of domestic bliss in my own family, I'd be more impatient about it, about, you know, about running out and getting married or something."

"What happened?"

"In my family?"

"Yeah."

"Hazel and my father fight all the time. You know. They aren't divorced, but they can't be around each other for five minutes without going berserk. Hazel starts throwing dishes. My father has to leave."

"Why does she do it? Because of what happened to her in Chicago?"

"No, not really. It's not all her fault." Pause.

It is hard to believe that Julie had been sitting in that same car seat not two months before and that now Sonya is here. Sonya seems far more gorgeous than Julie . . . from a purely physical point of view—he recognizes that now—it isn't really disloyal to admit that, merely a fact. Sonya is so . . . healthy and sensuous, so velvety and uninhibited. Her fingers and toes are works of art. Her proportions are so cleverly turned out, so remarkable. This was evidently what Keats had been talking about all along. Now he can feel it—now he understands.

"God, what a beautiful night. Why don't we walk?" Moke says.

"Great." She slides out of her sandals, pulls on the doorhandle and gets out. Moke pauses a moment, watches her get out, framed in the open doorway, a sleek Aphrodite, cunningly revealed in the same turquoise bikini she has worn all day but no less dazzling or intimidating in his eyes. Stunning. She turns expectantly, sees he has not moved, and smiles bewitchingly. She is a woman who does not mind being admired. All poise and feminine grace. Willowy animal vitality. Moke leaps out, slams the door harder or more zestfully than need be and joins the divine creature. Together they walk out on the municipal pier among the deserted picnic tables as far as the beach-end and lean there against the railing, the canvas roof gently flapping overhead, crumpled napkins—eerily white—stirring in the wire containers, the immense concave of black ocean and night sky, the surf sucking and squirting, the smell of salt and green peppers and night-blooming jasmine. "You know what?" Moke says.

"What?"

"I've got a feeling this is going to be a good night. I really feel like—you know. Tonight, I think, is going to be good." Sonya slowly unbuttons the last three wood-buttons on his Hawaiian shirt and presses the cups of her bikinied breasts against his bare flesh, sliding her cheek along his shoulder, pressing her closed eyes against his throat. "You angel," he says, kissing her. "You perfect beautiful angel."

"Let's go down to the beach," she says softly. They follow the railing around to the stairs, descend to the dark beach. Moke unties his shoes, throws them off. The tide is out; the beach is enormous, acres of dimpled and scalloped white sand slipping and sinking now between their toes. In the shadows beneath the pier they walk through a forest of pilings. Moke corners Sonya against one of the pilings, embraces her, squeezes her gently against the coarse wood. She melts, forgets herself, raises her turquoise nylon Mons against his hard thigh, shivers, rocks slowly back, touches.

They walk on out of the shadow of the pier into the moonlit fringe of glistening wet-packed sand close to the water; a lavish gush of foam bathes them to the ankles. They stroll steadily north past the "Swim at Your Own Risk" sign, past a large wash-in of beached debris, holding each other, stumbling, kissing, collapsing finally in a tangle of arms and legs.

"Oh, God," Sonya says breathlessly, "I never thought we would make it to Florida. It's so beautiful I can't believe it." She unsnaps her halter and flips it.

"*You're* so beautiful I can't believe it," Moke says, taking her left breast in his mouth. He is convinced it is the prettiest, most succulent he has ever seen, in or out of girly magazines. The nipple is as bulbous as the end of a knockwurst. "Oh, Moke. . . . Moke, what's that light down there?"

"What light?"

"By the pier." He turns and looks. A bright oval of light is visible beside the pier railing, perhaps near the roof.

"It's just a spotlight, isn't it? Wasn't it there before?"

"I don't think so," Sonya says. "I don't remember it."

"See if it moves," Moke says. They watch intently for a moment; nothing happens. "In the meantime . . . ," Moke says. He places her other breast in his mouth, resting his head against her belly, and trains one eye on the fugitive light. Slowly, the eye closes. Sonya is raised up on her elbows, staring toward the pier. Her skin is as sweet-smelling as fresh peaches, strawberries, raspberries, apples, boysenberries, rhubarb.

"Un-oh, that light's moving. I think it's coming this way," Sonya says.

"What would a light be doing walking down the beach?" Moke says. He sits up and looks. Sure enough, there's this frigging light down by the pilings, flashing around. Sonya stands awkwardly, breasts bouncing, and starts brushing sand off her legs. With just her bikini bottoms on, she seems suddenly very unprotected and bare-looking.

"Uh-oh, where's my bra," she says. Moke hops up on his hands and knees and feels around at every probable black object he can see in the dimness, a coconut husk, a piece of drift wood, several stiff, crackly sections of dried seaweed.

"Here it is," Sonya says. As he stands up, she already has it fastened. The damned light is bigger than ever, a huge cone of whiteness glaring in their eyes. "Oh, God," Sonya says. "I hope we don't get in any trouble."

82

"There's nothing illegal about walking on the beach," Moke says. They start walking.

"Who could it be?" Sonya asks.

"Probably just some undersea monster, or a motorcycle gang—or maybe your mother," Moke says.

"Oh, you," Sonya says.

A hundred yards on down they can see it is nothing but a cop with a big silver flashlight. They walk slowly towards him, holding hands.

"What seems to be the trouble, Officer?" Moke says. He is an old mother with white hairs growing out of his ears and a rudimentary mouth. He doesn't smile.

"That your car up there—'54 Catalina with a cream roof?"

"That's mine all right," Moke says, "the orange one."

"Let's see your license." Moke pulls out his wallet and hands him the license.

"What's amatter? Am I illegally parked? I didn't see any signs."

"You know it's after midnight, don't you?"

"Is it illegal to park here after midnight? Gee, I didn't know that."

"No, it's not illegal; it's just suspicious-looking. Just one car and so on."

"Sorry, I don't understand."

"Somebody might think it's a stolen car."

"Oh, I see. Well, it's not. It's *not* a stolen car. It's my car."

"*I* know it's your car. And *you* know it's your car. And *she* knows it's your car. But it looks suspicious, you see what I mean? Just one car and so on."

The cop hands Moke his license back. "I wouldn't park here after midnight if I was you."

"Right," Moke says. "Well, we'll just be moving right along then, Officer. We just thought it would be nice to take a little stroll along the beach here. It's such a nice spot and everything."

"Yeah, I know all about that," the Officer says. "You may not know it, but I know all about what you was doing down there. You may not know it, but I was young once. I know all about that."

"Fine. I'm glad to hear it. Well, goodnight now," Moke says. "It *is* getting late. Thank you for your trouble, sir."

"If it wasn't so sick, I could laugh," Moke says, turning in the entrance at the Terresonna Bible Ranch. The Bible Ranch buildings are all dark now except for the ornamental lighting at the Elijah Roark "All One in Christ Jesus" Auditorium and the scattered illumined trees in the Garden of Gethsemane Prayer Park, which contains every tree that is indigenous to the Holy Land—some one hundred and twenty-eight in all. Moke steers the Pontiac with its glowing Indian head twice slowly around the swimming pool area, the dark bluish platform of the ten-foot board rising above the palmetto hedge like a frozen, square-eared brontosaurus, its tongue elegantly displayed for some celestial dentist. "Where shall we go now?" Moke says. "You think Hazel's asleep yet?"

"I doubt it."

"How about this?" Moke says. "How about this?" He pulls off next to the hedge in a leafy inlet adjacent to the pumphouse, kills the motor, and kisses her, kisses her, kisses her. The kiss lasts twenty minutes. Sonya is trembling, then quietly crying? This is an amazing reaction as far as Moke can tell. Without breaking the kiss, Moke touches her cheek. Yes, he sees, it is definitely wet. He stops for breath and looks around. They are shielded on three sides by walls of vegetation; the fourth side offers a panoramic view of the Plain of the Burning Bush, a wide open field of crabgrass. "What's the matter, Sonya?" He holds her. She hides her face on his chest and presses close to him.

"I want to stay with *you* tonight. I don't want to go back."

"You don't have to go back for a while."

"I don't want to go back at all."

"Why? Where could we go?"

"I don't want to see my mother. I just want to be with you."

"You don't have to see her. She'll be asleep. I'll come over early in the morning and we can go some place and be alone." Pause.

"Moke, I have to tell you something horrible," Sonya says.

This is what she tells him, trembling and crying: Her father, she whispers, who is a beautiful, passionate Greek man, impulsive and loving and considerate, had *done* things to her when she was thirteen, things he should have done to her mother. Hazel knew about these things, which was a terrible, terrible burden, she whispers. But even more terrible, she whispers, was that *she* liked what her father did to her. This was why her father went away and why they could never live together again. This was why, she whispers, she tries so hard to get along with Hazel, whose life is such a terrible ruin, such a terrible, terrible ruin.

She has stopped crying. She is smiling ruefully.

Moke cannot help himself: He asks, "What did he *do?*" She says she can't possibly tell him, as much as she would like to tell him—it's too difficult. He asks again: "Tell me!"

Sonya whispers: "I would *never* tell you this except that I think I might just probably be in love with you." She kisses him—her cheeks are still wet. Her angelic face is radiant with intensity. She presses her tongue against the roof of her mouth.

"He kissed me here," she whispers—touching herself— "with . . . with the tip of his tongue."

The next morning, their third in Florida—wild with sunshine. Sonya's and Hazel's apartment is in the "celebrity unit" at the Bible Ranch—two big double beds, a kitchenette, deluxe bath, walk-in closet, terrazzo floor, impressive view of Garden of Gethsemane Prayer Park and sun splashing on Plain of the Burning Bush, vegetation in carefully tended brilliance by the door. For them, all this luxury for $20/week—the "celebrity rate"— thanks to Moke's father. Already Hazel is bored out of her skull. "You're always running off and leaving me by myself," she says to Sonya this morning. "What kind of vacation is that? Staying out til all hours of the night! Leaving me alone. Flouncing around in that skimpy little skintight bikini, popping everybody's eyes out of their heads. I want to be out of here and doing a few things myself! Did you ever think of that? No! Of course not." All of this is a preliminary to walking the six short blocks downtown to try to rent-a-car at Avis on Main Street, a tactful suggestion Moke has contributed two days before. Finally Hazel flops on her new bargain-basement Panama hat and minces out, nearly tripping on the sandy terrazzo in her toeless wedgies. The jalousies rattle as she slams the door and clack-clocks away.

"Whew," Moke says. Sonya, quietly at the stove in her turquoise bikini, is scrambling eggs barefooted. The sight of her velvety back and fantastic bottom against the white porcelain brings a lump to his throat. God is she beautiful this morning, a bright-haired thoroughbred with two dimples showing above her waist-band, the luscious bulging arrogance of her turquoise nylon polka-dotted panties, the leggy nonchalance of a *Vogue* model. Words form in his head: "For a transitory, enchanted moment, man must have held his breath in the presence of this continent"—some quotation he remembers from Freshman English—"compelled into an aesthetic contemplation he neither understood nor desired, face to face for the last time in history with something commensurate to his capacity for wonder." Smiling wistfully, he hangs his chin over Sonya's shoulder and peers down into the skillet. "Good morning, world." He kisses her ear.

"Good morning to you," Sonya says, sliding her hands under-neath his shirt and pressing herself full-length into his arms. He kisses her breasts; she touches him through his bathing suit.

"Uh-oh, better close the curtains if we're going to do this," Moke says. The erection inside his jockstrap is killing him. Sonya whirls to the big windows on the Burning Bush side and quickly pulls the drawstring.

"She'll be back any minute," Sonya says.

"I don't care," Moke says, yanking the front drapes at that end of the room. He opens the door, sticks his head out into the heat-thick morning chirping, eyeballs it in both directions—all clear—slams the door shut, locks it, fastens the safety chain. Sonya shakes her breasts loose, heaves the bra, peels herself free of her turquoise panties, kicks them across the room. "That's one thing I like about you," Moke says, dropping his shirt, collapsing with her on the bed, sliding his eyebrows along sumptuous belly flesh. . . .

"What?" Sonya gasps. He buries his face in her perfumy muff—the nearest he has ever been to such luxury.

"You're so modest!"

"Wait a minute," Sonya says. "The eggs are burning." She leaps up, sashays to the stove, deals with the egg problem by dumping them in the sink and flooding them.

"Uh-oh, we can't do it here," Sonya says in desperation. "I can see right through these jalousies." Moke leaps up.

"Put some towels over it," Moke says. "No, wait-a-minute," he says. Let's go in here." He runs into the bathroom and turns the shower on full-blast. "Lie down on the floor," Moke says. "If Hazel comes back, I'll duck out and close the bathroom door and you won't have to worry about your clothes or anything."

"Good," Sonya says. She turns herself around and lies down obediently in the middle of the bathroom floor. . . . Moke hesitates, kisses her belly, works his way down. Slowly and delicately, he French-kisses her. Sonya raises her bottom off the terrazzo, straining to meet him. The root of his tongue begins to ache; Sonya tastes more and more like fresh apricots; the shower water drums against the tub.

Sunday morning. Reeking of Mennen's, his father appears at the door of his bedroom wearing boxer shorts and a fancy dress shirt with upturned collar flaps and nervously tying his expert full-Windsor knot beneath his Adam's apple with his favorite red silk necktie.

"Get ready, Buddy. Service starts in twenty-five minutes. Mother has breakfast on the table."

"I don't think I'm going today," Moke says, squelching a yawn.

"Not going!"

"Sonya and I were going to the beach this morning."

"Get up and look out the window. It's too rainy for that. Call Sonya and her mother and tell them we'll be there in twenty minutes to pick them up."

"No, I don't think they want to go either."

"Well, I think you'd better try to talk them into it then."

"What for?" Moke jumps up and pushes the curtain aside, taking in—sure enough--a steady gray drizzle. He squeezes into his tight Duke Blue Devils t-shirt and looks around for his madras bermudas.

"For Christ's sake, Moke. I've gone to a lot of trouble to get these women special accommodations at the Ranch. The least they can do is show their faces on Sunday morning and express a little good will. I'd like to introduce them to Elijah, for one thing. You know he likes to meet everybody."

"But do *they* want to meet *him*—that's the question."

"What kind of attitude is that?"

"I really don't think Sonya and her mother realized that going to church every day was part of the deal."

"It's *not* every day. It's Sunday morning, and those women are special guests of the Ranch and friends of *my son*, and it's going to look funny if they don't show up."

"I don't see why *you* have to feel responsible for them."

"There isn't time to argue. Are you going or not?"

"I'm not even *awake* yet," Moke says.

"All right. But if you're not going, don't expect to use the car. That's all I need is for somebody to see you driving around with Sonya in that skimpy bikini on Sunday morning while they're on their way to church."

"Oh, that *would* be horrendous. How am I going to *get* there if I don't use the car, pray tell?"

"If you're too tired to go to church, you're too tired to go anywhere—as far as I'm concerned." Bill says this over his shoulder as he retreats back into his own room to finish getting ready.

"Well, terrific!" Moke says. "Since when has going to church become compulsory around here?" Moke yells this into the empty hall.

"Don't get smart with me, buster," his father says from the next room.

"Well, Jesus Christ! I'm going anyway," Moke says under his breath. He finishes dressing quickly, slaps his wallet, and storms out through the living room, grabs his London Fog windbreaker from the closet—keys heavy in the pocket—flips it over his shoulder like James Dean, and pounds out the front door into the teeth of the downpour. The orange Pontiac is parked where he left it on the circular driveway, its hood and fenders beaded now with rain, which he swipes at in a gesture of futility as he goes by, lifting a spray and leaving a single smear-mark across the metal like a half-hearted windowwasher. He fights off an impulse to unlock the car and climb in, feeling his father's eyes on him from the slitted bedroom jalousies, and instead trudges out across the mushy lawn, preferring the role of martyr to that of juvenile delinquent now that he has begun this fatal gesture and there is no turning back. The steady rain beating through his crewcut and running down his neck seems proof enough of the rightness of his wronged soul. He is willing to suffer for the misguided deeds and shameless insults of those he loves most and he knows he will go on doing it until they finally begin to see how insensitive they are being, until they find his waterlogged form face down in a ditch one of these days or maybe after he has spent the next three years sailing around the world on a sixty-foot sloop with only an occasional headline in the *London Times* or the *Tahiti Daily Register* hinting of his whereabouts.

It is at least three miles to the Bible Ranch, but once he passes through the A & W Rootbeer lot and crosses the main drag and some sub-divisions it is mostly open country, scrubby fields, farm fences, and an occasional wet cow to share his misery. He will keep to the back roads, he decides, come at the women's room across the Plain of the Soggy Bush, and thus avoid causing a stir among the migrating worshippers. It is the kind of minor strategic problem James Bond has coped with routinely for years, nothing to throw an experienced agent. Just as the hiking is about to seem impossible, he spots the distant rectangle of white stucco, navigates the marshy hinterland, and circles the building, grateful at last for the cement walk and the generous overhang to keep the rain out of his collar. As he taps on Sonya's door, he hopes he will find Hazel already out on some hectic errand, but as the door swings open he sees instantly he will have no such luck. Hazel is already pacing back and forth, carrying on like a banshee.

"Now here's Dr. Kildare himself," she says sassily, "looking like a drowned idiot, which means you are both going to desert the skaggy old lady in about five minutes and leave me alone all day in this ratty dump at the mercy of these fanatical Christian cocksuckers! I won't have it! I didn't come all the way down here to spend my vacation in a retirement village! I have needs the same as the next person! And I won't be pushed around and left behind and talked about and *deserted* like a piece of sagging, over-aged meat. Goddamnitohell!"

"Oh no," Moke says, "not this."

"Stay out of it," Sonya says, "she's pretty pissed."

"OOOhhh, I think I'm going to *strangle* somebody!" Hazel yells.

"What happened?" Moke says.

"So this is the famous Florida sunshine, is it?" Hazel says—as if he is personally responsible.

"I had a talk with God earlier this morning," Moke says, before he can stop himself. "But he said he couldn't do a thing about it."

"Oh, he's cute, isn't he," Hazel says. "He's as cute as they come! I always knew he would turn out to be a cute one, all right. Cute!"

"Your father called," Sonya says, "and tried to talk us into going to church, for one thing. Then a Mr. Roark called and invited us to lunch."

"Terrific!" Moke says, "some people never know when to quit. I'm awfully sorry about this."

"You think you're sorry," Hazel says. "You're aren't half as sorry as I am, I'll tell you that. What have you got to be sorry about?"

"So Hazel said she would go to lunch," Sonya says. "But now she's upset because she doesn't have the right sort of dress or anything and *I* said I wouldn't go."

"*You will go,*" Hazel says.

"You don't *have* to," Moke says. "Neither one of you has to."

"I really don't want to," Sonya says.

"*You will go,*" Hazel says, "*and that's final! I'm* your mother and I say you *will* go!"

"I was just going to ask you," Moke says to Sonya, "if you'd like to catch some breakfast somewhere."

"I'd love to," Sonya says.

"Oh no you don't," Hazel says. "You can't leave me alone in this room! I won't permit it! Absolutely not!"

"I certainly didn't pay Sonya's way down here," Moke says, "with the expectation that it would be like *this*. For God's sake, Hazel! Try to be reasonable."

"Now there!" Hazel screams. "I knew it would come to this! Pack the bags!" She yanks a suitcase from under the bed and nearly falls flat on the terrazzo floor. "Pack the bags! This is one twat that cannot be bought! Get out! Get out!"

Moke looks desperately at Sonya and says he will wait for her outside. Head bowed, he steps out and closes the door behind him. He leans against the white stucco and surveys his options: three dripping lawn chairs with puddles in their seats or Hazel's rented Nash Rambler. Muffled rantings resound through the wall. A bed of orange gladiolas soaks up the rain. He gets in the Nash and begins to wait, crossing his fingers for Sonya.

After several minutes Sonya comes out the door, waving a little v-for-victory sign at him. Hazel calls her back. In dread, Moke watches Hazel jawing at the door. Finally Sonya breaks away, leaps the bed of gladiolas, and runs to the car as if nothing had happened. She tosses her head as she climbs in, flipping hair back over her shoulder, and lays the keys in his palm like a promise.

"Hit it," she says. God is she beautiful. Moke's heart swells with love and relief. He guns the Nash, whips it around like a toy, and throws gravel for twenty feet going out the driveway.

"What did it take?" Moke says, fondling her neck.

"I have to go to lunch with them and be a good girl and let her wear my black dress. After that, we get the car and we can park it somewhere," she says, squeezing his knee, "and make love, like good Christians, until 2 A.M."

Three o'clock. The sun has broken through; the sky is bluing up. Big patches of brownish-green seaweed have washed up on the beach during the rain. Moke and Sonya have cleared a spot far down the sand past the "Swim at Your Own Risk" sign. Moke has stopped off during the luncheon and picked up his Japanese 35mm camera, a Petri 1.9, from the deserted house. He busts open one of the yellow boxes of Kodachrome, breathing in its special celluloid fragrance, drops it in the camera and threads it carefully along the delicate sprockets within. He will pretend he is the great outdoor nude photographer, Andre DeDienes, and immortalize Sonya forever. Except Sonya is not totally nude in her turquoise bikini because there really isn't that much privacy and Hazel, who has heard of this photographic scheme, has given them stern warnings—no beavers, no tit shots, absolutely none, just nice swimsuit shots like Esther Williams in *Dangerous When Wet*. Sonya has promised.

Well, in her turquoise bikini, she is *almost* nude, and quite heart-breakingly beautiful enough. He takes her silhouetted against the sky. He takes her in the water, like a mermaid returning to her undersea kingdom, looking back seductively over her left shoulder. He takes her laughing on her hands and knees on the beach towel with the lovely arch of her back, where you would touch her to gently roll her over onto the terry cloth, giving him a terrible erection in his tight guard-trunks, and the cold ocean swelling unexpectedly around his thighs could almost produce steam.

Already Moke anticipates the time when these slides will be the only tangible evidence that Sonya existed. He imagines himself back in his room at Duke, sad and alone at midnight with his slide projector, slowly flicking the advance mechanism and throwing glorious lifesize reproductions of Sonya onto the wall above his bed. . . . A sad, sad prospect.

Chapter Eight

All day, all night, Marianne,
Down by the seaside, sifting sand,
Even little children love Marianne
Down by the seaside, sifting sand. . . .

AROUND FIVE they stop in at the Elbow Room, an oceanfront bar and dance joint with a certain seedy intimacy all its own.

"You should have seen my mother flirting with Elijah Roark," Sonya says.

"My God," Moke says. "Was he scandalized?"

"Are you kidding. Hazel is dynamite when she wants to be. He ate it up."

"I can't believe my ears."

"Elijah was so overjoyed he invited us all to go out in their yacht tomorrow."

"Do you have to go too?"

"There's no getting out of it now. You're even invited."

"What did my father do?"

"Talked about what a gifted natural athlete his son is and how you were president of the National Honor Society and everything."

"God."

The waitress wants to know do they want any drinks—Sonya orders a pink lady and Moke orders a whiskey sour.

"Do you realize that we only have six more days down here?" Moke says.

"I'm going to miss you," Sonya says.

"What will your life be like when you go back?"

"School starting—it should be fun enough. It's a little hard to imagine right now."

93

"I'm going to miss you too," Moke says. "How would you like an extra member of the family for a while? Just to keep an eye on you, I mean?"

"That wouldn't be like having a chaperone, would it?"

"Heavens no. I could just stay in your room, silly. It would be like having a roommate. Then when you came home from classes, I'd be there and we could study together."

"What *kind* of studying?"

"Whatever kind you liked."

"I'm afraid I wouldn't get much studying done with *you* in my bedroom, *mon cheri*."

"Sure you would, Sonya. You'd have to. I'd insist on it."

"What will your year be like at Duke University?"

"Terrible." Pause.

"You never know though, you know?" Sonya says. "It might not be so bad. How can you really tell?"

"Organic chemistry. No Sonya. Quantitative analysis. Advanced calculus. Advanced German. And comparative anatomy?"

"I bet you'll be good in comparative anatomy. You have a real feel for it, baby."

"I'd rather be your roommate."

"Okay."

"Okay what?"

"Okay you can be my roommate!"

"You just bought yourself a roommate, kid. What will Hazel say?"

"She'll say. . . . We better not tell Hazel at all, I think. Just keep it between you and me."

"Fine." He touches her under the table. "That's just where it should be, right? As long as it's just between you and me, Sonya, everything's going to be all right."

"As long as it's between you and me . . ." She gasps. "I'll give you just about fifteen minutes, Moke Galenaille, to cut that out."

"Hey, you wanna dance?" Someone has dropped some quarters into the jukebox, which starts clicking like an automatic cement factory, and Sonya is already up and pulling him across the floor, ducking underneath these empty Chianti bottles the management has hanging from the rafters to sharpen up the decor. Sonya's shirt is tied in rabbit's ears at the belly, but aside from that modest gesture, she is still wearing strictly beach attire, the bikini, her flip-flops (which she walks out of), and an anklet. The bar is practically deserted except for a booth with three American Legionnaire types gumming stogies and a couple of tired half-drunk insurance salesmen. When Sonya moves across the room, their backs stiffen up like crows on a wire and conversation stops in mid-sentence. Chubby Checker says:

> Twist again like we did last summer
> Twist again like we did last year
> Do-you-re-mem-ber when . . .

and Sonya is doing it, doing it, saying, "Come on, *baby*," as Moke is backing away a comfortable distance, mumbling apologies, excuses, suddenly meek and embarrassed and bumping into barstools. He can dance "Ebb Tide" all night long, but this kind of thing is something he has never even seen before, let alone learned how to do, and it looks to him distinctly like a bur-le-que routine or what they used to call "dirty boogie." But Sonya looks as if she doesn't need a partner that awful-bad anyhow, the way she is getting into it. This girl just really loves to dance, Moke is thinking, just really lovvves it, and somewhere along the line she figured out that it made every man within gawking distance into a helpless voyeur.

"Jesus," one of the insurance salesman says to Moke, "where'd you ever get a chick like that? She your sister?"

"Nope," Moke says.

"She is sumpin else."

"Yeah, she sure is."

"What's at?"

"I said, '*yeah, she sure is.*' "

Sonya is gazing steadily at Moke as if there is no one else in the Elbow Room but the two of them. She unties the rabbit-ears at her midrif and lets the shirttails fly around loose a little while; then she wraps each tail around her body as far as she can, pantomiming distress that the material isn't generous enough to cover all the parts that modesty requires.

"Tsh-tsh," says the insurance salesman.

"Who *is* that girl?" the bartender says.

"She ain't my mother," says the insurance salesman. "And she ain't *his* sister," he says, pointing at Moke.

Sonya takes off the shirt—which brings a round of applause from the Legionnaires' booth—and dances in a large semi-circle towards them, using the shirt as a cape to tantalize the poor idiots. "Oh, God," Moke is thinking, "how much did she have to drink, anyway?"

"She'd better watch herself," the bartender says. "We don't allow that kind of dancing in this place. We could get canned for something like that."

"Oh, she's just having a good time," says the insurance man. "Leave her alone, why don't ya, for cryin' out loud!" He grabs a handful of beernuts and starts chomping away like a starved rat, rubbernecking back to Sonya with a look of adoration on his face.

"Take it *all* off, Baby, why doncha, huh?" says one of the Legionnaires, and the others clap in agreement.

"Ha-ha, fat chance of that!" says the insurance man, looking worriedly at the bartender. "My, she sure can dance though, can't she? She sure can."

When Moke looks again he sees that Sonya, in fact, has her hands placed seductively on the snaps of her bikini halter and is giving them the old "should I?" routine—force of habit probably. He is starting to get in the mood of this little charade of hers himself. Why *not* liven up the local bistro a little bit on a rainy Sunday afternoon, for God's sake? These poor jokers have probably never seen such gorgeous flesh in their lives. You could look at it as a charitable act on Sonya's part really, letting a little light into the squalid lives of these sorry old boys. She is such a warm-hearted, loving person. She *enjoys* being beautiful, but that isn't going to make her a snob; she wants everyone else to enjoy it too. God, what a woman, Moke thinks.

Sonya suddenly peels off her halter—swish, lookee, lookee—does a fancy rotation that gives both the bar viewers and the Legionnaires' booth a choice perspective on her delectable breasts as they swing around in slow motion, and then minces over and deposits the tiny catty-cornered piece of polka-dotted nylon in the beer slops on the black tabletop under the Legionnaires' noses.

They are so transfixed and breathless, they forget to clap for several seconds and then begin clapping and cheering simultaneously.

"Holy mother of God," says the insurance man. "This must be my day."

"All right, miss! All right, miss!" yells the bartender. "That's just about enough of that! Put that back on. Put that right back on this minute, you hear me?" He bulls his way out from behind the bar and rushes to the jukebox and jerks the cord out of the wall.

"Godammit to hell," says the insurance man.

"We don't run that kind of place here, miss. I can't permit this to continue," he says, shaking his head back and forth woefully. He looks a little like a bald Yogi Berra. Sonya is standing there with a hand on her hip and her halter strap hanging now from the pinkie of the other hand, making no move whatsoever to put on the halter (returned to her guiltily by one of the boys) and she has a surprisingly defiant, pouty expression on her face.

"God, there's always a killjoy in every crowd," says the insurance man. "You never get what you really want because some dipshit always comes along and ruins everything." The bartender is having a hard time approaching much closer than twenty feet to the suspect. He keeps looking as if he would like to shield his eyes with his forearm or run out the front door.

"Put it on or I'm calling the cops," he says in a loud voice. "I'm not putting up with some nutty slut coming in here and ruining my business."

Unbelievably, Sonya starts walking slowly towards him, sticking her tongue out and twirling her halter around like an airplane propeller.

"All right. That does it," says the bartender, hurrying back behind the bar. "I don't have to put up with this kind of crap!"

"Come on, Sonya, let's get out of here," Moke says.

"Hold it right there!" the bartender says. He pulls out a brown-handled Saturday Night Special from beneath the cash drawer and waves it around like some kind of cowboy.

"Come off it," Moke says. "You must be kidding."

"Name, address, and ID!" says the bartender. "Right now!— on the bar. And no more fucking around! You college kids think you can come in here and do anything you damn well please. Bunch of god-damned spoiled brat beatniks!"

"Just watch your language," says the insurance man. Moke gets out his wallet and carefully lays his father's American Express card, his driver's license, and his last year's University ID onto the black counter-top. Sonya pulls on her shirt and ambles toward the door, still unbuttoned up the front and the halter dangling over her left shoulder like a nice catch of fish.

"Where's she think she's going?" yells the bartender.

"Better wait a minute, Sonya," Moke says.

"I'll wait in the car," she says.

"Hold it right there, miss!" screams the bartender.

"Go ahead and blow my head off," Sonya says, "if you think it'll make you *feel* any better, you faggoty creep!" She walks slowly on out the door, with a defiant swing of her hips.

"I'll have her busted for indecent exposure!" The bartender is purple. "I don't have to listen to that from some two-bit whore!"

"She got a little carried away," Moke says. "She's a professional dancer, sir, and maybe she had a little too much to drink this afternoon. She's been under a certain amount of strain lately, but she's a good girl—really, she's a very good girl—let's just calm down and put this thing in perspective."

"I'll *bet* she's a good girl," says the bartender. "Good for about twenty bucks on the hoof."

"I *knew* she was a professional the minute she got out there on the floor," says the insurance man. "I knew it instantly. That girl can *dance*. Anybody can see that."

The bartender is copying down every number on Moke's driver's license. "All right, what's *her* name?"

"Her name is Sonya Velonis. . . . She's from Canada, but she's visiting with us . . . with my family, my parents and me. . . ."

"Spell it!"

"S-O-N-Y-A . . . V-E-L-O-N-I-S," Moke says.

Rubie-red to M-as-in-Magpie. Rubie-red to M-as-in-Magpie. Come in. Magpie, come in. Do you read me? Air Support Control, do you read me? Are you hit? Are you out there, Magpie? Do you read?

When he finally gets out of the Elbow Room, big cumulus clouds are again blowing out over the water like huge lumbering dirigibles and the palm fronds are whipping this way and that with the hint of more rain. There is no sign of Sonya in the car. Moke scans the beachfront and picks her out finally, sitting down near the water, hugging her knees, staring out into the misty deep. He walks slowly towards her.

After some burgers and fries at A & W, they drive out A1A to the nearest passion pit and see a flick called *On the Beach* about the end of the world. The nuclear holocaust had finally come, and everybody was dead except the Australians and the Navy men on an American submarine. Ava Gardner fell in love with Gregory Peck, who was the captain of the sub; but everybody had to die in the end anyway. Newspapers blew around the deserted streets of San Francisco; though, for some reason, there were no rotting dead bodies or exploded buildings or spark-popping electrical lines snaking through the trees that would surely electrocute a lot of people when the real holocaust came, not to mention firestorms, sheer blast destruction—try peeling your skin off the wall like wallpaper—brainrot caused by radiation sickness, falling hair, blood in the gutters, and invasions of locusts. Still, Moke considers it a pretty good movie, all in all. Something like that would probably happen some day, but it wouldn't be that hygienic. If it did, he would certainly never take a suicide pill like those cowardly Australians. He would never have left Ava Gardner either to return to the sea with his crew like Gregory Peck. What a waste! Moke imagines himself crawling heroically along the beach toward Ava Gardner covered with scabs and barnacles and seaweed like the Creature from the Black Lagoon.

During intermission, they nuzzle and touch as spotlights dance across the motionless image of a pizza pie and the low full moon rises over the concession stand, its flat roof trimmed in pale yellow neon. If the end of the world were coming, Moke feels he would commit himself to Sonya. He would not leave her for any reason. He would die in her arms, if it came to that. But until the radiation cloud descended upon them, he would fight to stay alive and he would fight to protect Sonya with every cell of his being. They would have to kill him outright to stop him, and in this instant, he feels particularly invulnerable. If it came to that, he feels he could save Sonya from the end of the world through sheer will and determination.

Moke tells Sonya: he thinks he is the kind of person who just naturally looks for a permanent relationship, not the kind who enjoys going from one new girl to another. He doesn't know how he got to be this way—it may be a form of mental retardation—but there it was. He hopes she understands why he is getting more and more attached to her in a primitive and desperate sort of way that may not even be terrifically healthy, for either of them.

Sonya says she thinks he has bedroom eyes and a really cute mouth and she has gone totally ape over his body, if he wants to know the truth. Then she takes his hand and directs his fingers up beneath her short skirt, where he is surprised to find she isn't wearing panties. "Feel," she says. "You make me wet, just thinking about you." The luscious slipperiness he encounters is like an electric shock. She presses his hand there and holds it and brings her nose next to his and stares longingly into his eyes. "But this is more than just a physical attraction," she says. She has never felt this way about anyone before, she says. She doesn't like to use the word "love," and she doesn't believe in underrating "the physical" either—because it's a lot more important than people are willing to admit, and, for her, the body speaks a certain truth about the soul. But, whatever it is, she feels she knows him better than she should, as if they had met in a former life. And what she knows, she loves. She takes his hand away and kisses his fingers. "Don't touch it again right away," she says, "or I'll come!"

It grows darker suddenly, and he kisses her. The second movie flickers on the screen, but they are too distracted to watch. The gears of the universe begin to slow down and stop as they make love. Moke imagines himself as one of the blind fishes in the underground river inside Mammoth Cave. Sonya is dark and gleaming and immense and wet beside him, her body tinctured with a glow of pure animal happiness. He feels the current of it flowing through him and back again. "Oh, God," she says. Together, they are the snake eating its own tail, the Yin and the Yang, ghost-dancers shambling through a moonlit garden, worshippers in a semi-religious trance speaking in strange tongues. Sonya begins to make breathy little noises. "Yeah," she says. "Oh, yeah." She is beautiful, just beautiful.

During the drive back alongside the eerie ocean, Moke muses: frankly it is hard to believe Sonya is as inexperienced as

100

she claims to be. She just seems too accomplished. Should it matter that she has probably screwed her way across half the continent?—what could you expect from a professional stripper, for God's sake, whose own father had molested her at the first tender blush of puberty—didn't that constitute incest at the very least? Think of the possible psychological consequences! What could you expect of a girl who had shaken her naked ass in front of every wino, seedy bum, horny bespectacled pharmacist, meatbanging corporal, and lonely ad exec from St. Louis to Baltimore? Who actually got sexually aroused by shoplifting and who gave herself spontaneous orgasms in church? What could you expect? Maybe she had withheld her final favor until now only as a form of self-respect or out of a desire to save the last mystery. Who cared? Maybe she was so advanced that all-the-way sexual intercourse just wasn't exciting enough! Who could say? His heart rises into his throat as he stops the car in the shadow of the flat roof of the Bible Ranch and kisses her goodnight. He decides he loves her anyway—what choice is there?—what is there to prevent it?—he will simply have to love her in spite of everything.

"Well, look what the cat drug in," says Bill Galenaille, as Moke comes in the house. They are sitting there in their pajamas, watching the Late News. Moke hangs his London Fog jacket in the closet and goes over and squats down on the edge of the rug and stares at the TV screen with them. When the commercial comes on, Moke's father says: "I'm sorry we had that little misunderstanding this morning, son."

"So am I," Moke says. "It's all right. How did your day work out?"

"Fine, just fine. Those women made a tremendous hit with Elijah. You wouldn't believe it. He wants to take us all out in the yacht."

"That's what I heard."

"Where have *you* been all day?" says his mother.

"With Sonya. . . . We went to the beach and drove around and stuff."

"Did you get anything to eat?" she says.

"Well, *of course*, he got something to eat, Honey," Bill yells. "He's a grown man, for Christ's sake. He ought to know enough by now to feed himself when he needs to!"

"I guess so," she says, smiling at Moke oddly, as if she had never quite noticed he is as big as he evidently is.

Moke gets up and sits down next to her on the couch and puts his arm around her shoulders, soft and fuzzy in the pink bathrobe. "I got enough," he says. "You don't have to worry," he says.

"He certainly is big, isn't he?" his mother says to his father, smiling back at him fondly. "He sure is. . . . I can hardly believe it sometimes. I can hardly believe my own eyes."

"And built like a horse," his father says. . . . "Say, that little Sonya's got a cute figure, hasn't she? *She* is really built."

"I thought you weren't supposed to notice things like that," says Moke's mother, giggling.

"When you're *living* with the prettiest woman in the whole state of Florida," Bill says, patting her on the knee, "you can afford to keep a critical eye on a few of the others. No harm in that, is there? It's when I *stop* noticing that you've got to be worried about!"

"I'm not worried," says Moke's mother, "are you?"

Chapter Nine

I wonder, wonder, wonder, wonder who
Who wrote the Book of Love?

THE TWO-CAR CARAVAN—Elijah's Imperial and the Galenaille's Oldsmobile—winds down the gently sloping marina road at eight sharp. All the way from Terresonna, the four of them in the Olds (Moke's parents, Sonya, and himself) have made cheerful, commonplace conversation, and Moke has been puzzling over the silhouettes of Hazel's frazzled mop and Elijah's bullethead in the rear window ahead, wondering what those two could possibly have to say to each other. The yacht basin—a generous nook along the Intercoastal waterway—gleams with white hulls and a forest of masts, and just before they drop down to the water's edge, Moke glimpses in full panorama the huge golden bar of sunlight splitting the bright expanse of Atlantic—the edge of the world—just a long stone's throw to the east.

The boat's name is *Impulse,* and Moke, ever suspicious of Elijah's and his father's talents at overstatement, is unprepared for its grandeur. It is no dinky motorboat. It really is a yacht, a big cruiser with broad decks, wraparound glass, a lofty flying bridge, and a surprising labyrinth of rooms, beds, and cubbyholes below deck. "It's as big as a house and twice as comfortable," Elijah rhapsodizes, conducting the compulsory tour, bow to stern. "It sure is," Moke's mother chirps, "isn't it? I've never seen anything like it. Have you? My gosh!" Hazel rolls her eyes appreciatively at each new revelation. Sonya's mother, buoyant and giddy, shows a distracting talent for fluttering her eyelashes that Elijah seems to find positively riveting.

"How's this as an example of the fruits of free enterprise?" Bill says, winking at Moke conspiratorially.

"Pretty impressive all right," Moke says.

"You know what I'd do if I was you?" Bill says.

"What?" Moke says.

"I'd try to find some way to get a good grounding in business and economics, pal. I mean—even if you stay in pre-med. *Especially* if you stay in pre-med. You never can tell when that kind of information might come in handy. You know these doctors rake in all kinds of money. One of these days you might start making money so fast you won't know what to do with it. I'm not kidding. If I had only known thirty years ago what I know today about economics, I'd probably be a millionaire several times over."

"You probably would be."

"I know you don't think it's such a hot idea, but think it over. Your old man isn't as dumb as he looks. Some of my advice might be worth thinking about." Bill chuckles in Elijah's direction. "What do you think of this fellow, Elijah? He's a pistol, isn't he?"

"He's a son to be proud of, Bill. Yes he is. And I know you *are* proud of him. He also bears a striking resemblance to his father, I'm pleased to say—more than you know, more than either of you knows."

"You really think so?" Bill says. "Of course, I always did think there was a certain resemblance between the two of us, except that he's better looking than I am!"

"Handsome is as handsome does," Moke's mother says.

"You can say that again," Hazel says.

Sonya looks at Moke sympathetically. "Hey, Dreamboat," she says, "when do we get to go swimming around here?"

"Let's get this show on the road," Moke says. "The guests are getting restless."

"Who wants to drive?" Elijah says.

"Oh, *you* do," Hazel says, enlarging her eyes, "you drive. No one else knows how to."

"I'll teach you how!" Elijah says. "It's as easy as pie. Everyone to the bridge!"

"We'll get our suits on," Sonya says, pulling Moke through a low doorway into the innards of the boat. "Duck, you big hunk." Her clothes are already falling off as he dips in behind her.

"How did we get ourselves into this?" Moke says.

"Life is too short to worry about it," Sonya says.

When they come out on deck, the *Impulse* is plowing along a broad, well-defined channel lined with expensive backyards. Everyone seems to have his own private little pier, runabout, and barbeque pit. Narrower canals lined with smaller pastel ranch houses connect to the main artery.

"It certainly puts Venice to shame, doesn't it?" Moke says, at which point they move into view from the flying bridge and Sonya's fluorescent yellow bikini elicits a loud wolf-whistle from Bill.

"Oh, for heaven's sake, Honey," Moke's mother says, "you'll embarrass her!"

"I doubt it," Hazel says.

"I'm just having a little fun with her," Bill says. Sonya does a cute parody of insulted hauteur out across the bobbing foredeck, then turns and winks and smiles at her audience.

"My, but she is a fine young lady though, isn't she," Elijah says, "a beautiful girl! So full of life."

"You're going to have to start fighting the men off with a club," Bills says to Hazel.

"I wish she wouldn't wear such skimpy bathing suits," Hazel says. "But like I always say, it doesn't last forever—if you've got it, you might as well flaunt it."

"That's for certain," Moke's mother says. "It doesn't last forever, does it? It certainly doesn't."

Moke watches the gentle current slipping beneath the bridges. Fishermen overhead are mostly stolid types who have seen a million boats go by and a million silly tourists. Already the sun is warm and full on their bodies, and the lemony, fish-scented breeze from the motion of the boat feels cool and nice in their faces—and blowing back their hair. "I'd like to get good and wet," Sonya says, just as a sheet of droplets sprinkles them. "Even wetter than that," she laughs. If he only had a picture of her laughing like that he could take it out and look at it in the fall at Duke when the black umbrellas are sprouting along the sidewalks and everyone is hurrying to the post office to find out what letters haven't arrived yet. If he only had that picture he knows he would never show it to any of the dopes on his hall, who would only make obscene remarks. He would keep it locked away for special occasions and try not to look at it too often so that it would always appear novel and not lose its sense of animation. He would write long letters to Sonya on rainy Sunday afternoons, staring at the picture every few lines, memorizing every detail until the picture begins to seem stupid and boring and he hates to look at it and the feeling is lost.

What a dismal train of thought! Maybe they should just make a clean break with their present plans and elope to Nassau. Ditch Hazel somehow and do what they really want. Find an old deserted beach house and live like savages, catching fish to live on, eating coconuts, and making love whenever they feel like it with nobody around to bother them. After a while Sonya could get part-time employment at some go-go palace if she wanted to. He could maybe find a job as a janitor or cabana boy at the Nassau Hilton. Terrific. He could carry suitcases through the lobby for fourth-rate gynecologists from Indianapolis. Seymour Kuntz, O. B., GYN. *"Boy, put four new tires on this Caddy of mine, will you. The damn things already have five thousand miles on 'em! And I'd like it washed, vacuumed, Simonized, and ready to go by nine tonight. You got that?"*

"Yessir."

"Here's five for your trouble."

Moke is beginning to have such a good time he is beginning to make himself miserable thinking how soon it will all be over.

Lunch break. They have hied into a tidy cove and dropped anchor. No alligators in sight. Plenty safe for a swim, Elijah assures them. Too near the ocean for alligators. Too near the waterway for sharks and barracuda. The four-member bridge crew have assembled aft on canvas deckchairs embossed with the *Impulse* insignia and are chewing on chicken sandwiches with chopped olives and nursing lemonades and early martinis. Moke is standing at water-level on a plastic flange clinging to the grab-rail while Sonya toes her way up the ladder to the single diving board. The water below is bluish-green and clear and inviting-looking. Now and then, the white bulk of a big Hatteras or Chris Craft will cruise past on the main channel like a small mountain passing in the distance, but their boat sits deep in the water—the wake plays itself out in wave upon wave of gentle laps and ripples, and the nearby palms quietly flap and sway in the heat like exhausted marathon-dancers moving through the last few bars of the last soft saxophone solo.

Sonya stands poised for a moment at the tip of the board, all eyes on her, then executes a neat jackknife, splashes, bobs up smiling and shaking her hair with half her bikini halter askew, one breast exposed, and water in her ears. Hazel eyes the errant breast in horror and squawks, "Sonya, for God's sake!"—doubly alerting everyone—but Sonya is back underwater swimming toward the ladder, arching up, catching ahold, swinging into perfect focus, still oblivious to her condition. Sonya's breast, with its bulbous tip and dark aureole, is truly lovely. Suddenly her attention is caught, like a high-wire artist at the peak of the bigtop by six heavy-duty klieg-lights—by Hazel's arm waving and Moke's mother's tsh-tshing and Bill's and Elijah's chortling—and she drops heavily backwards like a cliff-diver, arms clapped across her nipples, and smacks the water and somersaults under, swirling and bubbling, until she pops up again, this time all private parts strictly in order and Sonya smiling and even more delighted with herself than at the first surfacing.

"Hussy, would you watch yourself!" Hazel screams. "Where do you think you are!"

"Thank God, she got it back," Moke's mother sighs.

"Oh, it was an accident," Elijah coos.

"She didn't mean anything by it," Bill says, stifling a chuckle. "Are you all right, Honey? Come on up here and let us look at you." Moke climbs up and takes a lemonade.

"Sure," Sonya says, floating over. "Just a little accident is all—whew."

"No more diving for you today, Miss Priss," Hazel says.

"Oh, mother! I'll just have to tighten it is all."

"It's quite all right, Hazel," Elijah says. "Don't spoil her fun, for goodness sake. For goodness sake! It's not worth that. It was just an accident, after all."

"Accident, my sore foot," Hazel says.

"Come on up on deck," Bill says, "and let us have a look at you." Sonya climbs out dripping and flops onto a pile of warm life preservers.

"That was pretty cute," Bill says, "I'd like to see you do that again, as a matter of fact."

"Oh, Dad!" Moke's mother says. "You'll embarrass her!"

"She sure is as cute as a bug's ear," Elijah roars. Hazel looks utterly disgusted.

"You can say that again," Bill chuckles. "But what I want to find out, Sonya," Bill says, winking and offering her a glass of juice, "is—how much for the one with the pink nose?"

"Sorry," Sonya says, not batting an eyelash, "but these pink little pussycats aren't for sale. They belong to my friend here," she says, clapping Moke on the back, causing him to cough into his upraised glass and shoot a spray of lemonade out over the side, after which he turns as red as his bathing suit.

Cocktail hour. Bill and Elijah, Hazel and Moke's mother are stewing about aft—distracted by their own rituals. Elijah's distant har-har is heard as he produces an ice bucket, much to everyone's feigned surprise, and threatens to slide ice down Hazel's back. Have their elders regressed into adolescence, Moke wonders, or never emerged from it? A coral-pink sun is dipping toward a stand of feathery pines that rim the distant shore, and from the four or five sloops and yawls anchored nearby only the occasional clink of dinner cutlery or glass ripples the silence across the water.

He and Sonya decide to slip below to shower and change. She bumps the Coppertone bottle accidentally getting up; the liquid glops out into a creamy puddle. They leave it spilled. Sonya hurries through the narrow passage, through one of the bedrooms to the relative safety of the tiny closetlike bathroom. Moke pulls the door shut and locks it as Sonya sits on the lid of the commode, stretches her slippery legs out and slides the elastic-looped bikini bottoms down and away. He kneels and slides his cheek along her trembling flesh, sticky with coconut-oil Coppertone, and locates the holy fount with his lips and kisses it. Hello, you beauty. "Oh," Sonya says. Words pass through his head: *This is My Body given for you . . . that you might have Everlasting life . . .*

There is something so open and innocent and direct about Sonya, Moke marvels. Her hedonism is not the least bit embarrassing to her. Somehow the Canadians must have bypassed that scrawny strain of Puritanism that corrupts the collective psyche south of the border. The French influence possibly? Life-affirming instead of life-denying. Yes instead of no. Brigitte Bardot instead of Norman Vincent Peale.

Sonya lets out a little breathy scream. She comes convulsively, gasps, opens her eyes and rolls slightly towards him, smiling, her moving fingers visible now in the shadow of her mound, gasps, "Oh, I love you," in a higher voice, and comes again, and a third time. "Oh, whew. Oh, whew. Oh, God! Here comes another one. Oh, Moke! Oh, Jesus! Ohhhhhh"—and a fourth time. "Ohhh."

Sonya is brushing her hair vigorously with a lavender hairbrush. Moke lies on the bed, his hands cocked behind his neck, elbows pointing at the ceiling. He wonders if he should broach the subject of Nassau yet but doesn't know quite how to begin. "I know you wouldn't want to get married or anything, Sonya, but. . . ." No—terrible! "I hear Nassau is quite nice this time of year, Sonya. . . ." "You don't say." Horrible—too British. . . . If he doesn't think of something soon, it'll be too late. Probably already too late. Probably she wouldn't want to do it anyway. She has her fall plans already laid out—starting into college at McGill, for God's sake, big plans, old friends to see and compare notes with, clothes to buy, books to read, new Kingston Trio records to listen to—a whole matriculating herd of carefully selected males with impressive SAT scores and extracurricular activities to their credit, not to mention athletic accomplishments, chess and debating victories, fluency in several languages, trophies for body-building, brand-new wardrobes in the latest styles, extensive experience with women, Porsche 356-B Roadsters or Austin-Healeys with wire wheels and reclining bucket seats. Why would any woman with all that waiting for her want to go screeching off to Nassau and the Bahamas with an unknown sophomore from Duke with a 1954 Pontiac Catalina (that needs a valve job), less than eighty dollars in his checking account, and one drip-dry suit to his name? It doesn't make sense. It isn't even a remote possibility. She will never do it.

"You have an electrically charged tongue, you know that?" Sonya says. "You ought to patent it, Dreamboat."

"Sure."

"You're such a sweetheart," Sonya says, dropping her bikini bottoms again, for the shower, and then adding her halter to the small pile of clothing on the carpet. Moke slides out of his guard trunks and flips them as she falls into his arms and squeezes her breasts against his chest. "Mmm, you're so scrumptious."

"So are you," Moke says.

"Do you love me?" she says.

"Yes." She sits above him, forms her lips into a perfect pouty "O," slowly brings the tip of his erect penis toward this gross succulence.

"Wait," she says, "they might come down. . . . Where—the bathroom?"

"No—I know." There is a hatched locker in the forepeek he has already checked on . . . plenty roomy enough to curl up in. He falls off the bed and knees his way over and unsnaps it, a trapezoidal doorway in the teak cabin wall like a secret panel opening into a large crawlspace, almost empty inside except for some slickers and flippers, a couple of face-masks and snorkels, a can of Teak-Bright, and a bunch of bulky life-jackets, which he begins to unfold and spread around the floor for padding.

"Perfect," she says, squatting down girlishly like a child eager to play house. "What a neat hideout!"

"After you," he says, smiling in expectation of the lovely compromising view of her, crawling in on all fours, that this order will present. Maybe dogs know what they're doing, he thinks, but immediately squelches the flippant vulgarity of such a thought as he admires the breadth and roundness of her entry, so heartlike and smooth and feminine it gives him unanticipated pain. She rolls over in the dimness and holds out her arms to him. He rambles towards her. They embrace. "You're beautiful," he croons.

"Wait," she says. She climbs over the tangle of legs, pushing the hatch-door fully open again, jumps up and struts with leggy nonchalance to the vanity, where she uncaps and twists a tube and quickly, expertly smears her lips with the pinkest lipstick Moke has ever seen. Then she is back with him, her hand firmly gripping him, her lips back in the "O" and ready. She adjusts the hatch-door so that it is slightly ajar, tight enough to conceal them but open enough to allow the light to penetrate their cave. "Now!" she says. She kisses his cock. "Do you love me?"

"Yes," Moke groans. She takes him into her mouth and sucks. She takes him out.

"How much?"

"Oh . . . God." She kisses him back in and sucks. And out.

110

"Tell me how much."

She's going to get pink lipstick all over me, Moke thinks abstractedly. "More than . . . anything," he says, as his penis is again enveloped with moist warmth. I wonder how many cocks she has sucked in her life? he thinks. Or are they born knowing how to suck cocks like this?

"Tell me exactly how much," she says, "or I'll stop!"

"Okay, silly," Moke says. "But it's pretty hard to put into quantitative terms. . . ."

"How much!" she says.

"Okay," Moke says. "More than . . . more than all . . . the silver ships sailing to Nassau . . . at midnight . . ." Where did that come from? he wonders. "That's how much."

"Hey, that's pretty good," Sonya says. "I think I like that. I think I like that a lot. And here's how much I love *you*, you big Dreamboat." She makes a pink pouty "O" and brings him into it slowly and hungrily, closing her eyes and working at it, pushing against the teak, until he comes heavily into her mouth. He wants to say, "It's all right, Sonya, you don't have to . . . ," but, as he watches breathlessly through half-closed lids, she swallows his outpourings and keeps swallowing and swallowing, like a drowning woman who is dying of thirst.

"When I was thirteen back in Kingston," Sonya is saying, "my cousin Arlene taught me to strip. She had been making a good living out of it for twenty years. . . ." Her head is nestled in the cleft of his arm, her mane of hair tangled along his cheekbone, as she sends words up toward the dim ceiling of their locker. "She said you'll never have to go hungry as long as you know how to shake your ass, sweetie. She was older than Hazel is now, but she had some bod. She was a piece. When I watched her, she'd laugh. She'd say, 'That's all right, sweetie, sex is sex. It don't matter one bit if you do it with collies or cocker spaniels as long as it feels right.' That woman loved to dance." Moke envisions himself as a cocker spaniel. Or is he more of a collie?

"You think you'll make a career of it?" Moke says.

"I could," Sonya says. "You get immune enough to the sordid aspects after a while. . . . But I want to try a lot of other things too, just a whole lot of other things."

111

"Have you ever been to Nassau?" Moke says tentatively.

She squeezes his thigh. "Shh, I think I hear someone coming."

"Oh, Christ." The cabin doorhandle rattles, the door swings open, and Elijah Roark lumbers in. Moke's eyeballs stiffen through the crack in the doorhatch. His throat goes dry, like a cocker spaniel with a long thirst. His father will blow a gasket if he finds out. How is he ever going to explain how he and Sonya got into the forepeak locker-hold with no clothes on? Oh my God! Roark will never understand. Sex is too unthinkable for people like Elijah Roark. He will expire with apoplexy he is so full of sanctimonious bullshit. He will bellow like a wounded rhino. He will burst several cranial blood vessels and collapse and start twitching around on the shag carpet.

But so far Elijah Roark is acting quite oblivious to their presence, as a matter of fact. He opens and shuts a drawer. He seems to be making himself at home. He takes off his trousers—too much!—and pokes around in a pair of baggy boxer-style shorts with a red-and-blue sailboat motif. He examines his pouchy, well-porked mug in the vanity mirror at some length, alternately smiling and scowling at himself, patting his jowels with Mennen Skin Bracer, and scratching his dangle. *"Oh, hello, sir,"* Moke will say, *"we were just looking for the skin-diving gear, sir, and then we starting doing a little skin diving of our own—har-har. . . ." "Oh, hello, Dr. Roark. I bet you wonder why little Sonya and myself are in here thrashing around with our pants off. . . . Well, sir, it's a long story. Now, if you'll just calm down and listen to my side of it, I'm sure you'll. . . ."* Unbelievably, Elijah Roark discovers Sonya's swimsuit in the middle of the rug, parked at his toes. Uh-oh, Moke thinks and completely stops breathing. Roark towers above the yellow cloth momentarily as if listening to the faraway voices of angel choirs, then stoops awkwardly, collects the fragile things in his meaty paw, and—without hesitation—begins sniffing greedily at the crotch of Sonya's bikini bottoms, like a man who has just discovered his nose.

During this blatant behavior of Roark's, a light rattling noise issues forth from the near bathroom, the creak of the outer door perhaps, then the slow percolation of someone urinating in the commode there. Roark cocks his ear and shows all the signs of a keen interest in this development. The bikini drops suddenly to the rug, and the broad expanse of sailboats trundles toward the wall, beyond which the unknown occupant of the bathroom is ensconced; and then, incredibly, Roark removes from the cabin-wall a framed life-like technicolor print of Christ (pictured staring earnestly toward the Heavens) and presses his eye to a hidden peephole!

"Tsh-tsh," Sonya says in his ear.

"Shhh," Moke says, as quietly as air escaping from a tire.

"I'll bet it's *my mother*," Sonya says.

They continue to squint out through the crack in the door for some minutes at Roark's inert hulk. "He's going to give himself an eye-ache," Moke whispers.

"What could she be doing in there so long?" Sonya says.

"Maybe she knows something we don't." Suddenly Roark backs up, hangs Christ quickly back on his nail; the bathroom door opens a crack from within, and Roark slides through the opening with astonishing agility, sailboats flashing.

"I'll be damned," Sonya says. "That bitch. That good-for-nothing shameless whore."

Moke and Sonya waste no time crawling out of their hole, snapping it tight, dressing in fresh clothes, and collecting their scattered towels and suits and stuffing everything into Sonya's duffel bag. They start to leave, but Sonya says, "Hold it, I forgot my brush and comb." She retrieves them from the vanity and unzips the bag again and tucks them inside.

Just as they are finally escaping through the doorway, the *Impulse* lurches wildly abeam, tipping them suddenly to starboard. Moke catches at the doorframe. Sonya tumbles back into the room, sprawling on the carpet, the louvered door bangs against the wall, the picture of Christ bounces smartly to the floor, spraying glass, and a scratching, grinding noise resounds in the hull as the boat stops dead in the water and the engines stall out.

"Holy mackerel," Moke says, "What was that? Are you all right?"

"No problem," Sonya says, crawling to her feet. "Must have hit something out there."

"Felt like a small whale."

The starter whirs several times, and the engines growl and rev up and sputter from the stern.

Elijah Roark explodes through the doorway from the adjacent bathroom and bellows, "What in God's name is going on up there?" as he begins hopping madly into his discarded trousers, ignoring any potential inferences concerning the impropriety of his behavior or attire by cleverly diverting attention to the emergency at hand.

"We were just going back up to check," Sonya says.

"Tell them I'll be right there," Elijah says. "Tell them I won't be a minute."

"Sure thing," Moke says, scrabbling out the door.

When they reach the bridge, they find Bill and Hazel (who must have taken the back stairs) hovering over Moke's mother, who is hunched over in one of the deck chairs sobbing into her folded arms as if the world will end. Hazel is patting her. "It was just an accident," Hazel is saying. "It wasn't your fault, was it?"

"It's all right, Honey," Bill is saying. "No damage done."

Sonya goes to her mother, and the men fall in together, all with serious looks on their faces.

"What happened?" Moke says.

"Ran into some bad water," Bill says. "She just shaved off the end of a shoal." Moke is not clear whether by "she" he means his mother or the boat. He presumes his mother was attempting to steer at the time.

"Probably just sand," Elijah says, "but you never can tell."

"Right. We better head on in," Bill says. "The engines seem to be holding."

"Right," Elijah says. "Scared her pretty good, all right. . . ."

"Well, these waterway markers are sometimes for the birds," Bill says. "It's best to give them a wide berth, but every once in a while, they expect you to pass close abroad one side to keep you out of danger on the other. About all you can do is check your charts and keep an eye on the water."

"It's clouding up anyway," Moke offers.

"Well, I hope Mom doesn't feel too bad about it," Bill says. "It could happen to anyone."

114

"I should have stayed on the wheel myself," Elijah says absently. "I hope there wasn't any coral in the shoal. Could cost a mint to fix it. Probably ought to radio the Coast Guard and tell them we'll be limping on home."

"Roger," Bill says. "I'll handle that." He turns abruptly and disappears up the ladder to the bridge. Moke and Elijah stand together for a moment, gazing out across the water at the beginning of a narrow band of irrepressible pink sunset forming itself somewhere over the mainland and the Gulf of Mexico beyond. Elijah sighs and shakes his shiny Skin-Bracered mug at the clouds.

"Sometimes the Lord speaks in strange ways," he says. "Yes he does."

"I guess so," Moke says uneasily, wondering if Elijah figures the boat wreck is his punishment for whatever he was trying to accomplish below deck, and is suddenly grateful he had tentatively decided to become an agnostic second semester.

The first peculiar thing Moke notices when he jumps off and then finishes tying up the rope and looks up across the wharf and the sweep of pavement is a cop-car in the marina lot with its bubble-gum-machine spinning around. Two of Terresonna's finest are ambling toward the *Impulse*. They come up alongside just as the Bible Ranch party is preparing to disembark. Hazel and his mother, still hunched up and sniffling and cradling Hazel's arm like a true shipwreck victim, shuffle on by, making a beeline for the Galenaille's Olds. Up close Moke sees the cops are young and smooth-faced and have their sideburns lopped off at an uncanny height. One of them looks something like Tony Curtis.

"We have a warrant here for the arrest of a Sonya Velonis on the suspicion of indecent exposure," the Tony Curtis copy says. He is obviously the one who does the talking. The other cop has a crueller, less communicative scowl . . . must be the muscle, Moke figures.

"Oh, NO," Sonya says.

"Why that's impossible and ridiculous," Elijah says, taking a minute to puzzle over the situation. "That was merely an accident. How could anyone be offended by such a thing. No one in the world could have seen her without binoculars. No, they couldn't."

115

"Says here she was carrying on in a lewd and lascivious manner," the cop who can talk says.

"I was *there* myself," Bill says, "and I can testify that there was nothing improper about it. Now you fellows listen to me: I don't know who brought this charge, but, believe me, it'll never hold water."

"That may be," says the cop, "but we'll have to take her in on this warrant, sir, and see what we can find out. Is this the young lady in question?"

"This young lady is a guest of the Bible Ranch," says Elijah, "and she is a personal guest of mine. In her conduct, I'm quite sure she abides by the highest moral standards, as does every person associated with the Terresonna Bible Ranch, Inc., and I will not tolerate any innuendoes being made about her character."

"And what is your name, sir?"

"My name is Dr. Elijah Roark, President of the Terresonna Bible Ranch, and I'm a friend of the Mayor's."

"Is this young lady Sonya Velonis with a V?"

"Yes I am," says Sonya in a small voice.

"You want to come along with us, Miss?"

"Now just a minute here," Bill says. "You fellows just hold on one god-damned minute. Pardon my language." He walks with them a little ways over toward their squad car. "Frankly, I thought you were here to help us. We've just had a bad boating accident and are lucky to be alive. I thought the Coast Guard might have called you. None of us are in any condition to go down to the station right now, I can tell you that. We're all in pretty bad shape. Now I know you have your job to do, and I respect that; but just do this one small favor for me, will you. You get on your radio over there and call up the Chief for me and let me talk to him. He knows who I am—we've played golf together on several occasions, and we're both members of the Rotary. I just want to talk to him and explain the situation to him, so that he has the full picture in mind. You tell him Bill Galenaille of WTSF wants to talk to him on the radio and he won't give you any static about it, I promise you."

Bill walks to the cruiser with them, out of earshot. "If anybody can get this cleared up in a hurry," Elijah says, "Bill can. He could sell snowballs to Eskimos and make them come back for

116

refills." His father seems so brisk and earnest in the twilight, every bit the Marine Corps captain, taking command from these amateurs, good old solid Magpie with his reassuring, confident voice talking them in, a ramrod up his backbone, big capable arms pumping at his sides, grasping the plastic mike—the arms and hands and knobby knuckles that wouldn't have been out of proportion on the village blacksmith if he were six inches taller and fifty pounds heavier than Bill. Moke's heart quietly glows with filial pride. His old man sure can be a brick—though Moke is also worried that Bill might find out about the Elbow Room if he talks to them much longer. It is all-too-obvious that Yogi Berri bartender has kept his vicious promise—that fanatical fascist bastard.

"I wonder what they can do to you for indecent exposure?" Sonya says.

"Make you wear clothes for the rest of your life," Moke says, trying to cheer her up.

"I'd rather they just take me out and shoot me."

Why is it, Moke wonders, that he has been dogged by the fuzz ever since getting to know Sonya? Is America turning into a police state or is there something so basically anti-social or dangerous about Sonya herself that the cops can smell it out like those insects that are so attuned to a certain molecule they can detect it from miles away even though, for all intents and purposes, they can't smell anything else? Maybe she gives off a fragrance which they translate roughly as "female-in-heat," which seems likely to attract, confuse and stir up every fevered male within a seven-block radius. Now would be the time for taking Sonya by the hand, fading away into the shadows, slipping quietly into the water, and breathing through two reeds as they begin their long, green underwater butterfly stroking to Nassau, leaving all this incredible bullshit behind them.

Moke's father is finishing up with the radio, leans deeper into the vehicle and appears to hang up the apparatus, stands up beside the shiny cruiser, the red revolving light flickering across his earnest weathered brow, and says a few final words to the cops. The talkative cop says something back and laughs and gets in the fuzz machine and guns it into life. Bill gets almost to them with his toothy grin and jaunty gait before Sonya waylays him, encircling his neck with her arms, and plants a relieved thank-you kiss on his collarbone. "It's all right, Honey," Bill says with a paternal tenderness in his voice, "we got it all straightened out. You don't have anything to worry about as long as the old Kentucky Galena-illes are looking out for you." He winks at Moke.

"So what's the deal?" Moke says.

"What did I tell you," Elijah says. "Is this man a salesman or not?!"

"Sometimes, Buddy, *who* you know matters a whole lot more than what you know—remember that—not always, but at least half the time."

Elijah wraps his enormous arm around Bill's shoulders like an enraptured elephant.

"So are they dropping the charges?" Moke says.

"You fox," Elijah trumpets, shifting his portly gray bulk, "You sly fox."

"Well, we don't know yet, but we got a little bit of luck working for us too. Weather Bureau reports another hurricane blowing this way—news just came in—everybody's going to be pretty busy, it looks like, whether it hits or not. I guess the boat ought to be put up, Elijah. If the storm hits, we'll all have our hands full. If it doesn't hit, I've got a little golfing date set up with the Chief for along about Saturday morning."

Chapter Ten

Was it someone from abo-uh-ove?
Who wrote the Book of Love?

"GOOD FRIENDS, we are gathered here today to pray with all our hearts for the safe passage of our state and region through the oncoming ravages of this terrible hurricane. We know that, with *Gawd's* help, we will all be spared from the fury of the storm. With *Gawd's* intervention, our homes and families and places of worship will all be protected and safe from harm. With *Gawd's* guidance, we will all—some day—find our way through the glorious clouds above to His Promised Land. . . ." Elijah Roark goes on and on in his unctuous baritone. . . .

Seated next to Moke is Sonya—in a yellow taffeta dress and a wide-brimmed sunhat—her Southern belle costume, she calls it. Moke is wearing his light-blue seersucker suit, feeling cleancut in his crewcut; and when he looks over at Sonya, she rolls her eyes meaningfully to indicate her opinion of the service. They have come to pacify their elders, pure and simple—who are seated in the same pew—and because today is the day that Hazel has decided to accept Christ as her Savior, to be Born Again, and to be officially and publicly baptized in His Name, Amen. In her purple dress, Hazel stares hypnotically up at Elijah Roark and the impressive stainless steel cross above the altar where he stands. She gapes at the words "All One in Christ Jesus" in silver-glitter high up on the blue velvet curtain beyond with its border of potted palms, their branches nodding ever so slightly in the air conditioned currents of the hall, as if in placid assent.

Sonya is of the opinion that Hazel is only going through with this ludicrous ritual in order to make up some brownie points with

119

Elijah, but Moke is not so sure. The beatific expression on Hazel's face almost convinces him of the sincerity of her conversion. There is something poignant and lost about Hazel, some essential confusion that might be seeking remediation; and Elijah has, after all, bathed her in attention, focused all the wattage of his considerable persuasive powers in her direction. Roark's drive for converts seemed as deeply seated, as intense, as an instinct. "Let us pray," Elijah says. They bow.

"Lord, we beseech thee, to remember us now in our time of need. We are the sheep of thy flock, the white sheep who have tried so hard to do thy bidding, though we have sometimes failed so miserably. We beg thy forgiveness for those times when we have tried and failed to do thy work. We are not so strong or perfect as thy Majesty, but we are so thankful for thy mercy and devotion to us. Yes, we are. So terribly thankful, Lord. Without you, we would be nothing at all, less than the grains of sand upon the beaches of this marvelous world you've given us, less than the insects, less than the lepers, or the crustaceans of the ocean deep . . . ."

"And today, Lord, we have a *special* offering to make, another new lamb for your flock, a poor lost soul who yearns to be saved. Yes she does. While the demonic winds of Hurricane Hazel stir up the waters of the gulf of Mexico and threaten us all, we are so pleased to be able to bring this mortal woman—also named Hazel—before thy throne as a convert and a disciple. Yes we are. Thy servant Hazel has lived a hard life, Lord, a hard and bitter life. And her temptations have been great. We must do our best to help her overcome the afflictions of her difficult past so that she may receive Your Holy Mercy and be cleansed, both now and forevermore. *Amen.*"

"Will thy servant, Hazel, please approach the altar?" Hazel arises shakily and wobbles up the center aisle toward the Great Man in his bluish robe. While she is approaching, the curtains open magically before her, revealing a large glass tank of the kind usually used, on a smaller scale, for tropical fish. It is filled nearly to the brim with glittery water through the surface of which beams a striking mosaic of sunlight rotating slowly and eerily from above, as if the heavenly hosts themselves are aiming their purest and most worshipful thoughts on the ritual about to take place in the Bible Ranch auditorium. Bill turns toward Moke and winks conspiratorially—as if to say, "We both know this is just clever show-manship (not real angels) but it sure is good P. R. for our buddy the Lord, don't you think?" Moke looks hastily away.

"Well-beloved, you have come hither desiring to receive holy Baptism," Elijah says. "We have prayed that our Lord Jesus Christ would vouchsafe to receive you, to release you from Sin, to sank-ti-fy you with the Holy Ghost, to give *unto* you the Kingdom of Heaven and Ev-er-las-ting Life." With this, he beckons to Hazel to climb the steps, mount the altar, and approach the celestial fishtank. As she does, Elijah raises his arms aloft as if to implore the spirits on high and then brings his enormous arms slowly and dramatically downward to rest tenderly, paternally, upon Hazel's shoulders.

"Dost thou, Hazel, renounce the Devil and all his works, the vain pomp and glory of this world, with all covetous desires of the same, and the sinful desires of the flesh, so that thou wilt not follow, nor be led by them?"

"I will," Hazel says meekly, the wings of her back heaving noticeably with emotion.

"Jesus Christ," Sonya whispers in disgust.

"Praise the Lord!" someone yarps with enthusiasm. At this point, Elijah escorts Hazel around the fishtank and up some steps, and the two appear on a platform above the water. Then Hazel removes her shoes and Elijah assists her in climbing over the rail-ing into the angel-lights, which play briefly over her white feet and the billowing flower of her purple dress as she frantically tries to hold it down. When Hazel and her dress have settled, belly-deep now in the tank, Elijah cups some of the water and, leaning over, sprinkles it into her hair.

"O Merciful Gawd!" Elijah says. "Grant that like as Christ died and rose again, so this thy servant Hazel may die to sin and rise to newness of life. Grant that she may have power and strength to have victory, and to triumph, against the Devil, the world, and the flesh. *Amen.*"

"Especially the flesh," Sonya whispers to Moke.

"And now," Elijah intones—and tips Hazel adroitly at the waist and dunks her brow, then her entire head like a doll—"I baptize thee In the Name of the Father, and of the Son, and of the Holy Ghost. *Amen.*" Hazel, who, underwater, has been making the astonished, agonized face of a dying guppy, suddenly explodes out of the tank, barking and choking and spraying.

"We gladly receive thy servant Hazel into the congregation of Christ's flock," Elijah says, smiling hugely, patting her on the back to help clear her lungs, "and do sign her with the sign of the Cross"—touching her forehead—"in token that hereafter she shall not be ashamed to fight under Christ's banner, against sin, the world, and the Devil. *Amen.*" Hazel looks ready to fight immediately, if necessary. The curtain sweeps mercifully shut as she begins struggling to get out of the tank.

"Has the Lord ever asked you for a 'loan'?" Elijah resumes, while the organ plays a soft obligato accompaniment. "If this statement surprises you, it is probably because you have failed to recognize in the needs of others, a direct request from Gawd. James warns us against the sin of neglecting Gawd and of uttering pious words while keeping too tight a grip on our purse strings: 'What doth it profit, my brethren, though a man say he hath faith, and have not works? Can faith save him?' Depend upon it—bread cast upon the waters *will* return, though it may be 'after many days.'"

> Give as you would to the Master
> If you met His searching look;
> Give as you would of your substance
> If your hand His offering took!
> Remember: When Christian love stirs you to generosity . . .
> The more you *give*, the more you *gain!*
> Give the Lord a Loan today!

"What will you give me," Sonya whispers in Moke's ear, "if I can come before the collection plate gets here?" Moke finds this kind of talk, in this context, acutely embarrassing—he blushes—though he too is repulsed by Elijah Roark's santimonious hypocrisy. He keeps his eyes directly on the four elderly deacons just now fanning out, one on either side of the two long banks of pews, wielding their shining golden plates. They could wear the plates as hats and do a soft-shoe routine, but instead, they pass them slowly back and forth, their faces expressionless, across the rows among the heads of the mostly blue and purple-haired little ladies and seedy-looking trailertown converts with big hands clutching coins and wallets and local small businessmen and their families. The plate-bearer coming closer on Moke's side is a little overcooked fellow in an open-necked Hawaiian shirt with a snazzy Texas-style string-tie decorating his shirt-front and "If-ever-there-was-a-time-when-our-country-needed-divine-healing-now-is-the-time" written in a scowl across his face. Sonya is holding Moke's hand. He can begin to feel her fingers tighten and her thigh tensing against his pantleg. She is kidding, of course. She is obviously upset and angry about Hazel's conversion, both because she thinks it is phony and because she dislikes Roark. Also, it scares her—she thinks her mother is finally losing her marbles.

Just as the plate comes drifting towards them on a current of hands, bills folded into its velvet-lined center, like a birthday cake buoyed up by a row of bakers, Sonya secretly moves his hand beneath her many bright folds of cloth and pushes his fingertips to softly touch her wet lips. It seems to him, in the instant of recognition, perhaps a pious gesture—as if to say: *the Body of Our Servant Sonya, which was given for thee, . . . preserve thy body and soul into everlasting life. . . . For this only is holy. This only is the Lord. . . . Glory be to God on high, and on earth peace, good will towards men. We praise thee, we bless thee, we worship thee, we glorify thee, we give thanks to thee for thy great glory, O Lord God heavenly King, God the Mother Almighty.* But Moke is so shocked and embarrassed, reflex alone jerks his hand swiftly away from under the dress, and his flying knuckles nick the golden plate smartly; the plate rises into the air and seems to hang momentarily (but out of reach) before clanging and clattering to the floor with a rain and roll of coinage that turns heads in every direction.

"When I was in the Marine Corps stationed at Orlando in the early forties," his father is saying, "a hurricane passed almost directly through the place. The wind was so ferocious it picked up little pieces of straw and grass and drove them like nails into telephone poles! All the telephone poles looked like pin cushions!" He has just returned from the Terresonna Lumber Co. with a load of pre-sawed ¾" plywood sheets, and he and Moke are systematically nailing and screwing them in place over the picture windows of the L-shaped ranch house—one in front, one in back, plus the sliding doors leading to the patio.

Overnight, the sky has turned to slate, and already the wind is gusting up to thirty miles-an-hour, whipping the palm fronds like crazy, riffling the grass, and catching at the edges of the plywood with a strange, almost willful, mischievousness. All over the neighborhood there are signs of desperate preparations for the storm: people scurrying about like ants, banging shutters closed, lowering awnings and antennas, tacking up plywood, collecting hoses and birdbaths and porch furniture and picnic tables and garbage cans and decorative rocks—any potentially lethal flying objects—and trundling them into garages.

Secretly, Moke is hoping the storm does not veer away. He hopes it blows right down the main drag of Terresonna with record winds wrecking half the town and ultimately destroying all means of transportation to the north for an indefinite period. He enjoys this heady sense of apocalypse in the air—it fits his mood; it brightens his outlook. Considering the past few months of his life, it seems more than fitting. It seems . . . almost predestined, though he reminds himself he doesn't believe in predestination. They lug another heavy sheet from the garage around the side of the house and press it into place above the concrete sill. His father pounds. The field of tall yellow grass undulates eerily like a body of water. Something resembling a tumbleweed flicks past his eye's periphery and disappears behind a row of bushes. "Just what exactly *did* go on in this bar you took Sonya to, son?"

"Oh that. I figured you would hear about that sooner or later."

"Your old man wasn't born yesterday—I can tell you that." His father's tone is light and conspiratorial—no anger—strictly man-to-man. Moke is relieved to have the subject out in the open.

"Well, she did get a little carried away, I'll admit. She had a few drinks and, you know, she likes to dance and everything."

"Yeah."

"She just did this seductive sort of dance and the bartender really over-reacted for some reason."

"Did she actually take anything off—any clothing?"

"Just her bra."

"Uh-*huh!*"

"But it was no big deal—it really wasn't. She was just having a good time, and everybody enjoyed it."

"Except the bartender."

"Except the bartender."

"Just exactly who is Sonya?" Bill says. "Is she a prostitute?"

"Are you kidding? Of course not."

"You're sure?"

"Of course I'm sure! You think I'd bring a prostitute to stay at the Bible Ranch? I don't even know any prostitutes."

"Who is she then?"

"What do you mean, who is she? She's a girl."

"You think you're serious about her?"

"Serious enough."

"Hunh!" Bill takes all this in with a "just asking" and a "well, I'll be" tone of voice. His muscular forearms work steadily. "Tell me," he says, "what do you think little Julie Greenway is going to have to say about all this?"

"I doubt if she cares at this point, frankly."

"I wouldn't bet on that. You never can tell about women."

"Maybe so. . . ." Moke rubs his chin and sighs loudly. "I've been thinking I might drop out for a while," Moke says. His father stops pounding.

"You'd be crazy to do that now, son. For Heaven's sake! I wouldn't even consider it. With your brains and good grades, you could be sitting pretty in just a few more years if you can stick it out. . . . Why, there are a thousand young men out there right now who would give their right arms to be where you are."

"I know. I wouldn't leave permanently . . . just take some time off. . . ."

"To do what?"

"To get away from school for a while—the steady grind of it—and find out what I really want to be. It seems senseless to be working for something I'm not even sure I want."

"You don't even know what's good for you. How would you support yourself?"

"Get a job."

"What kind of a job?—you don't have any qualifications for a good job. You have to have a college degree to carry out groceries at Kroger's in this day-and-age."

125

"I know. I know."

"Of course, it's hard work in pre-med—no one said it was going to be easy. But it's work that will pay off in the long run, pal. Look at me. Just look at me"—his father's blue eyes penetrate hypnotically into his own. His father's weathered, troubled face so near his own—he is such an earnest man, so certain of what he believes. . . . "I never even graduated from high school. You didn't know that, did you? Well, I didn't. I never even graduated from high school, and I'm making more money today than a lot of college graduates. That's a fact. But it wasn't easy, and I *wouldn't have done it* this way if I'd had any other choice, believe me. Who knows what I might have become if I'd had a college education? I'll never even know what I missed!"

"You've done fine *without* one."

"That's not the point. . . ." His father pulls out his cellophaned Camels, hits the pack with its blue stamp on his left-hand knuckle and extracts a cigarette and tamps it furiously on the windowsill. "My father was a drunkard most of his life, Moke." Inserted in the corner of his mouth, the Camel bobs up and down unlit as he talks until he jerks the huge orange flame of his pocket lighter within an inch of his half-slit eyes, inhales sharply, and erupts with smoke. "If I looked at him cross-eyed, he'd whip me with a belt. When I was sixteen, he threw me out of the house and I *had* to make it on my own. When I was nineteen, I was the manager of a Kroger's store. I made good money for those days . . . before I went on the road . . . and I made good money afterwards too . . . selling vacuum cleaners door-to-door."

"You've told me this story a hundred times!"

"I want you to remember it. . . . I sold vacuum cleaners all over Ohio, Kentucky, and West Virginia. Eventually I had a hundred men working under me, and my district sold more vacuum cleaners than any other *two* districts in the country. I wanted to *be* somebody, and I thought I was. But I found out that without a college degree, all I was was *a god-damned vacuum cleaner salesman!* I wouldn't want you to go *through* what I had to go through. I did it so you wouldn't have to, son. Think about it."

"I thought you had stopped smoking."

"Just while I was recuperating. I'm back to normal now. I try to keep it down though. It's awfully hard to quit when people blow smoke in your face all day long. When you've been smoking for thirty years like I have, it's hard to give it up."

"You think you can get Sonya off the hook?" Moke says.

Bill places one of his heavy blue-veined hands on Moke's shoulder, then squeezes the back of Moke's neck. "You're a good one," he says. "I wouldn't let you down after all these years, buddy, now would I? You're my own flesh and blood, for heaven's sake. But I want you to know—I wouldn't do it for just anybody, I'll tell you that. I sure wouldn't." He winks and goes back to the pounding, lipping the Camel and squinting as the smoke trail rises across his eyes.

Bad weather brings out the pack instinct. Bill invites the women to move out of the Bible-Ranch unit temporarily and spend the night in the relatively greater security of their L-shaped white concrete walls and boarded up and shuttered windows. They agree readily and gratefully. Hazel is scared shitless. When everything is set—late in the afternoon—Moke and Sonya decide to take a spin over to the beach to see how the ocean looks. The wind is getting fierce and portentous, gusting up to seventy-five, according to the radio, blowing the Pontiac around like a toy. The roads are nearly deserted. They pull up the hill and around the circular drive at the Terresonna Municipal Beach and park and get out and walk slowly across the shaggy planks of the municipal pier to the railing.

Someone has already lowered the canvas and taken in the wire trash baskets and the place looks bare and desolate and hazy. The breakers are enormous and wild, reminding Moke of a terrifying dream of tidal waves, as he squints out along the horizon almost certain, almost hoping, he will see the great crushing twenty-foot-high wall of water that will surely annihilate them. Sonya's hair blows straight back from her skull as if she is Wonder Woman in flight, or some angel of mercy come to save him from a watery death. The thrashing of the waves and the rush of the wind are so loud it is impossible to talk and be heard, a fact he notices when he licks his lips and discovers them coated with salt and tries to tell Sonya. The words "lick your lips" rattle in his throat and are literally blown away into the grey sky.

Sonya's mouth moves to reply and she smiles forlornly when she sees the effect, as if they are cut off behind soundproof glass, already strangers to each other, already ghosts in two different cosmic dimensions across which sound will not travel. The thought could make his eyes water even more than they are already watering from the wind. They hold each other—her warmth envelops him. For a moment it is as if they are standing on the prow of some clipper ship, setting off into a gale, in the middle of some hopelessly sentimental sea-voyaging movie. When they return to the car, the Pontiac's windshield is so cloudy with salt deposits he has to skim it off with his handy ice-scraper before starting the drive home.

It is a cozy evening, closed into their tightly boarded fortress, candles and flashlights and transistor radios at the ready, the wind lashing and whistling and thumping outside as if ghouls and demons are dancing across the lawns. The bigger wind that will sweep them all away may be arriving at any moment. Then the man on the Late News reports that Hurricane Hazel has skidded off to the west somewhat and it now seems unlikely that Terresonna will receive the full brunt of the storm. Hazel and Moke's mother actually clap when they hear this news. In the middle of their clapping the electricity suddenly dies and the TV screen fades away into a white dot and Moke begins clapping. "Now this is more like it!" he says gleefully. "Oh, no!" Hazel says.

"Get the candles," Moke's mother says as Bill simultaneously pops a match and holds it to a wick in front of them.

"Probably just a line down in the wind," Bill says reassuringly. "Nothing to get excited about. It's about time to go to bed anyway, gang." He lights another candle and a third and places the first next to the delicate hurricane lamp on the end of the piano, whose cut glass surfaces reflect flame and shadow about the room in spooky flickerings. Sonya and Hazel and his parents say their goodnights, and his parents go off to their room and Sonya and Hazel go off to Moke's, each of the two nursing their umbras of departing candlelight as if completing some somber religious ceremony, leaving him the single remaining candle there on the dark piano. Earlier he has made Sonya promise to sneak out to him if she can, not to the Hide-a-bed where he would ordinarily sleep surrounded by open jalousies, but to his sleeping bag pressed into the well-protected hallway at her door. They both understand she will not—there is not enough privacy; Hazel is an insomniac—but he wants to take the fantasy to bed with him if he can, so they leave the possibility open. He unrolls the bag, still smelling faintly of woods and canvas and the boxes of Tide in the utility room where it is stored, and flops it into place.

"I wonder why it's called a hurricane lamp?" Moke ponders, walking over to extinguish the candle. It wouldn't last a fraction of a second in a real hurricane. No practical use whatsoever. Still, the fragile elegance of the lamp appeals to him. The two hurricane lamps, one situated at either end of the piano, have followed them from house to house and era to era. They are his mother's idea of beauty and culture and part of her effort to civilize them.

The other two glass adornments there—shapely blue vases with minute orange and green stenciling in a floral design—are his father's contributions, the only remaining war mementos he has not sold or given away. They are decorative vases removed from either side of a walk-in mausoleum in Okinawa. His father, who is not one to relish telling war stories around the coffee table or in any other context, once told a story about these vases. He was muddy and feverish and under fire in the story. He ducked into this immense white tomb (with the two vases) for cover. Something moved in the darkness, surprising him, and he blasted away into that corner with his 45-revolver, the same one he now keeps on a hook in the back of his closet behind his business suits. There was a yelp of pain. After several tense minutes of waiting, he lighted one of the votive tapers and saw, to his anguish, that the person he had inadvertently murdered was an unarmed and quite lovely Oriental woman.

Thinking about this faraway dead woman, Moke absently puts on his pajamas and returns to the black hallway, sliding over as near to Sonya's door as he can get, and after what seems like hours of turning and sighing and listening to the wind, he falls into an uneasy and difficult sleep.

Chapter Eleven

When you walk through a storm
Hold your head up high

IN THE DREAM, Sonya is walking slowly towards him on the dark, deserted beach. She is almost too distant to be recognizable. But as she comes closer, he sees she is naked and is crying—crying resolutely, her head thrown back, hair billowing out as if attracted by small electrical currents in the night wind. The tears migrate slowly back across her cheeks in rivulets as the rain bears down upon her body in the eerie light. Her breasts, as they swing in their elegant arcs, are wet and erect. She holds out her hand to him.

There is a sound like several boxcars slamming together and a scream and the prolonged swooshing of an enormous SAC squadron that fills the night-sky above the house as far as the eye can see in every direction. Then someone is shaking his shoulder, and he wakes up and realizes it is his father kneeling over him in the corner of the black hallway and speaking. The drumming of rain and wind on the roof and its buffeting on the plywood and walls are deafening. *How did the storm get tuned up to this pitch?* he wonders all in an instant. He must have slept through it. His father, still in his pajamas, is standing and knocking on the door to Sonya's and Hazel's room. . . .

"What *time* is it?" Moke says, sitting up groggily.

"After three," his father says.

"What *now?*" Hazel says, cracking the door. "There's no sleeping in this madhouse!" Sonya slips out in a pink nightgown and sits on the edge of Moke's sleeping bag, hugging her knees.

"The storm has veered back this way," Bill says. "I just heard on the transistor that they expect the water to begin rising. We might be smart to head for higher ground before it gets any worse."

"Oh, my God, my God, my God!" says Hazel. "We can't go out in this!"

"We may have to," Bill says. "I don't know."

"Sounds pretty hairy out there," Moke says.

"We can stay buttoned in here," Bill says, "and take our chances with high water, or we could get in the car and try to drive to the high school. This close to the waterway, it could be bad. I'm not talking about water around your ankles. Hell, it *could* rise twenty or thirty feet."

"Oh, my God, my God, my God," Hazel says. "I knew this would happen if we came down here."

"I don't want to alarm you unnecessarily," Bill says, "but we have to be realistic . . . Mom's getting dressed. I think we all ought to. Get dressed and we'll talk about it some more."

"I'm not leaving this house!" Hazel says. "Not for any amount of money. You can all go if you want to and leave me here to die."

"Oh, mother!" Sonya says.

"I mean it," Hazel squawks. "I'll get dressed, but I'm not leaving. Never in a thousand years!"

Moke is in the utility room looking for his combat boots in the darkness when his father comes in carrying the big flashlight and a yellow slicker. Bill roots around in one of the foot lockers until he finds what he is looking for—an old toy flak-helmet of Moke's, which he adjusts and slaps on his head.

"Maybe the thing to do," Bill says, "is head down the block a ways and have a quick look at that water. That way we would know one way or the other." He slides the slicker on over his khaki shirt and zips himself in. "I'll stay to the leeward side of each house as I go down, Moke, and I shouldn't be long. You make sure the women are all right, and if I'm not back in about half-an-hour, pack them all in the car and drive them to the high school, okay." Standing there in the semi-darkness in the flak helmet, his father looks ready to invade the beaches on Okinawa.

"Wait a minute. I'll go with you."

"No, you won't. I appreciate it, son. But we need to dividethe labor in this case. You tell the women what I'm doing. I don't
want to argue with them again too!"

"Or I could go instead. Why don't we do it that way?"

"No. This is the best, Moke. Do it my way this time." His
hand is on the door to the garage.

"Okay. You're the boss."

"I'll go out this way. I think it's the safest." He moves
quickly out and clicks the door shut behind him. Moke listens for
the swoosh of the outer door opening and closing. His father is
gone.

He decides not to worry about Hazel just yet. He takes his
candle in and checks the kitchen wind-up clock—3:21—and sets
about packing the car. He assumes they will need blankets, soap
and towels, the first-aid kit. His father has taken the one and only
flashlight. His mother, he finds out, already knows about the plan.
He tells Sonya. He decides that if his father is not back by 3:40 he
will go out looking for him. He tells Sonya to pack her bag and be
ready to do what she can to pacify Hazel and get her prepared.

At 3:40 he is tightening a pair of blue diving goggles around
his ears, standing in the dim utility room, his head pinched inside
his old Cincinnati Reds batting helmet, preparing to launch himself out into the night. Sonya, in Levi's and one of his Duke
sweatshirts, is watching him grimly, warily. Suddenly she hands
him her small candle and surrounds him with her arms and begins
kissing him. "Now is no time for this," Moke says, awkwardly,
holding the candle out and away from her. "What are you doing?"

"You don't want to go out there, Dreamboat. You want to stay
here with me."

"I won't be gone long." He feels her trembling along the
length of his arms and her hands on his neck. She is really shaking all over. "It'll be okay. I'll be right back."

"No, Dreeamboat, nooo."

He kisses her hard on the lips. "I'll just run out and check
the yard and come right back, Sonya. We can't just *leave* him here,
for Heaven's sake."

"Noooo."

"You go in the other room now and help my mother with
Hazel." He pats her with his free hand.

"Nooo."

"Let go now."

"Nooo."

"Sonya! Stop it." He pulls himself free, hands her the candle and pats her again on the shoulder, saying "Come on, you can do it," then moves quickly out the door into the garage. He adjusts the goggles and squints out one of the small unboarded windows, exclaiming, "Jesus!" at the sheets of blowing rain, then cracks the outer door, zips through, fights it closed, and begins to trot tentatively along across the puddled yard. Almost simultaneously, he is blinded by rain and wind and soaking wet to the bone. He struggles for every inch against the incredible wind. At the corner of the house, he collides with several garbage cans and falls down. The instant before they had seemed to be marching in formation across the expanse of sod between their house and the next; now the cans are suddenly becalmed, as if keeping him company. He stands up quickly and snatches at one of the lids, reaching it just as the galvanized body of the can catches a gust and bangs away into the road end-over-end. He has the idea that he can hold the lid up like a shield as he crosses between the houses to ward off the rain and any lethal flying objects. Uncannily, the streetlights are still on. The goggles are hopeless. He rips them off and fights the blowing rain out across the marshy land, holding the lid up against the wind. Just before he reaches the cover of the next house, the lid suddenly takes off into the black sky, like a frisbee thrown by a gigantic hand. He watches it sailing away in disbelief, thankful his fingers were not tangled up in the handle. He crouches against the wall and holds his curved palms against his cheek and forehead, trying to penetrate the opacity beyond the yard—nothing visible. A loud crack, like the sound of a baseball bat slugging a rock, startles him into further cramped movement along the wall. He does a fast do-si-do around the concrete stoop at the front door and then sees a pale hulk in the adjacent flower bed—his father half-crouching there in his flak helmet, like William Holden in *The Bridges of Toko Ri*.

"Are you all right?" Moke grabs his arm, and his father rises shakily.

"I can't hear you!"

"What are you doing here?"

"Something took my leg out!"

"We'd better get back!" Moke pulls his father's arm over his shoulder and turns him back toward their yard and muscles him away. Their feet sink ankle-deep in a low area of sand and muck. They struggle to free their feet at each step. His father does a gimpy-legged waltz-step, hanging onto Moke's back and shoulder like a man about to be machine-gunned behind German lines, hugging him manfully in a desperate last embrace. Their shamble towards the nearby Galenaille garage seems a slow-motion odyssey toward an ever-receding point of light, walking sideways through a long tunnel.

"God, what a night!" his father growls as they explode back into the garage.

"Jesus, I lost my hat," Moke says absently, feeling his head, pushing his back against the door, snapping it shut. His father sits and begins rolling up his soaked pantleg, revealing a purple lump on his right shin the size of a small walnut. Hazel is standing there with a horror-stricken expression on her face.

"God-dammit-to-hell!" his father says.

"Where's *Sonya?*" Hazel screams. "My baby girl?!"

"She's inside," Moke says.

"No!" Hazel squawks. "Nooo, nooo, nooo, nooo! She ran out looking for you! She's *out* there! She's *lost* out there! She's probably dead by now! My little *baby!*"

Without thinking, Moke yanks the door open and catapults his body back out into the howling rain.

He runs out towards the main drag, letting the wind carry him, carry him, reasoning that if she has gone the other way he would have seen her before now. Up past the dark and deserted A & W, he can see flashing lights, so he navigates, hobbles, sprints, and half-flies across the sand, muck, and splashing asphalt until he can just make out what it is—a couple of cops in fluorescent slickers hanging from the door handles of a black patrol car waving big yellow spotlights at a thin stream of traffic. Moke puts his head down and barrels toward them.

"I'm trying to locate . . . ," he starts to yell, but the drumming of the wind converts the words into a meaningless hum. The nearest cop makes a motion for him to get into the backseat of the car, so he wrenches open the door and climbs in and slams it shut. The cop does the same, careening into the frontseat.

"I'm trying to locate a missing person," Moke says into his wet, curious face.

"A Caucasian chick about twenty years old looking for her boyfriend?"

"Could be."

"Nice buns."

"Could be her."

"Who are you?"

"I'm the boyfriend."

"Live around here?"

"Yeah."

"God-*damned*. You ought to know better than to be out in this weather. I wish you kids could just hang it up on a night like this. Someone could get hurt! This is serious business if you want to know something. She was just here a minute ago and crying her eyes out. They took her down to the station."

"How can I get there?"

"You can't."

"How did *she* get there?!"

"Christ!" the cop says and gets out angrily and slams the door. Moke can see him gesturing broadly to the other cop. He reaches for the door handle, but the first cop sticks his big red face back inside and says, "We'll get you a ride down with one of these tourists. But the next time, kid, try to keep your girlfriend indoors, okay?"

"You bet," Moke says. "I sure will."

When Moke walks into the Terresonna police station, Sonya is seated alone on a bench over against the far wall, across an expanse of black-and-white tile, like the only girl in the junior high gym who no one will ask to dance. The room is bathed in watery white light, whiter than daylight, from banks of egg-crate fixtures overhead; and the deadly smoke from several hours of lung-pulling drags is swirling like fog. Two cops are leaning on a plywood counter near Sonya's position. They ignore him until Sonya suddenly sees him and leaps from her seat and rushes over and embraces him ferociously.

135

"You'll get wet."

"Oh, Dreamboat," she sobs. "I'm already wet." She buries her face in his neck. "Is that all you can say?"

"I was terribly worried about you."

"I was terribly worried about you, too." Now that he looks at her, he sees she is nearly as wet as he is, and incredibly bedraggled-looking.

"You have to promise never to do this again."

"I promise."

"You'll always do exactly what I say during hurricanes."

She laughs a thin little laugh into his collarbone, then sobs all the harder.

"It's all right," he says. "Everything is going to be all right."

One of the cops saunters out from behind the counter with his thumbs sticking through his belt loops. Up close, Moke recognizes him—the Tony Curtis cop.

"I wonder," he says, "just what relationship are you to the suspect?"

"What suspect?" Moke says.

"Well, I mean, to this young woman right here?"

"These meatballs tried to *feel me up*," Sonya says. "Just keep your miffty grits off the merchandise," she says petulantly into his face.

"Routine frisking procedure," says the cop.

"You frisk hurricane victims?" Moke says, in astonishment.

"Only if they're women," Sonya says.

"Now just hold it one god-damned minute," says the cop, raising his finger and pointing it at Sonya. "You're lucky we didn't do a strip check on you, honey. We have a warrant for your arrest right over there in that drawer. We could have you in the slammer in five minutes if you think you might like the weather better in there. What do you say to that?"

"I say, 'Up yours,' " Sonya says.

"And just for good measure, we could add 'resisting arrest' and 'insulting an officer' to the charges."

"See what I mean," Sonya says, looking back at Moke, her eyes filling again.

"Is the Chief here?" Moke says.

136

"No *the Chief* is not here!" says the cop.

"I thought we had this straightened out before," Moke says. "I don't get it."

"Well, let's put it this way," says the cop. "The teletype never lies and the teletype never forgets. Miss Velonis here has a record as long as your arm, and that may put the whole business in an entirely different light. It just might."

"What sort of record?" Moke says.

"A little of this, and a little of that," says Tony Curtis, "and to think that a person like you is a resident of the Bible Ranch—tsk-tsk. I hope you've found religion, honey, because you're gonna need it. I didn't have any idea what kind of place they were runnin' out there. My, my!" Sonya starts sobbing vehemently into Moke's chest. The cop sucks his teeth emphatically and an expression which says "oh-God-what-an-act" passes across his mouth.

"Could I see the charges," Moke says.

"What charges? The charge is indecent exposure."

"Could I see a copy of the record you mentioned."

"Sure—glad to!"

"I don't have any record," Sonya says faintly.

"You sit over there," Moke says and follows Tony Curtis behind the counter, where a fortyish female dispatcher, wearing a bun and headphones, is plugged into a switchboard and a tired-looking blond woman is scribbling onto a clipboard. Tony Curtis walks over to a big table and lifts up a roll of pale lemon teletype paper and folds back two or three sections and points with his big blunt forefinger.

"Right here," he says. Moke reads: *Velonis, Hazel Sonya. Chicago, Illinois. Jumping bail, 1948. Disrobing in a public theater—lewd and lascivious charge. Loitering for the purpose of prostitution. Suspicion of prostitution. Soliciting. Petit larceny, 1945. Flight to avoid prosecution.* "Quite an incriminating list, wouldn't you say?"

"It's not the same person," Moke says. "The dates are wrong. She was only two years old then."

"Oh, the god-damned dates are always wrong—the keys misfire—that doesn't mean anything."

"Check it out," Moke says. "Sonya's only seventeen, you know. I think this is a mistake."

"You bet it's a mistake. What did you say your name was?"

"Moke Galenaille," Moke says. "G-A-L-E-N-A-I-double-L-E."

"Slower," the cop says. He begins writing it down.

"Even in 1955, she was only twelve," Moke says, "even if the numbers are wrong. And 1965 is not here yet, right?"

"I don't want to talk about it," the cop says.

"How would you like to talk about gross misconduct?" Moke says, raising his voice, surprising even himself. "How would you like to talk about a lawsuit? I thought the exposure charge had been suspended or postponed—am I right?"

Tony Curtis thinks for a minute. "We've got a hurricane to worry about here—in case you hadn't noticed."

"Are there any charges then? Or are we free to go?"

Tony Curtis decides it is time to consult a colleague. He leaves Moke standing by the teletype table. The two cops speak in low tones, eyeing him but turning their mouths away confidentially.

The blonde with the clipboard wags her head in Moke's direction. "It's been a pretty hectic night," she says. "I've been here since seven last evening and so have most of these people."

"How's the storm coming?" Moke says.

"Some real damage," she says. "Some bad damage from what we hear. I think I heard you mention Bible Ranch? We heard there is some terrific devastation out on that side of town—whole blocks blown out."

"Really!"

"Did you come from over there?"

"No. We live fairly near here."

"It's been a real bad storm," she says.

Just then Bill, Elijah, Hazel, and Moke's mother file into the station. In his yellow slicker, his father marches to the desk. Hazel, wobbling and swooning like a mad woman across the expanse of tile, embraces Sonya and sinks to the nearest bench in a fit of choking sobs, still clinging to Sonya's shoulder, nearly causing Sonya to roll onto the floor. Sonya fusses at her, pats her, then settles down beside her on the seat. Elijah puts his arm around Hazel and coos quietly into her upturned face.

"Are you all right?" Bill says to Moke.

"We've got a little problem here," Moke says. He shows Bill the print-out. The Tony Curtis cop appears quickly at Moke's elbow.

"No, it's not a problem. It's evidence in an ongoing investigation. The suspect seems to be the same person we discussed earlier, sir. She has a record, including flight-to-avoid-prosecution."

"What do you intend to do about this, officer?" Bill says.

"The Chief is not here right now, sir; but, according to the book, the suspect must be incarcerated until bail is set."

"I thought we had this settled," Bill says.

"I thought so too, sir."

Suddenly, Hazel erupts from her bench and starts towards them. "You god-damned pigs, it's *me* you want! It's not Sonya. Let me see that paper." She grabs it off the counter, tearing half the page from the folded print-out, and stares at it fiercely. "This is me, and this isn't half of the awful things I've done. Here—take me away." She holds up her crossed wrists in the melodramatic gesture of a Christian martyr going to the lion pits. "I give up. I'm the guilty one. Take me away. Put me in prison where I belong. I'll go quietly."

"Hazel, this is not helping," Bill says.

"Is your name Hazel Sonya Velonis?" the cop says.

"Yes," Hazel says. "And I'm guilty of terrible crimes."

"Mother," Sonya says. "Would you stop fooling around."

"There's no need to confess, Hazel," Elijah offers, "to something you didn't do. These men understand you're only protecting your daughter, which is perfectly natural."

To everyone's surprise, Tony Curtis snaps a set of cuffs on to Hazel, takes her by the arm, turns resolutely, and leads her out and through a steel door toward the cellblock.

Chapter Twelve

You're a thousand miles a-way-ay
But I still have your love
To re-mem-ber you by. . . .

OUTSIDE, the storm seems to have passed. The air is calm, the trees stiff and quiet in the rain. The sidewalk and street and parking lot are littered with debris, but aside from that and some shocking dents in Elijah's Imperial, it might be an ordinary 5 A. M. in downtown Terresonna. Sonya leans on Moke's shoulder drowsily as they settle into the backseat. "My mother is famous for her brains, but this just about tops it all," Sonya says into the roof. Elijah starts the engine and they glide smoothly away.

"Don't worry, Sweetie," Bill says. "We'll get her out first thing tomorrow. It's just some damned administrative mix-up."

"She might be better off in a safe, secure place like that on a night like this," Moke's mother says. "Don't you think?"

"When the House of God is ravaged," Elijah says, "no place is safe. Only God can protect her or any of us. But she is a member of His flock, and I'm certain He is well aware of that fact and will protect her from harm's way, just as He protected us all tonight."

"What sort of damage is there out at the Ranch?" Moke asks. "We heard it was pretty bad out that way?"

"Total devastation," Elijah says. "As I drove away, there were trees flying through the sky like guided missiles. The roof of the auditorium blew off. The windows blew out. It was terrible, a terrible sight."

"What are you going to do now?" Moke's mother says, meaning where was Elijah planning on driving the five of them.

"Rebuild," Elijah says, still in a glassy-eyed funk. "And we welcome this opportunity, this test of our faith." In a few minutes, he slows down, and Moke sees through the rain-streaked window that they are already adjacent to the entrance of the Bible Ranch, though the Bible Ranch sign above the entrance is missing. The car stops, pointed toward the opening, and Elijah clicks the headlights on highbeam and directs his small auto spotlight out across the expanse of real estate that was formerly his headquarters as a mute testimony to his words. Even in the darkness, one can get an immediate impression of the uncanny extent of the destruction caused by the storm, for extending out for their view is a collection of wet rubble, broken beams, and wrenched forms that resembles nothing Moke remembers ever seeing in that spot. To his tired eyes, it seems, momentarily, to be a vision of the shadows and huddled shapes of gnomes and goblins, dispossessed creatures like themselves from some errant dream, vexed and miserable, conspiring in the rain. Elijah Roark folds his enormous head across his arm on the steering wheel of the Imperial and begins to blubber like a child.

The next day the sun comes up in all its Floridian splendor, blazing and generous and restorative. The storm seems a cruel memory, even to Moke with his heightened readiness for apocalypse, but there is a giddy sense of exhilaration in the air. Surprises are everywhere: lawn furniture dangling from rooftops, trees festooned with welcome mats and garden hoses, and a new *horizon*, entire blocks rearranged. There is work to be done, and a powerful sense of community spirit and cooperation, neighbors out picking up their yards and exchanging garbage can lids and assessing damage, insurance adjustors prowling the streets in their black-walled company cars, newspeople and photographers and camera crews, the mayor and his contingent shaking their heads and taking notes they hope will prove that they are a "major disaster area," eligible for Federal money.

The Chief is unable to see Bill about Hazel's case until later in the day, so Moke helps his father take down all the plywood from the windows. Then they all drive out to the Bible Ranch to see Elijah and the mess in the daylight. The place is crawling with parishioners. At the entrance, several members of the flock are struggling to resurrect the battered sign above the gateway. Others, in groups of three and four, are standing waistdeep in the tangled remains of the headquarters building, lifting chunks of concrete and broken jalousies, banging with sledge hammers to loosen twisted reinforcement rods, moving the shards of rafters from where they had crashed. Still others are uncovering desks and filing cabinets, stoves, beds, refrigerators, tables, and chairs from the debris and dragging them to separate spots on the lawn. The pool area and one wing of the motel building seem relatively unscathed. Luckily, Sonya and Hazel had taken their luggage (and themselves) to the Galenaille's because the motel unit where they had been living was blown away except for the terrazzo floor. Moke and Sonya pace the floorspace in disbelief. Sonya seems quiet and vulnerable; her large eyes search his face as if to say, "Do you realize that except for sheer luck, either one of us could be dead right now?"

Elijah bursts from one of the doorways in the section of the motel that is still standing, and he is beaming and holding out a copy of a newspaper. "We're setting up the new offices in here," he says. "Everything is going fine. Take a look at this," he says to Bill, pressing that day's "hurricane" edition of the Terresonna *Plaindealer* into Bill's hands. Moke suffers through a weak moment when he imagines what *might* be in the newspaper—FORMER PROSTITUTE ARRESTED AS PART OF BIBLE RANCH SEX RING. STRIPPER'S DAUGHTER INDICTED ON INDECENT EXPOSURE CHARGE. DUKE STUDENT IMPLICATED IN INTERSTATE TRANSPORT OF SHAMELESS HUSSIES. BAIL SET AT 100M. But Elijah's mood seems to belie such newsflashes from Moke's conscience; and, in fact, when his father hands him the paper, he sees it is only a story about the hurricane and Elijah's plans for reconstruction.

Immediately after the storm, many of the environs of Terresonna resembled the wrecked church-auditorium building at left. Only the Christian education wing of the Elijah Roark Bible Ranch Auditorium remained intact. But Dr. Elijah Roark has vowed to "restore every brick, jalousy, shrub, and hymnal" to its rightful place. "The Lord has provided this new challenge for us to test our faith, devotion, and resourcefulness," Roark said. "We must all pitch in together and rebuild God's house, making it an even finer dwelling than the previous structure. God has indeed worked a miracle of blessedness out of the heartbreak of destruction, and out of that miracle I already see an excitement, a new birth of Christian commitment. Yes I do. Praise be to the Lord!"

Though insurance will pay full coverage of the loss, plans are already under way for a $4-million dollar fund-raising campaign, Dr. Roark proclaimed, "that will make our own Bible Ranch the most splendid Gospel-facility in all of the southern United States. The town is truly awakened now," he continued. "The community and the congregation have been united and purified by this storm as never before. It's one of the most stimulating developments I've ever encountered," Dr. Roark said. "Though some 25 members lost their homes in the devastation, temporary housing is being provided on the Ranch-grounds. And we have already taken in some 40 new members and look forward to a true resurgence of our mission."

"Good job," Bill says. "A terrific write-up." The two men walk together toward the new headquarters building, yakking happily.

The afternoon passes swiftly. Trucks begin to arrive and line up to transport the rubble to dumpsites. Finally, Elijah and Bill depart for the station to meet with the Chief in their effort to spring Hazel from the jaws of the law. Sonya doesn't want to go along, so Moke and Sonya grab some extra workgloves and wade into the wreckage, looking for ways to make themselves useful. After what seems a long time, the battered Imperial pulls back into the compound and Hazel is in it, along with her rescuers. Getting out of the car, Hazel does not look nearly as elated as Bill or Elijah.

"So," she says grimly, approaching their work space surrounded by piles of broken lathing, "This must be where the forced labor begins."

"Oh, Mother," Sonya says, rushing over to embrace her. "Did they get you out for good?"

"No," Hazel says, "I'm still in prison."

It turns out that the Chief has agreed to release Hazel into Elijah's care and with the understanding that she will participate in a "rehabilitation program" sponsored by the Bible Ranch. She will be required to work her ass off helping to clear up the rubble at the Ranchgrounds along with the legions of the devout. If she behaves appropriately, she will have her record wiped clean, especially since there is some question about the statute of limitations in her case. Bill and Elijah think they have worked another miracle; Hazel thinks the whole deal is disgusting and insulting. She is interested in catching the next bus for Montreal.

"If you had only kept your mouth shut, you wouldn't be in this predicament," Sonya says. "Mr. Galenaille could have gotten me off, and they never would have known it was you."

"I doubt it."

"Sometimes you're just totally irrational."

"I suppose that's the thanks I should expect for saving your neck. I should be used to it by now."

"But who's going to save *your* neck, huh? Did you ever think of that?"

"My neck isn't worth saving."

"Oh, mother. It is too."

"My neck is about as valuable as an old chicken's with wattles." Sonya drops the board she is holding and puts her arms around Hazel and hugs her tenderly. Hazel starts to cry.

"Would you just stop talking like that. You're a beautiful woman with a lovely neck, and we're going to get through this just fine. Everything's going to be settled, and you won't have to worry about your damned record anymore. You'll be a free woman. Doesn't that sound like an improvement? It *will* be, believe me."

"I'll be so glad to get back home, Honey. I don't know why we ever came down here to this roach-infested wilderness. It's a virtual police-state, and the weather is the absolute pits, if you want to know my frank opinion."

"Do you see any roaches around here?" Moke says. "I don't see a single roach."

Later that day, Bill pays a visit to the Elbow Room and talks the Yogi Berra bartender into dropping all charges against Sonya.

For four days, they sweat through the clean up, sorting, lifting, loading, raking, returning at dusk coated with powder and grit. At first, Hazel fumes about in a cloud of resentment, working slowly and resting often and scowling at anyone with enough foolish disregard for their own safety as to make the mistake of speaking to her. But, gradually, even Hazel falls into the rhythm of the labor, catches the infectious sense of ant-like purpose permeating the flock; and especially after the hot, windy, exhausting days, and two early evening prayer sessions and private conferences with Elijah—part of her rehabilitation program —Hazel's aspect begins to brighten somewhat.

Sonya and Moke move through a daze of love-sickness. There is only the physical, the sweating, the bending, the lifting, the sitting around in the heat drinking cold Cokes with Sonya blowing hair out of her eyes, but always the recognition that the other is nearby. Each moment together seems precious, and it hardly matters that the work is back-breaking, the days long, and that they have no privacy.

With less than a week left, Moke is still in a quandary about what he will do next. He could go back to Duke or he could go to Nassau with Sonya, if she would be willing to go to Nassau, which she probably wouldn't be. If she wouldn't go to Nassau, he could always go to Nassau by himself. But, for some reason, nothing sounds more boring and meaningless than to think of going to Nassau by himself. If he goes to Nassau, his parents will be disappointed with him and he will be throwing away his future, and if he goes to Nassau and doesn't even take Sonya, he will be doing it for no good reason. He decides not to go to Nassau without Sonya.

As long as he doesn't ask Sonya whether or not she wants to go to Nassau, he avoids finding out the bad news that she can't go but he also diminishes his chances of ever going to Nassau, which are definitely not very good to start with. He also avoids finding out the bad news that she wouldn't even want to go to Nassau if she could plus the almost equally bad news that he might definitely have to throw away his future and disappoint his parents and ruin his life if, by some incredible miracle, she says yes she wants to and will go to Nassau and when should they leave and why did he take so long to ask her in the first place. If he were twenty-five, this might be an easier decision. But he is only eighteen.

Moke and Sonya drive to the beach, for maybe the last time, to see what damage Nature had done there. They find that the current has piled up huge rows of lush tangled kelp and seaweed along the sand and kicked up zillions of dead sea urchins, and the whole mess is starting to decompose in the sun. "Symbolic of the way things are turning out," Moke thinks, but keeps the thought to himself as they meander through the surf, hand in hand.

Their last few days in Florida pass, and Moke is feeling more and more blank on the subject of Nassau. Without deciding to, he stops thinking about it. Everyone, including Sonya, assumes that he will be going back to Durham. He begins to assume so himself. The travel plan, finally evolved, is that Moke will drive Sonya and her mother as far as Duke and Durham, his hypothetical destination, where they will catch the Greyhound to Montreal. This will save Sonya and Hazel some trouble and some money, and it will give him some traveling company and postpone a little longer the agony of having to say goodbye to Sonya.

He spends the better part of that Saturday just laying things out next to his suitcase on his bed and rummaging around the house, while Sonya sunbathes under the sprinkler in the backyard in a lather of Baby Oil, her closed eyelids glistening. More than once, he stops momentarily by the patio door and looks out at her and feels a sense of endless sadness that is not unlike a physical pain.

On impulse, he carries his dissecting kit out to the patio to show it to her. It was a going-away-to-school present last fall from his Uncle Doc, the one Doc himself had used in medical school. Moke had had to replace the scalpel with a new changeable blade variety, but otherwise the instruments were perfectly workable and even pleasant with their quaintly elegant lightweight wooden handles and their alligator-hide case. No one else had had anything like them. He tells Sonya how he would sometimes study this case, handle these instruments of his chosen profession, watching carefully how they moved about in his hands, and ask himself: "Is this what I am destined to *do* with my life? To cut up things?" It seems possible but not exactly probable, a kind of accidental alternate life.

He has an overpowering feeling during such moments that his hands are capable of doing something consequential, that they even yearn with an independent will to locate their proper use and get on with it. Last spring he had been the only student in his zoology lab who had managed to successfully dissect a chick embryo without breaking the delicate amniotic membrane—*that* had pleased him at the time. It seemed evidence of a certain talent. But, for some reason, he persists in doubting whether by manipulating these particular tools he will ever be able to truly realize himself—whatever that is.

Sonya says she doesn't have any doubts at all. She is certain he is going to be a great doctor some day and she hopes that when he is he will let her be his patient. That makes him feel better—momentarily—until he starts estimating the chances that he will ever see Sonya again after next Tuesday, whether he is a great doctor or not. By the time he is a great doctor she will probably be married to someone else and living in Saskatchewan!

The orange Pontiac is packed and ready by late Sunday. The three of them start north bright-and-early Monday morning—after excessive and drawn out and embarrassing good wishes and good-byes from Moke's parents, who stand waving from the frontyard of the L-shaped ranchhouse until they are out of sight as if Moke were going away to camp for the first time.

Tuesday night at around 9:30 they reach the outskirts of Durham. Moke is eager to impress them with a leisurely drive around campus, but Hazel is nervous as a monkey and insists on going straight to the bus station to find out about the scheduled departures for Montreal. Moke tries to talk her out of it—they are tired; they should take their time—but finally relents when Hazel promises they will absolutely come with him as soon as they have stopped and found out the bus schedule.

The Durham terminal is a dark, dusty building of beige, porcelainized brick surrounded by an acre of pavement and reeking of bus exhaust. They all get out and go in. Hazel immediately shuffles into line at the ticket window and he and Sonya sit dumbly on a shabby bench. The waiting room seems surprisingly crowded considering the hour; it is smoke-filled and smells of cigars and newsprint and chewing gum balls in little red machines and bad breath and sweat and rancid popcorn and month-old candy bars.

"Oh, I feel like I'm still moving," Sonya says.

"Try to get some sleep on the bus tonight," Moke says.

Hazel joins them, clutching a fistful of red-and-blue slips of cardboard, and informs them that a bus is leaving for Montreal in half-an-hour.

"Oh," Sonya says. Hazel picks an imaginary piece of lint from her dress and arranges her ugly straw pocketbook in the middle of her lap, obviously her waiting-for-a-bus posture.

"So you mean you won't be able to go with me after all?" Moke says.

"It doesn't look that way, does it?" Hazel says, not meeting his eyes.

"There's no reason to be so irritable about it," Sonya says. Hazel glares at her, then looks away and doesn't say anything—she is clearly the picture of a woman who is waiting for a bus and has no other immediate interest.

"There really isn't time, I guess," Sonya says to Moke with an embarrassed, pitiful look.

"You don't think there might be time for *you* to come at least?" Moke says.

Sonya eyes her mother. "The bus will be here shortly," Hazel says.

"Not this time, I guess," Sonya says.

Moke knows it is silly of him, but he is furious, livid with the injustice of it. Isn't it a matter of the commonest human decency to honor a promise, or at least to offer a polite apology, for God's sake, if circumstances change and the conditions under which the promise was made no longer apply? Anyone but a rude, hopeless, insensate cretin like Hazel would realize that! He finds himself standing up, his ears burning.

"Well, in that case," he says with mock cheerfulness, "I guess I'd better be going. I wouldn't want to complicate your departure plans and I'm not very good at saying goodbye anyway."

He jiggles the change in his pocket, then reaches out and shakes hands with Sonya and says "goodbye" to her in a softer voice and she says "goodbye" to him, and he turns and walks away and almost trips over someone's suitcase and keeps right on going out the door past a crush of bodies and a monstrous heaving open-mouthed whale of a bus that says ALBUQUERQUE and out across the pavement, telling himself what a relief it is to have all this foolishness behind him, what an incredible relief!

He practically blows a rod through the bug-spattered hood of the car, flooring it in neutral, then, feeling suddenly overwhelmed with reluctance to leave at all, embraces his head and allows the wheels to creep slowly toward the exit until he can collect his wits and decide what to do. As he raises his head from the wheel he can see a girl running toward the car—it is Sonya—running awkwardly in her shorts and sandals, her tanned legs, her beautiful hips, her sandals falling off, Sonya still running barefoot to the car, the car stopping, Sonya sobbing convulsively against his bare arm, reaching in to kiss him with her helpless face. He is thinking "Don't cry" so loudly he fears he has spoken it. Sonya whimpers an incoherent little noise and tosses her hair and runs part way back toward the terminal as the car begins moving again, her weeping image in the side mirror becoming smaller and smaller and blurred with the dark shapes of telephone booths and parked buses. As Moke steers dizzily up Main Street toward campus, the streetlights and the distant illumined spires of the University buildings appear to become minute garish astral bursts as if the night overhead is suddenly melting through the windshield.

Chapter Thirteen

Round this time of day I gets to feelin' low
And I wonder who's my baby's latest beau-o-o-o-o. . . .

MOKE WANDERS NUMBLY through the labyrinth of dormitory halls, searching for his new room. He locates the correct number and unlocks the door, swings it open and turns on the lightswitch. The room is bare and cramped with a diagonal slab of overhanging ceiling, painted an institutional green, and with one window, containing squares of wavy leaded glass, and one small bookshelf barely three feet high. He had requested a single, but this cubbyhole is a disappointment. An empty dormitory room is a depressing sight. He heaves his suitcase onto the bed and shambles back to the car for several more loads of gear. He hooks up the portable stereo and listens to Johnny Mathis singing "Warm," but that only makes him think about Sonya, who is no doubt on the bus by this time, heading north on some desolate highway, staring at her lovely, miserable reflection in the tinted glass of the dark bus window while twenty-two thousand totally deserted acres of black pine forest whiz by in the night.

After walking around some more and then slowly unpacking and starting a letter to Sonya, he raps on the door across the hall with the idea of introducing himself. The person answering his knock is an enormous hairless, shirtless youth lugging a huge dumbbell in his free hand. He sets it down hard on the oak floor with an elephant-like exhalation and offers what proves to be a knuckle-breaking handshake. "Kent Masterson," he says. "From Dallas. Pardon the sweat. I like to lift weights." He rests his arms against the doorjamb like one of the great apes. He is probably 6' 4".

"Moke Galenaille," Moke says. "From Cincinnati. I guess we'll be seeing quite a bit of each other. I live across the hall." Masterson makes no effort to move back or invite him in.

"Nice to meecha, Galenaille. I'll be finished with my routine here in about fifteen minutes. Then we can go down to the slop-shop for a snack. You et recently?"

"No." Masterson laughs loudly as if something one of them said had been funny.

"Well, *all right* then. See you soon then, ol' buddy." Moke turns to go back to his room, but Masterson says something else he can't hear, which sounds like, "I guess you're the serious-type."

"What's that?" Moke says.

"I said, 'My roommate's not here right now.' But you'll meet the bastard soon enough. He's a nigger."

"Oh."

"Isn't that a pisser!"

In the dope shop Moke learns that Masterson is also a pre-med—in fact, Masterson's father, he says, is an alumnus of the Med School—and Masterson says usually two-thirds of the sopho-more class "starts out" in pre-med and they have to "wash 'em out early" in Comparative Anatomy to get the class down to a rea-sonable size. Masterson has already bought one of the new-style Duke University T-shirts, with blue piping around the sleeves, and every time he takes a handful of potato chips or moves his arms, the incredible bulk of his biceps and pectorals strains at the cloth. Masterson says weight-lifting is about the best exercise there is because you can get more accomplished in a shorter time and re-ally increase your strength and improve your definition. Masterson keeps 500 pounds of Joe-Wieder-brand barbells in his room and says he lifts weights for two hours every day, which isn't hard to believe.

Masterson says he can't figure out why they had given *him* "a jungle bunny" for a roommate. But he guesses, as long as the bas-tard keeps to his own side of the room and doesn't try to borrow his hair oil, he isn't going to make a big issue out of it. This too is funny, for some reason.

151

Moke decides that Masterson is a hardcore bigot. He feels impelled to state a position or challenge Masterson in some way. He imagines what might happen if he suddenly raises up and throws the heavy table, spilling the dishes, platters, and catsup bottle into Masterson's lap, like an angry gambler who knows he's caught someone cheating at poker on one of the late-late movies.

"Maybe you'll like him better after you get to know him," Moke suggests calmly. "Give him a chance, for heaven's sake. Think how he must feel."

"Yeah, you're right," Masterson says. "He may not even *be* a nigger, for all I know. Maybe he's just got a fantastic suntan!" He laughs uproariously and slaps the tabletop. Another semester is under way.

In fact, Masterson's roommate is not a Negro. His name is Norman Adujabi, and he is a helplessly shy, somber boy with dark almond eyes, olive skin, and a slightly foreign, Mideastern look, whose boney knuckles are always straining around the handle of an enormous briefcase that seems too immense and weighty for his slender body. Norman is the only other one who ever stays regularly after the 4:30 Zoology/Comparative Anatomy bell or comes back to the lab after dinner. He is also the only other one who ever gets up regularly by 6 A. M. and takes himself to the sophomore lounge to watch the special chemistry program on educational TV recommended by Dr. Portier.

When he encounters Moke for their early morning vigils, he seldom speaks but smiles politely and prepares his clipboard and expensive-looking pen for the onslaught of information from the TV. Whoever arrives first, by tacit agreement, gets the set warmed up and the chairs arranged. The two of them seated there morning after morning—in the deserted lounge with its baronial splendor in red leather chairs with deluxe rivets before the flicker of the television and the steady grey early morning light from the high Gothic casements—cement a relationship. Norman's usually stolid features always bend into a shy smile of recognition and greeting if he passes Moke coming out of the Chem Building later in the day, lunging to pull his gargantuan briefcase past the doorjamb before the heavy door swings shut upon it, or later yet, in zoology lab again, where Norman works methodically on numerous careful drawings of all their assigned dissections. Norman becomes a kind of standard those first few weeks for Moke to measure himself against. Above all, he is determined not to fail in the pre-med program from sheer laziness, and he knows that if he works as hard and as earnestly as Norman is working, he can work no harder.

Moke haunts his mailbox, hoping for word from Sonya. Maybe she will not like McGill and will transfer to Duke and study to be an X-ray technician. He has the slides from Florida developed. But when they are ready, he flips through them quickly and without feeling. They seem like pictures from some other time-warp or some other planet. The colors are unreal, and the people are smiling so expansively you would think they were actually happy, but the happiness seems false. The girl is impossibly photogenic, with a quality of beauty and raw glamour and sensuality that men would kill for. The boy is loose-jointed and cocky and embarrassed-looking and has a foolish, hysterical grin on his squirrelish face, like some third-string batboy for some hopeless bush-league team, who has just been fired for incompetency. Moke tucks the small yellow box into his desk drawer out of sight. Already Sonya is beginning to seem like a stranger, and he doesn't want to ruin his memory further or make himself miserable. He is miserable enough as it is.

The Zoology/Comparative Anatomy lab is an amazing and horrifying place. Arranged in old oak-lined glass cases around the perimeter are specimens of snakes and internal organs and insects of hideous proportions, even the embalmed spiral of a sixty-foot-long human tapeworm in one corner. On top of the cases are perched, most prominently, the complete reassembled skeleton of a mountain goat and various fossil skulls and, elsewhere, skeletons of smaller animals, mostly mammals. Wall-charts on two walls display gigantic enlargements of hydra and paramecia and jellyfish and cross-sections of the human eyeball with all its parts labeled.

The eyeball looks faintly bloodshot, and when Moke looks up from his work he frequently stares at it. It makes him think of all the other eyes he has studied so far in zoology: the eye of his dogfish shark, carefully dissected from the peeled chondrocranium on the tip of a scalpel, lovely and transparent as a marble, precious vitreous fluids tenuously immured in a delicate spherical membrane one-cell deep; the eye of the honey bee that perceives ultraviolet as a color in nature and the sky as the under-surface of a tesselated dome, checkerboard squares of grey and white and black shifting with the sun like stars in a planetarium, a built-in sextant; or the compound eyes of the ordinary housefly that must see the world as if through twin kaleidoscopes. Who is to say how the world actually looks?

Moke continues to work late in the zoology lab, hoping for word from Sonya, and occasionally imagining his own eyes growing as bulbous and bloodshot as the one on the wallchart.

Though it is still early in the semester, Moke's professor in Religion/Philosophy 201 assigns a topic for the mid-term exam. It is to be a single question upon which they are to come prepared to write for three hours without notes. The question is: *What is life?* A collective groan goes up from the class, but Moke thinks he likes the idea. The more he considers it, the better he likes it. They will have plenty of time to prepare; there will be no anxiety about having to regurgitate segments of the textbook they have already covered. No ridiculous cramming. He can just systematically research the question when he has time and think about it in the meantime. And what a question! *What is life?* Perfect. This is what he has come to college to think about, the ultimate questions. This is why he is supposedly interested in medicine, after all, isn't it? Because it has to do with life-and-death issues.

His Zoology/Comparative Anatomy textbook itself, he finds, which is entitled *Life*, discusses the question of *What is life?* but only in terms of biological processes. Surely a religion/ philosophy professor will not be satisfied with a merely physical or mechanistic definition, and it does not satisfy Moke either. *The living organism maintains itself, grows, and reproduces its own likeness.* But to what purpose? Why should it bother?

Searching through the library stacks for a better answer to his question, Moke begins to encounter varieties of information, speculation, dogma, and enquiry he had not hitherto known existed. He begins to read eclectically and, as time leaks away, a little desperately: *Philosophic Classics: Bacon to Kant, Philosophy Made Simple* (covertly), *What Is Existentialism?, Leviathan, The Humanity of Man, The Meaning of Meaning, Beyond Good and Evil, Lady Chatterley's*

Lover, *Civilization and Its Discontents*. He discovers he is part of something called "the human condition."

Dr. Vernon returns the lab tests on Thursday. He is a compact, formal, muscular little man who wears navy three-piece suits, gestures impressively with his broad, short-fingered hands, and is almost completely bald. The lab tests are notoriously difficult. Comparative Anatomy is notoriously difficult. Masterson had been right, he guessed. They are trying to weed out the lightweights.

When Moke sees the 69 on his paper, his heart grows weak. He folds the quiz quickly away into his briefcase, his ears turning hot. If he fails Comparative Anatomy, his life will be over—his image of himself, his chances for medical school, everything. God, a 69, and he thought he had done reasonably well. He tries to concentrate on Dr. Vernon's instructions for the lab assignment on chick embryos. With each point made, Dr. Vernon pounds his square-tipped forefinger rhythmically into his left palm for emphasis. As soon as the brief lecture is over and the class has started to work on the dissections, Moke goes up to the blackboard and stands around until Dr. Vernon is free. "Could I talk to you . . . privately, I mean?" Moke says.

"About the test?"

"Yes." Vernon walks with him into one of the nearby supply rooms and shuts the door. The space is lined with jars and reeks of formaldehyde and embalming fluid. It seems a little embarrassing to be suddenly shut off from the others with this intense, hawklike little man, who stares at him sharply and waits for Moke to speak. "I was wondering if I might do something extra to make up for the quiz?" Moke says. "I can't believe I did so poorly."

"We don't keep you busy enough, is that it, Mr. Galenaille?"

"I've been working on it very hard, I really have. I wouldn't want any special treatment, but I know I can do better than I did. I think I just need more work . . . or . . . ." He feels his eyes begin to cloud over slightly, irrationally, a sensation of self-pity he has not felt so strongly since childhood. He is furious with himself.

"That's all right, Mr. Galenaille. You needn't worry yet. In fact, your score was twenty points higher than anyone else in the section. I doubt if you need any more work for the moment, but if I detect later on in the semester that you seem to be running out of things to do, I'll be certain to let you know." He claps Moke manfully on the shoulder and ushers him back into the laboratory.

As the semester picks up momentum and they all begin to feel swamped under the load of work, Masterson still spends hours clanging around his room with his weights. His apparatus takes up so much floor space that he has, more or less, driven Norman into the least desirable third of their room. As Moke passes the open door of Norman's and Masterson's room in his hectic comings and goings, he often sees Norman huddled in his corner, his determined features focused above the cone of light from his study lamp and his hands clamped over his ears. Eventually Norman takes to wearing a pair of earmuffs to block out Masterson's constant huffing and crashing and inane monologue.

Masterson has quickly learned to wear this year's ubiquitous light beige London Fog windbreaker and chinos and no socks with his penny loafers and has become an adept at frisbee. He oddly persists in pretending that Norman is Black and in baiting him with racist insults. Moke never responds to these gibes and is made so uncomfortable by them that he imagines Masterson does it partly to insult him as well. Later on Masterson grows somewhat friendlier and refers to Norman in all conversations as Nerman-the-Herman. Several others on the hall, mistaking Masterson's maliciousness for wit, or actually mistaking the name, start referring to poor serious, dignified Norman as Nerman. "How ya doin', Nerman!" "See yaroun', Nerman."

Then one day, Norman is abruptly absent from the morning TV session. Moke is mildly pleased at first, thinking he has outlasted even solid Norman and taking this as evidence of his own virtue. But he is vaguely uneasy; he keeps expecting Norman to come in late, excusing himself for this tardiness, and to start right to work, copying formulas as before. The next day Norman's absence begins to seem more permanent and alarming. Norman isn't the sort of person to give up so easily. Moke frankly misses his companionship. He finds himself growing drowsy and paying little attention to the program and worrying about Norman. It seems pointless to get up at such an ungodly hour if not even

Norman is there to witness his act of sacrifice. He decides to stop coming. Norman is absent from Comparative Anatomy lab too and from the hall.

The following Friday he chances to eat lunch at a table where Masterson is holding forth. Masterson has a black eye and a bruised-looking purple mark on the side of his face. Moke isn't thinking about Norman at the time, but Masterson brings it up: "You hear what happened between me and Nerman?" he says. The way Masterson tells it, Masterson had been lifting weights, clanging around the room as usual, and was just stooping over to try to clean-and-jerk 280 lbs., a new personal record if he had only done it, when Norman suddenly sneaked up behind him clutching a 10-pound dumbbell weight and (for no reason at all) brained him on the side of the head. "I didn't know I was livin' in the same room with a homocidal fuckin' maniac!" Masterson says. Masterson slipped to his knees but quickly recovered himself, shook his head two or three times like a slightly stunned wounded animal, and went after Norman roaring and cursing and swinging. He caught Norman with a shot that "pulverized" Norman's cheekbone and then he chased him around the room and up and down the halls and finally treed him in the quad, where Norman climbed to the shaky top branches and "squealed and carried on until the Dean showed up and then the little men in the white coats came and carried the son of a bitch away to the looney bin, I swear to God," and Masterson pounds the table with his sense of this evidence of divine justice. "And now I've got that whole gorgeous double *awll* to myself!" he adds idiotically.

Whether or not Norman is in the looney bin, he has certainly been absent from his usual classes and schedule, and Moke continues to wonder about him. One night in the deserted lab while he is returning his microscope to its cabinet, Moke is struck by the impulse to check Norman's cabinet to see if it has ever been cleared out. Sure enough, the lock is missing and there is no microscope—it was a university microscope; the lab assistant must have taken it back to the supply room. Curiously, Moke opens each of the little wooden drawers in the cabinet, hoping for some evidence that Norman has once used this particular locker. In one of the drawers, he finds something that makes his hair stand on end. It is a cylindrical plastic vial containing clear formaldehyde, and floating in the formaldehyde like a piece of half-chewed pork-chop is the perfectly dissected brain of a frog. They had not worked at all on frogs' brains. Norman must have dissected it on his own. He never saw Norman Adujabi again.

The letter from Sonya finally comes, a bluish envelope with a purple portrait of Queen Elizabeth in the corner, and the Montreal postmark.

> Dear Dreamboat,
>
> How are you? I never thought I would miss anybody as much as I've missed you the last few weeks, even as busy as I've been. But I've tried to be hard on myself and hard on you too, I know, by not writing and not giving in to my real feelings. I'm afraid I'm not much of a letter writer anyway, as you can see, certainly not one who could ever satisfy your appetite.
>
> Florida was a beautiful moment in my life, a beautiful interlude, and I know I'll never forget it and never forget you. It doesn't make sense to cry over a past you remember with such great pleasure, so I won't, I keep telling myself. Life is too short to play the wilting wallflower crying into your beer.
>
> How are your classes? How are you doing in Comparative Anatomy?!! I have such a horrible load of work at McGill! My favorite so far is Biology, of all things. I never thought I would enjoy it, frankly, until I saw our lab instructor. He's twenty-eight and has cute curly hair, and already he's been giving me special tutorials. Don't be jealous! I'd never be able to get through it any other way. I'm just not an academic slugger like you are, Dreamboat. I still love you as much as ever, just remember that, and if you were here I would much rather have tutorials from you, believe me, especially in Biology!
>
> All my love,
> Sonya

A snapshot falls out of the envelope as he tilts it against the light. It is a picture of Sonya taken at some ball or formal dance, almost a kind of prom picture—if they *have* proms in Canada. Proms in October? His heart melts at the sight of her. She is posing in a white, off-the-shoulder satin dress, a corsage pinned at her waist, and wearing white gloves, nylons, and shiny high heels. In the background are a couple of large Japanese umbrellas, crepe paper streamers, and what looks to be a wicker perambulator. Looking at her now, no one would ever suspect she was the notorious Suzi Sinzinnati. She is prim and wholesome—an ingenue— her cheeks like apples. There are no signs of tear stains or baggy eyes. There is no indication of who snapped the photo, but it was probably the lab instructor. Who else? Ladies do not go to balls unescorted. *Oh, Sonya, how could you? On the other hand, how could you not?*

It is during this time that Moke decides to start lifting weights. He orders 500 pounds of Joe-Wieder-brand iron—dumbbells, barbells, collars, wrenches, a "Samson twister" for "putting knife-sharp definition in arm, chest, and shoulder muscles," and a subscription to *Muscle Builder* magazine. When the shipment arrives at the University post office, it takes him six trips to lug the equipment back to his room. Before he does, he makes sure Masterson is nowhere to be found and the hall is deserted. He doesn't want any extraneous comments from *any*body. What he does in his room is his business.

He starts working out with a vengeance, reading and studying the muscle magazines. He concocts a powerful porridge of wheat germ, Special K, and brewer's yeast that he consumes in gigantic portions at bedtime after his work-outs. Only last year Julie Greenway's mother had referred to him as "skinny Moke," not exactly to his face but to Julie's, and Julie hadn't hesitated to pass on the insult. Moke ruminates about this morosely as he sweats through his routines, then frequently takes out the tape measure and measures his biceps, his forearms, his chest-normal, his chest-expanded, his thighs and calves—to see if he has gained any new bulk. He gives himself burning-hot sunlamp treatments in the nude, screwing the conical bulb into his study-lamp socket. He writes to Sonya.

His mailbox is a constant disappointment except for weekly letters from his mother, talking about the weather, her allergies, and his father's escapades. In Comparative Anatomy lab, the dissections move speedily along from the dogfish shark to their large project—the housecat. His cat-specimen, skinned and swollen from the embalming tank, is as big as a cocker spaniel and the most hideous beast he has ever seen or imagined. Each lab day he has to fish for it by plunging his arm up to his bicep in cold formaldehyde and pulling up plastic bags full of dead cats until he can locate the one with his name on it. He spends so many hours with this same horrendous cat, picking away at its organs, that he can eventually identify it by the shape alone, even inside its bag. Breathing the stench of it for three hours at a sitting leaves him with whanging headaches. His attitude towards the cat changes from contempt and loathing to guilt (at the desecration he is forced to enact), admiration, and a kind of friendliness verging on tenderness.

It rains for a week. Walking from chem lab and zoology/comparative anatomy lab to the post office to his room, dodging the hoards on the broad, uneven flagstone sidewalks, there is no way to keep from splashing water in his sock. The imposing neo-Gothic edifice blots out all horizons, all sunsets. Two more weeks go by and still no further word from Sonya. Could she have lost his address? Moke decides to grow a beard. He will never shave again. He will take on the look of some returning Arctic explorer or some bushy disciple of Sigmund Freud. He becomes one of three beards on all of West Campus.

Late at night as he studies quietly in his room, drunken fraternity goons ride by in convertibles and yell: "Hit dem books, assholes! Hit dem books, you muthas!"

He begins taking long late-night walks to look at the girly magazines at one downtown drugs and sundries and spends sometimes forty-five minutes flipping through the pages before buying—first superstitiously hoping to find a picture of Sonya, finally settling on the loveliest women available—testing his powers of discrimination quite minutely—then rushing back to his room and masturbating with pounding heart and hand in rapt admiration of their various beauties. How he loves women! He loves them in every posture, in every light. He loves every ridiculous thing they do in the magazines and he never tires of their antics. They are always available, always willing, always his alone.

One night in the shadow of the cigarette factory a dusty overloaded car rattles past and some nut yells, "Hey, Castro, go back to Cuba!" and hits him hard in the back with a half-empty beer-can.

Only later on would he realize that his confusion and increasing frustration over the question *What is life?* are partly the result of his unconsciously extending the question to include, too intimately, What is *the* purpose of life? and What is the purpose of *my* life? But the question *What is life?* begins to seem utterly burdensome to him. He would prepare his other work, his German translations, his calculus, comparative anatomy, and chemistry exercises—everything straightforward and neat—and then he would still have this monumental conundrum to face, which begins to seem more puzzling and immense than the riddle of the Sphinx. What *is* life? What is *life?* It begins to seem either sheer nonsense or the most important question he has ever asked.

Next to his desk in the library is a botany section containing, to his amazement, *The Weeds of North Carolina* in seventeen volumes; and this workmanlike little series bound in light green boards begins to symbolize the absurdity of existence, the uselessness of all human effort, and the futility of his ever knowing enough to answer *the big question* on his philosophy mid-term. To *think* that someone probably devoted his entire life to classifying weeds, and to think that weeds grow in such profusion that it would take seventeen volumes just to identify the ones in North Carolina! "Life in the state of nature," he reads, "is solitary, poor, nasty, brutish, and short." But wouldn't the case be worse, he thinks, if it were nasty, brutish, and *long?* Sometimes he feels as if he might be near the edge of some important breakthrough, some ultimate postulate he cannot quite comprehend or articulate. If only he can . . . dig deeper, have more time to prepare, . . . *think.*

It occurs to him that maybe medical school isn't the answer. That had been Julie's idea anyway, hadn't it? Maybe Duke isn't the answer. Maybe he needs to "find" himself first. Sometimes he can see himself just hitchhiking west, working his way, maybe, picking grapes for a few weeks in some small mountain town in California, just stepping aboard any bus that happens along, not knowing where it is going or where he will end up. Occasionally, when he thinks about Sonya and Julie, he begins to wonder if what happened with Sonya was just too fast and uncanny to be taken seriously. He had read about something called "transference" in a psychology text, and he begins to wonder if that might have been what had happened to him, almost a form of temporary insanity. Physically, she reminded him of Julie. So, because of his grief about losing Julie, unconsciously he transferred his affections to Sonya. But who was Sonya? Some mysterious girl he had met under incredible circumstances and had known for a little over three weeks, and that was about it. He hardly knew her at all. He had no basis for the depth of feeling he entertained concerning her. He had let himself be swept away by some cheap, semi-pornographic fantasy of femininity: a burlesque girl, for God's sake, an Arabian princess. What a cliche. All she really was was a girl who had happened to take off her clothes at the right moment.

That afternoon, in front of the union, while he is passing from the chem lab, tired and hungry at five o'clock, he sees Sonya turning up past the library. He stops abruptly in the middle of the walk and stares back across the quad. Could it actually be Sonya? Whoever it is disappears into the library. Someone bumps into him and says, "Watch out," and brushes past. Moke hurries across the quad, dodging in front of some hotshot in a Porsche who almost mows him down at the crosswalk, and follows the girl, a girl with long hair and a marvelous walk, who resembles Sonya, into the cavernous grey bowels of the library. She is gone by the time he gets inside. In the undergraduate reading room, one girl, wearing a black turtleneck with a purple seed necklace, could be the one. He walks slowly toward her as she folds herself into the cushions of a couch in the Browsing Room. But, up close, she does not look that much like Sonya. Reluctantly, he turns around and heads for the Periodical Room. If Sonya is here, at Duke, looking for him, surely she will eventually find him. There is no need to wander around the library and the stacks, checking out every hidden carrel, for three-quarters of an hour with an empty, desperate feeling when he should be eating dinner and getting back to work.

Rain drips past the lab windows all afternoon, forming in puddles on the walks and spilling out into the bright grass. Students coming out of the Chem Building across the quad snap out black pushbutton umbrellas or run like madmen toward the library. When the bell rings at four-thirty, the doors begin thumping downstairs and everyone leaves the lab except him.

Moke squeezes the bulge the small bottle of sperm makes through his shirtpocket and lays a clean slide directly in front of him on the desk. He feels a little like a mad scientist who is about to inject himself with an unknown disease in order to try to discover its cure. (He is going to have one hellava time explaining where he got this stuff if somebody catches him and wants to know what he is doing.) Quickly he slips the bottle out, uncaps it, pours a little of the sperm onto the slide and places a glass cover on it, recaps the bottle with lightning speed and jams it back into his pocket. He fastens the slide to the microscope and focuses in, keeping both eyes open (as he has recently learned), his left eye over the eyepiece. The field sharpens, sharpens, and there they are, unbelievable zillions of them! Even after about seventeen hours most of them are still alive and eager! Well, there are a few dead ones, yes. *But, my God, look at them! They have different length flagella! They are so different from one another! Live creatures from my own body! My God, who would ever believe such a thing!*

It is the morning of the mid-term exam on "What is life?" and Moke goes down to the head with his soap dish, washrag and towel over his arm, toothbrush, Crest, hairbrush, and scissors—feeling like a monk-with-begging-bowl, ascetic and worn out—and steps in line with Masterson, Clark, Gallagher, and McNally in front of the big row of mirrors and lavatories. Steam hovers near the ceiling over the shower stalls, and odors of Old Spice and Listerine mingle with the harsh laundry-soap pungence of their towels and the stench of Masterson's hair concoction. Masterson has his elbows positioned carefully above his head, raking and shaping his miserable mop with an Ace comb into his idea of debonair colle-

163

giate insouciance. Moke washes his face and starts to brush and clip at his beard.

"Why in the world do you *have* that thing?" Masterson says. "Why don't you *shave*?"

"I don't think it's any business of yours what I do," Moke says. Gallagher, who is busily shaving on Masterson's left, says, "Yeah!" Gallagher is in Moke's chemistry section and is his wrestling partner in gym, due to sheer alphabetical proximity, even though outweighing Moke by seventy pounds. Gallagher has received offers of football scholarships from forty different schools before choosing Duke and is considered a celebrity.

"It may not be my business," Masterson says, "but I still have to look at the rancid thing every day. It looks like some kind of god-damned cabbage growing out of your cheeks." He winks in Gallagher's direction, evidently thinking this sort of kidding will appeal to Gallagher's sense of the rightness of things.

"Your whole *head* looks like a god-damned cabbage to me," Moke says.

"Watch it, you fuckin' Commie, or I'll use your face for a toilet swab."

Moke's right arm swings like heavy rubber around Masterson's porcine neck, and Masterson's uplifted comb falls away and glances off the rim of the lavatory. He forces Masterson's huge off-balance bulk across the room and slams him hard against the marble shower stall.

"Ouch," Masterson says. "Now you've done it." His face shows utter astonishment. Someone grabs Moke's arm from the rear and prevents it from punching Masterson's scowling mouth.

"I'm not Norman!" Moke yells. "So don't think you can push me around!" Two of them are restraining Masterson too, who is rubbing the back of his head and not trying to pull loose.

"You're asking for it, Santa Claus," Masterson says. "You're asking for a knuckle-sandwich, and you're gonna get it."

"From you and who else?"

"All right, you guys, cut it out!" Gallagher yells.

"As soon as I put Galenaille's head in the toilet," Masterson says, starting to reach out with his ape-like arms.

"Cool it, Masterson," Gallagher says. Masterson squirms and fights, and the next thing Moke knows, Clark and Gallagher are forcing Masterson into the toilet stall and Masterson is screaming, "Nooo, noooo!" and Gallagher is saying, "Kneel down, you bastard, before I break your arm," and then slowly squeezing Masterson's bullet-like head toward the bowl and saying, "Take a drink, Queerbait, *You heard me, drink it*! And then you can sit up and apologize like a good boy."

Moke has spent more time and effort preparing for *What is life?* than on any other single subject, but when he comes to the examination room that morning, edges into the hardbacked seat, and stares at the first page of the blue-book, something freezes within him. The lines of the booklet seem too widely spaced. *What is life?* he writes. But his hand will not make the necessary motions across the page to fill in any further lines. Other students seated nearby are already scribbling furiously. What can they be saying? he wonders. The feat of moving a pen across a page at such speed seems as absurd, as impossible as frogs juggling beachballs. His hands are like ice. The image of Masterson with his head bowed toward the toilet bowl flashes through his mind. The fact is that in weeks of struggling and digging, he has not succeeded in discovering any satisfactory answer to the question *What is life?* His present position is somewhere between a sort of humanist-agnostic-existentialist and a pantheistic-hedonist.

Spermatozoa dancing in a field of light—he writes—*are they conscious? Can they feel? What can they know of the world beyond themselves, of their creator, or their ultimate destination? One in millions will survive until the end of the journey, to the egg gleaming larger and more radiant than the Taj Mahal at the end of the Fallopian tube. With what yearning does that single potent spermatozoan swim leapingly toward this awesome and gigantic pearl while his fellows fall away and drop on every side, their short lives forever spent. And what unique message does he whisper to her in order to gain entrance to her palace within? Suddenly, he sees, the walls recede—he is bathed in light as if entering the sun itself in a chariot drawn by golden stallions. . . .*

For mid-term, he receives A's in all his pre-med subjects and a C– in religion/philosophy.

Chapter Fourteen

Send my mail down to Bimini
This town is weary, son. . . .

Moke enters the undergraduate reading room and meets the bored eyes of several students who hope he will provide some sort of diversion. The eyes follow him until he finds an open space at one of the oak tables, lays his books down, and settles into the hard-backed chair. He seats himself so as to be in perfect line to see her if she is there this time, but he has no intention of looking up until it will appear quite natural and unplanned. He pretends to read two pages of comparative anatomy, and his imagination pictures the red couch where she will or won't be lying just inside the arch of the reading lounge when he looks up. He pictures her face and lips and the way she slouches down into the couch with her legs stretched out across the rug. She might not be there—he knows that too—so he imagines the couch empty or with someone else sitting there, some hairy football type, in order to prepare himself for the worst.

He is in luck, he sees, after a furtive rolling of his eyeballs. She has again monopolized the red couch, scattering books from one end to the other and a boxy leather purse near the armrest and a burlap serape balled up in the corner. Her posture is so incredibly flagrant it gives him another paralyzing erection. If she starts out sitting up straight, it never lasts. Within seconds she begins sinking, extending her long tense legs out across the purple nap of the carpet, fluffing it and caressing it with her toes. Her soft breasts rest against her propped up book, and she is constantly licking and mouthing her pen lid between note-scribbling as if it might be raspberry-flavored.

She is not *that* attractive in the conventional sense, Moke tells himself, not as attractive as Julie or Sonya, whom she does slightly resemble, but there is something so careless about her, so apparently unselfconscious and inviting. She exudes sensuality like an air-borne chemical. Could she possibly not realize she is upsetting the study habits of half the men in the reading room? Or is he the only one? Today she is wearing the black turtleneck and a long necklace of red seeds, and her dark hair is piled on top of her head in what strikes him as an absurd but sophisticated hairdo. Her tan is an all-body Florida-or-the-Bahamas tan most probably. She looks rich and bitchy, but who knows?—she might be very nice. Slowly she turns her head in his direction and her large icy blue eyes meet his and linger. Uh-oh, he *thinks* she is trying to tell him something. She looks away, lets her eyeballs coast along the shelving, around the paneling on the arch, across the ceiling, then snaps back to him, as direct and steady as laser-light.

Moke is having an identity crisis, and he knows it. He spends two days pouring over college catalogs in the undergraduate reading room. Sometimes he can see himself at some radical beatnik school like Antioch or Berkeley, just sitting under a huge sycamore or eucalyptus tree with a guitar in his lap, a big ugly White Owl ceegar in one hand and a blonde in the other. She would be wearing black fishnet stockings and a turtleneck and have pierced ears and long straight hair and a striking resemblance to Julie Greenway and a personality something like Sonya's. They would sip red wine from a Dixie cup and after a while he would play and sing "Love Me Tender," sounding quite a bit like Elvis and a little like a combination of Fats Domino and Ricky Nelson.

The letter is from Julie Greenway of all people—he'd recognize that handwriting anywhere!

Dear Moke,

The reason I'm writing is to warn you that Craig may be stopping in Durham on his way to the Virgin Islands. He has really flipped out this time, I'm afraid. My father sent him his tuition money at the usual time, but instead of paying the bursar at Princeton he's beat it out of town. He sent my father a telegram saying he is going around the world and will drop us a line from Hong Kong! We don't know where he is or what he's doing and my mum is so worried it's like premenstrual tension week 24-hours-a-day around here—tearful phone-calls and imprecations in the middle of the night, etc. Some guy he met down there last year was looking for a crew to help sail his boat (a 40-foot ketch), and we think that may be where he's leaving from . . . the place from where . . . from whence . . . he is leaving . . . anyway . . . you get the idea. If he does stop there, the elder Greenways would give almost anything to hear some word about their errant offspring. Could you, would you, interject a note of simple reason into our lives?

Sincerely,
Julie

P.S. How are you anyway?

Moke reads the letter over three times, then unscrews the lid from his handy Kretschmer's Wheat Germ and eats a mouthful of the tan flakes straight from the bottle. He reads Sonya's old letter over two times and Julie's letter over three times very slowly, fiddling with the Kretschmer's lid and rocking slightly on the creaky back legs of the wooden deskchair. The noteworthy part of Julie's letter, as far as he is concerned, is the P.S. What does it mean? Had she had a falling out with the physicist? Maybe she was lonely back at school, or maybe Northampton had revived some memory of him and she was having second thoughts? And that last line! What did she mean by that? On the other hand, maybe it *was* just a business letter—he merely happened to reside somewhere within a two-hundred mile radius of her brother's march to the sea—and she felt a little guilty asking him a favor without including some personal note. It is impossible to tell really. He seriously doubts if Craig would be at all interested in including him in his itinerary.

By Friday he has more or less forgotten about the Craig part of the letter and is still worrying about the P.S. and whether or not he should risk writing back to her to try to explain how he is. How is he anyway? He isn't at all clear about that.

So when this weird character with a scraggly beard and shades steps out in front of him in the hall as he is exiting from German class and says, "Hey, brother!" Moke starts to duck around him, thinking the guy is talking to someone else in the mob. Then Moke pauses for an instant, giving old scraggle-beard a chance to move past him, slightly off his bearings for a minute because there is something oddly familiar about this person and he doesn't, in fact, proceed to move out of the way at all. He just stands there looking directly into Moke's face. With a rush of recognition and surprise, Moke realizes he is face-to-face with the fugitive himself, Craig Greenway, who is just getting ready to guffaw at him for being so foolish as to fail to recognize a person of his obvious importance, even if he is in disguise.

"Whatsamatter, shitface, ain't you never seen a beatnik before?"

"Jesus, Craig, is it really you?" Craig pulls down the black sunglasses and glowers at Moke over the nosepiece. "God, your eyes are bloodshot!" Moke says. It just pops out.

"Your eyes'd be bloodshot too, brother, if you'd just driven eight hundred miles with nothin' but a gallon jug of Paisano to keep you warm!" They drift out with the crowd and start ambling down the flagstone walk in no particular direction.

"Julie wrote me that you might be stopping by."

"Yeah . . . yeah. I guess I did hint to her that I might stop in if I ended up coming down this way. Yeah . . . okay with you if I sack out on your floor or somewhere overnight?"

"Sure. Sure."

"I got this important appointment to make with this cat in the Virgin Islands. She tell you about that?"

"Well, yeah. She mentioned it. She didn't say anything much about it though. She didn't give any details at all. She said you dropped out of Princeton."

"I didn't drop out, man. I just left. I just hauled my ass out of that sorry place, that third-rate finishing school for drunken preppies. I got so I kinda outgrew that Ivory League nonsense, you know what I mean? All those blond boys in their Brooks

169

Brothers outfits and their classic profiles and their mediocre intelligences. Jesus, what a drag! Who needs it?"

Craig heads toward a white Oldsmobile parked beside the curb, punches the door button, and flings open the door. It is filthy with road grease, about four years old, and has a pair of expensive-looking skis fastened to a rack on the trunk lid. "How do you like my new wheels?" he says, extending his arm mock-heroically toward the hood as he skips around the front towards the driver's side. "Get in. I'll take you for a quick trip to the car wash." When Moke gets in, he is horrified to see Craig snatch a gallon jug of wine off the floor in the back of the seat. Drinking on this campus is an expellable offense. Craig uncorks it and swirls the three inches of purplish fluid around in the glassy bottom, holding the cork in his teeth.

"You want some?" he says, through the cork.

"No, no thanks," Moke says, looking around worriedly in case the Dean of Students might be walking by.

"Go ahead, brother," Craig insists.

"No, that's all right. Thanks anyway."

Craig takes the bottle in the crook of his arm, throws back his head, and gulps several mouthfuls, holding the jug up in plain view of everyone within a quarter of a mile. The bottle makes a loud sucking noise when he withdraws it from his mouth and some of the wine dribbles into this beard and bounces onto the seat. "Aaaaah," Craig says, wiping his lips on his forearm. He hands the cork to Moke. "Help yourself, brother." He guns the car to life and pulls away from the curb. "This car has been on every god-damned back road in the entire state of Vermont," he says, looking at Moke steadily instead of where he is going, which makes Moke distinctly uneasy on the narrow campus road.

"Where are you headed?" Moke says.

"To the nearest carwash, man."

Moke can't remember the location of any carwashes in Durham. This is the first year he has brought the Pontiac back with him, and it hasn't been here long enough to get dirty. He has never seen any carwashes at all. He thinks this over carefully.

"Where is that?" Moke says.

"How the hell should I know! I'm not one of the resident aliens, for God's sake. You tell me, shitface!"

The carwash they find is elaborate and quick: the Oldsmobile is vacuumed on the inside, jerked through explosions of water and brushes on a chain, then dried by a crew of black carwash employees with white terrycloth towels. When they leave, Craig complains about the "fascist redneck pigs" who run the carwash, sit around drinking Coke, and make the blacks do all the menial work. The South, it seems, is such a cesspool of corruption and discrimination that any right-minded person is morally obligated to condemn it, and someone who stands by passively and fails to cry out against such behavior—let alone someone who actually goes to school here—must be either a collaborator in evil or a pure nebish. Moke begins to suspect that he is being personally accused of responsibility for the South as a whole—but he doesn't say much at all, just lets Craig rant on for a while, and by the time they get back to campus, Craig seems to have calmed down enough to be interested in dinner.

They line up with the usual dinner traffic outside the cafeteria, and if Craig is at all impressed by the Gothic splendor of the hall, its rosewood beams and stained glass, he doesn't show it except by saying "humph" and mumbling something about "an imitation of Princeton." They slide their trays along the metal railing in front of the meticulous stainless steel cafeteria counter, Craig heaping his tray with food as if he hadn't eaten in a while. Then when they get to the end of the line he does a little dance, feeling in one pocket and then another, and is able to produce only $.28 for the dinner. He has left his wallet in the Olds, he says, and the line is backing up impatiently, so Moke pays for Craig's dinner as well as his own.

Back at the room, Craig eyes the W. R. GALENAILLE, U.S. Marine Corps, printed in fading black ink across the foot of Moke's blanket, and snorts. He also snorts at the nude Moke has taped to the bookcase and then trips over the tennis racket and knocks the stereo speaker off its shelf. Moke shows Craig his copy of Eric Hoffer's *The True Believer* in hopes of keeping him occupied while he tries to scrounge up an extra mattress from one of his friends on the hall.

Carl McNally's roommate is away for the weekend, so Moke is able to persuade McNally to let him borrow his mattress overnight. They grab hold of the ends of it and cart it back to Moke's room. Moke introduces McNally to Craig, who shakes hands rather condescendingly, then throws Moke's copy of *The True Believer* over into the corner on Moke's bed and informs them both that the book is nothing but "warmed-over sociology" and sits down and leans back in Moke's desk chair and puts his hands behind his head and his feet up on the desk as if he dares either one of them to attempt to persuade him otherwise.

"I hear you're from Princeton," McNally offers. "That's a pretty good school."

"Yeah," Craig says, staring off into space and sucking his teeth. "It's one of your red-hot contacts with the military-industrial complex. Just plug right in and ride it for all it's worth. They'll be happy to set you up with a six-figure salary in the suburb of your choice." McNally is at a loss as to how to reply to this. He is the only son of the village doctor from a swell town in rural West Virginia with a population of 782.

"But, personally," Craig says, "I'm not ready to settle down yet. You let some Jezebel domesticate you and the first thing you know she has these little porcelain god-damned nicknacks sitting on every windowsill, a crib full of brats, and three boxes of fucking silverware in the closet, every piece of it getting more tarnished by the minute, and then you notice this little velvet bag hanging on a chain around her neck, and you look inside, and, by God, it's got your gonads in it, one right next to the other like two oysters!"

McNally blushes from ear-to-ear and squats down suddenly beside the bureau to cover his embarrassment. He looks as if he might be getting in position to draw some battle plan on the rug if Craig will join him and suggest a strategy and tell him who the enemy is.

"I never thought about it quite like that before," McNally says. "I think it might depend upon the girl, I mean, just who the girl is and everything, don't you think?"

"You serious about some chick?" Craig says. "I bet you're serious as hell about some dumb cunt right this very minute, aren't you?"

"Well, I am sort of engaged to this girl back home named Ag . . ." McNally looks over sheepishly at Moke, as if he might have every reason to be ashamed of this revelation. In fact, he writes to the girl daily and is always gloating over the scented purple letters he receives from her and will frequently wave the stationery under Moke's nostrils or show him choice passages about what feverish designs Ag has on McNally's body and how she intends to put these into practice as soon as he comes home the next time.

"Another sucker bites the dust," Craig says. "Take my advice, man, and start wearing a steel jockstrap. Those little tentacles you feel crawling up your leg are holding a butcher knife! Wham, wham!" Craig makes several wild stabbing motions towards the crotch of his chinos and yells, "Get that mutha!"

When McNally has recovered from his amazement at this, he says: "Well, I know what you mean all right. But this girl, Ag, she's not like that at all. She's just a small town girl, you know what I mean? She's never even known any other guy except me; and she thinks I'm *it*, poor thing; and I'm sure as hell not going to tell her otherwise."

"You poor deluded son of a bitch," Craig says. "I feel sorry for you. She's making mincemeat out of you so fast you can't even feel the grinder moving. Now Moke over there—he used to go out with my stupid sister—*he* found out about women. And I don't care if she is my sister because as far as I'm concerned they all belong to a different *species* and they're all the same."

"What do you mean by *that?*" Moke says.

"She wasn't satisfied until she had your balls, brother. And if it wasn't that, it would have been worse! She would have tried to domesticate the piss out of you and you would have ended up with three bushel baskets full of silverware in some crappy mobile home way the hell out in the boondocks and you could kiss goodbye to medical school after that. So long, Medical School, it was nice knowin' you!"

"Oh, I don't know about that," Moke says. "We could have waited. We still might—who knows?"

"You really ought to dispose of these silly-ass ideas about romantic love, brother, or you're wasting your expensive education. Man is basically the hunter. His impulse is to leave the home territory, to conquer, rape, and pillage. That's all I'm saying."

"What a bunch of bullshit!" McNally says.

"It might be bullshit to you, you feeble-minded rube, but one of these days you'll find out the hard way, take my word for it. How do you know that little ol' Ag isn't out in some rancid barnyard right this instant making it with the whole fuckin' football team. I bet she is! And you wouldn't even know the difference, you horse's ass!"

"I don't have to listen to this," McNally says. He stands up with considerable dignity, rolls his eyes at Moke, and slams the door.

"That's *his* mattress you'll be sleeping on," Moke says, hoping to set the facts straight and thus awaken some glimmer of generosity toward McNally and open Craig's eyes to the realization that he hasn't been very appreciative so far.

"Hope I don't catch hoof-in-the-mouth disease," Craig says and spits viciously into the waste basket.

Moke wants to ask Craig about Julie and the physicist to find out if Julie's P.S. might have meant something serious, but he doesn't know how to broach such a subject without eliciting a lot of abuse, so he doesn't say anything.

Craig unrolls his sleeping bag and lays it on McNally's mattress. Moke goes on down to the head with his soap dish, Dial shampoo, his toothbrush, Crest, and his pj's, robe, towel, and washrag folded over his arm like a French waiter and showers and brushes his teeth in front of the row of immense mirrors and lavatories—his nightly ritual—and when he comes back Craig is already tucked away in his sleeping bag with the light off. Moke hangs his clothes carefully and quietly over the back of the desk chair, lines up his toilet articles neatly on top of his bureau, and gets into bed.

"I knew this girl once," Craig says across the darkness . . . , "and I was staying at her family's summer home on the Cape, you know, for the weekend, and this girl was really too much! Now here's a good example of exactly what I was talking about. This broad! See, she invited me out and everything like it was going to be this big romantic tete-a-tete and we went through this horrible long boring evening scene making chit-chat with her parents and so I go on up to my bedroom finally and get in bed and pretty soon I hear this weird noise and I realize it's somebody coming into my room and Jesus-Mary-mother it's none other than Eunice herself—I'll just call her Eunice for the sake of the story. (That wasn't her real name, but I'll just call her that.) So, here comes ol' Eunice herself and all she's got on are these tiny little shortie pajamas with little pink pussy-cats all over them and I think, 'Jesus Christ, I'm really going to lose my virginity this time if I'm not careful.' I mean, Eunice has never acted this way *before*. This is a totally unexpected development in our relationship. Eunice is acting like a different woman all of a sudden, purring and fussing around and obviously trying to get me to unbutton her pajama buttons in the dark. Well, I start feeling kinda sorry for her after a while, you know—I mean, I *was* a guest in her house and everything—so I finally take pity on poor ol' Eunice and help her off with her pajamas. Now here's the part I can't figure out. The next thing I know she gets up and turns on the bedside light and there she is totally dressed again! I mean, she *has on* a pair of bermudas and a blouse and she takes one look at my face and cracks up into a hysterical laughing fit, collapses on the end of the bed and just does nothing but snort for about fifteen minutes. Now what do you make of that? Isn't that a pisser?"

"How did she get her clothes on so fast?" Moke says.

"She *had* them on the whole god-damned time *underneath* her shortie pajamas. It was a totally premeditated act. Some women get their jollies in very strange ways, don't you think?"

"Jesus, Craig, I think she wanted you to take her bermudas off too. That's all."

"Holy shit! I never thought of that! You think *that* was it?"

"What did you do?"

"I told her if she wanted to laugh at me all night to get the fuck outa my bedroom. She took off. That was *it*, baby. We had what you might call 'a falling out.' She wouldn't go out with me anymore after that. Of course, I didn't want to go out with such a screwed-up broad anyway. Who would?"

"Huh! Were you serious about her before that?"

"I learned a long time ago, man, that it's better not to get too serious about anything, especially women! That's one reason I decided I had to split. I got a little tired of seeing Eunice, for instance, taking *herself* so fuckin' seriously, driving off with some

Beta to Vermont every weekend. 'Oh, hiya, Craig ol' boy, ol' buddy, ol' friend!'—as she slowly tightens the vice on your balls another micrometer—and then speeds away in this asshole's MG with her scarf flying out behind like the Red Baron. *That* I could do without."

"Yeah, I can see what you mean all right," Moke says. Speaking of people riding off in sports cars, Moke might have said, was about to say, what's new with your stupid sister and the physicist? But there is a knock at the door. It is John the chemist peering around the doorjamb, some strange guy who has been bugging him for months, with another invitation to a meeting of the Inter-Varsity Christian Fellowship. Moke starts to thank John and is about to close the door when Craig, who has overheard, yells, "Invite the fucker in! We'll have a prayer meeting right now. Tally-ho!"

"Oh, it's pretty late, Craig," Moke is saying, but John the chemist is already inside the door with his hand out ready to do battle for the Lord, yesiree.

"I'm an atheist from Princeton," Craig says, introducing himself cheerfully.

"Okay, if you guys want to talk, be my guest," Moke says, "but don't pay any attention to me if I sack out, okay." Moke crawls into bed and turns his face toward the wall, pulling the covers up over his ears. The two on the floor quickly launch into a heavy philosophical and theological discussion which Moke knows he doesn't want to hear. The last thing he remembers distinctly is Craig saying: "God and his miracles! What absolute bullshit! Gawd! If Gawd jumped out of that bureau drawer right there and started performing miracles, I'd tell the son-of-a-bitch to go down the hall and do his fucking miracles some place else!"

Moke has a dream about riding away on an ocean liner, and he is waving to a distant figure silhouetted on the high cliffs overlooking a town. At first he can't make out who it is. He squints through the sun glare and mist and diesel smoke, and first the figure seems to be his father or Craig and then it seems feminine with a flowing white gown and long hair, Julie or Sonya. Luckily he is able to borrow somebody's binoculars in the dream so that he can find out once and for all who he is waving to and who is waving to him. He raises the binoculars to his eyes and presses the eye cups tightly into his sockets and stares fiercely out across the bay, but in the instant he has taken his eyes away from the cliffs to borrow the binoculars the figure has vanished. There is only a cloudy pasture and a bare rocky coast and a deserted little village, which seems indescribably sad.

When the broomsticks and mophandles hit his door at 7 A.M. and the maid starts hawking and spitting in her closet, he awakes slowly as if swimming upward through layers of green water and peers for several seconds at the strange shape of McNally's vacant mattress in the middle of the floor before he remembers what it is doing there. Craig Greenway, he speculates, is already back on the road by this time, making his way feverishly—in his clean white Oldsmobile—in the direction of the Virgin Islands.

Chapter Fifteen

Tho' we're a-part
You're part of me still
For you were my thrill
On Blueberry Hill. . . .

Dearest Julie,

Well, I do have some news for you about Craig, though I'm not certain how reassuring it might be. He stopped here overnight and he *is* on his way to the Virgin Islands. He sponged a meal off of me and a place to sleep and seems in a pretty foul frame of mind, though otherwise okay. Tell your parents not to worry. I don't understand Craig that well, but I do think I understand why he's taking off. I feel like taking off myself part of the time, just hitchhiking west, working my way, maybe picking grapes for a few weeks in some small mountain town, or washing dishes—anything—then moving on until my money would run out, just stepping aboard any bus that happened along, not knowing where it was going or where you were ending up, not having to be responsible to anybody. Maybe you would get off and find yourself in Albuquerque or Montreal—who knows where?— and you would just have to make the best of it. Frankly, it sounds to me like a terrific thing to do to try to sail around the world in a 40-foot ketch. If Craig had asked me, I might have gone along with him.

On the other hand, I'm still thinking seriously about Johns Hopkins Medical School. I found out they have this special admissions program. You can start *into*

Medical School after only two years as an undergraduate. I'm going to try for it though it's very competitive. I have to take the MCAT next week. I'm cramming in every chemical formula I can lay eyes on—like one of those lizards with the lightning tongues . . . zick, zick, zick! I'm a walking memory bank. Just think! If I could get into Johns Hopkins, I would be out in only five more years. That's not so long. By that time maybe you would have had ample opportunity to get over your silly infatuation with the physicist. What do you think? How are you two getting along these days anyway? Not too well, I hope.

I dreamed about you last night . . . again. God, I miss you. I miss not getting your letters. If you only knew how much I enjoyed your Craig letter even, which was hardly personal, you might take pity on me. (If you knew how much psychic energy I expended on the P.S. alone!) You wouldn't even have to write anything every time. You could just send me empty envelopes—as long as they had your handwriting on them—and I think I would be quite satisfied. It's so lonely around here these days . . . so crummy and rainy . . . you don't know what it means to find a scrap of paper in my mailbox. I even enjoy getting advertising circulars for things I know I'll never buy or details of contests I'll never enter. Nothing is worse than an empty mailbox. Please consider writing to me again. We can still be friends, can't we? No one will ever love you as much as I have. I miss you so much, Julie.

> Love always,
> Moke

Maybe the letter is a little too blunt and self-revealing, but how can she fail to write back? She will have to write back if only to explain why she can't write back again. Maybe she has already had a falling out with the physicist. Maybe she has finally come to her senses, for God's sake, and only needs to be reassured of his loyalty and unswerving devotion.

179

Now that he expects news, he haunts his mailbox with high hopes. There are two and only two daily deliveries from the outside world, but because of the irregular habits of the mail sorters a letter might turn up at any hour. So he checks his mail twelve to fifteen times a day probably—before and after each meal, before and after each class, or whenever he happens to be going through the Union, past the Bookstore, or toward the Library. His mailbox is almost always empty, which he can see perfectly well through the small glass window in the door; but he flips the combination-pointer around-and-around and opens the door each time anyway and bends to squint into the void in case a letter might be pressed flat against the top of the box in such a way as to make it invisible with the door locked, even though this has never yet happened in over a year of using the box. He has become such an expert at working the combination that he can open it by touch alone with his eyes closed. He can work it so fast that nobody else in sight who happens to be opening their mailboxes at the same moment can come within three seconds of his time. If there were only an Olympic Mailbox Opening event, he is certain he would be world-class. Most of the time, however, he prefers to prolong the occasion and to savor it, so he deliberately slows the turning or causes a mistake by moving past the crucial point which necessitates going back to the beginning. Or he will open and close the box too quickly and walk away only to have his mind call forth the delayed retinal image of a letter, and he will be forced to retrace his steps past the case full of "WANTED" notices, again open the box, more slowly this time, and double-check the fact that it was indeed as empty as he thought it was the first time. There seems to be a magnetic field surrounding his mailbox that prevents mail from landing in it. He grows suspicious of the mail sorters—maybe they are putting his mail in somebody else's box! He has a recurrent ecstatic dream about his mailbox. He goes to his box and finds it empty as usual, but as he is leaving he suddenly remembers his *other* mailbox, which he has forgotten about. He goes to that mailbox and finds it stuffed to overflowing with mail, lovely crisp envelopes, some of them with exotic postmarks.

The only letters he receives all week are not letters. One is his admissions permit for the Medical College Admissions Test (MCAT), which he leans in a conspicuous spot against his study light. The other seems to be a letter and, ironically, it contains the Montreal postmark and even the purple stamp with the picture of Queen Elizabeth so that he mistakes it for a letter from Sonya and saves it like a promise until he returns to his room after chem lab and dinner. Then he removes a puzzling piece of paper from its envelope and reads:

Turn off the TV! Turn on your libido! This weekend see real, live 8 mm Love-Making on Your Bedroom Wall. By projecting these movies in the privacy of your own home, you and your wife will be able to shed the last of your inhibitions, try advanced new techniques you never dared discuss—and make her do the things you've always craved! Medically approved!

Nothing but a crummy sex ad! and a hypocritical one at that! He tears it into small pieces and throws it into the wastebasket and stays up until 3 A.M. smoking and cramming for the MCAT. If he can only get into Johns Hopkins, he decides, his life will be vindicated. He may have to give up some of the simple pleasures —like eating, sleeping, and women—but every worthwhile life requires some sacrifice.

The wedding invitation arrives in the late afternoon mail on Friday, the day before the MCAT. It is not even in Julie's handwriting and it is, of course, engraved on beautiful rag paper and appears to be quite permanent and irrevocable, more permanent and consequential and irrevocable than it has ever seemed to him before. "The pleasure of your company is requested"—ho-ho! His recent letter to Julie now seems foolish to the point of idiocy! How could he have sent such a letter? How could she have answered with this cold-blooded cruelty? On the other hand, why should he be so surprised after all? It was probably true that people who were engaged to each other usually did go ahead and get married eventually. It wasn't as if he hadn't been warned.

He stares out the Gothic casement at the milky pink light beyond the dark woods, a sunset like phenothalene poured out of a bottle, and the ruby taillights of the cars passing on the distant campus road and a few students taking themselves off to the cafeteria for dinner. How could he face that chortling mob again?—no chance. He walks quickly out, down the stairs, out across the well-kept lawns and the parking lot and chugs away in the orange Pontiac, driving down back streets, turning down any dim avenue he has never noticed or driven on before. It is a pristine twilight hour, the air smelling faintly of magnolia blossoms and quiet families enjoying hamburger dinners. If only he could make a home for himself in one of these humble bungalows . . . what a ridiculous idea. He thinks of the Platters singing "Twilight Time" and wishes himself back in Indian Park, then fantasizes driving all the way to Montreal to surprise Sonya and to upbraid her for not writing.

Julie had been so lovely when she surprised him spring of freshman year. "Some chick is out here calling for you," McNally had yelled through his door. She had staged her appearance on a whim to shock and flatter him. She wasn't due for two more days. Moke thought McNally was bullshitting him. He looked out through McNally's window, which faced the inner quad, and there she was all right, like an apparition framed by the Gothic arch, her mane of hair blonder and somehow curly, heels and all as if she always came dressed to the teeth expecting to be introduced at the President's reception for visiting celebrities from Massachusetts. She laughed uproariously when he showed himself and slunk toward her to be kissed to a chorus of wolf whistles from the quad windows—he must have looked flabbergasted and gray with fatigue—he was trying to finish all his work before her arrival.

"What are you *doing* here?" he said.

"I *came* to help you study for mid-terms, silly," she said, cocking her hips seductively. "Anybody can see that." Oh, brother, he was thinking. Still, there was no way he could be upset with her.

"Hey, we need some help up here too," somebody yelled.

"We need all the help we can get," somebody else moaned in a breathy voice.

"Oh, mama, I feel so faint!"

Girls were not allowed on the hall or anywhere in the freshman quad. Moke walked her around West Campus a little awkwardly, like a prize mare, her red leather heels clicking sharply on the flagstones, drawing all eyes. She liked Smith better, she said, but was still upset with her performance except for psychology, which she enjoyed. She was devouring Freud. She was horrified to discover that Moke didn't know what a "phallic symbol" was yet. She pointed to the chapel tower and said: "See that. *That's* a phallic symbol. Almost everything is a phallic symbol! You just have to be on the lookout."

They had gotten over their squeamishness about walking together through hotel lobbies by then. The Washington Duke was a bigger, more populated hotel than the one in Northampton—it was easier to feel anonymous. They moved into a room on the seventh floor, having lugged her bags and his portable stereo all the way from campus on the bus. The instant the door was closed and locked they collapsed on the bed, kissing, writhing, and tearing at each others' clothes. She was even wearing nylons and a tricky garter belt. She was silky and lovely. Later they got the stereo uncoiled and kissed and talked to the strains of "I'm in the Nude for Love"—its main asset was its voluptuous jacket—and Sigmund Romberg's "Deep in My Heart, Dear."

> We'll be close as pages in a book
> my love and I
> so close we can share a single look
> share every sigh. . . .
> Our dreams won't come tumbling to the ground
> we'll make them last. . . .

His problem was that he had believed all that sentimental crap, he really had. He still wanted to believe it, dammit!

> Give us some men
> who are stout-hearted men
> who will fight for the right they adore!

She taught him a new Kingston Trio song called "Rioting in Africa," which she kept humming and singing obsessively. It was all about how nobody really liked anybody—hatred was rampant and the world was falling apart—but soon nuclear destruction would wipe out the human race and good riddance.

Its cheerful nihilism appealed to her and appalled him. After she had taught it to him, he said: "If you don't like an-y-bo-dy ve-ry much, how come you tolerate me?"

"I don't tolerate you. I eat you up."

"How come you eat me up?"

"I wonder sometimes."

"But do you *like* me?"

"Do I like you?" She arched her eyebrows and pursed her lips as if she had to give this some careful thought. She whistled a few bars of "Rioting in Africa."

"That's not very nice," he said.

"Do I have to be nice?"

"When you're with me, yes. I like you best when you're nice."

"How do you like me when I'm not nice?"

"I still like you all right. You're nice most of the time, I guess."

"So it doesn't really matter whether I'm nice or not?"

"Yes, it does. I like you better when you try to be nice. But I do wish you *would* stop singing that song! I've got work to do."

"I don't like *you* when you're not nice!"

"At least I try to be nice."

"Sometimes I try *not* to be nice?"

"Well . . . let's just both *try* to be nice, okay?"

"Okay, we'll be as nice as we can. I can be very nice when I want to be."

"You're so damned nice I'm never going to get all my work done." She nuzzled his shoulder while he studied his zoology text, *Life*.

"Look," Julie said, cracking up. "They have a picture of us!" It was a picture with the caption "frogs copulating."

"That *does* look familiar. I wonder which one is the female?" Moke said.

"The one on top, I think," Julie said.

Moke studied the photo for a moment longer, then turned to look at her face, her smiling olive-drab eyes beneath the blond bangs, and ran his finger down the length of her ski-jump nose. "I'd recognize you anywhere!" He burst out laughing. She promptly clobbered him with a pillow.

Julie didn't want him to spend the night in the hotel—some lingering superstition or bit of puritanism. But it was already one o'clock. The buses had stopped running. She patted him on the head and said she would walk him part way back. They had only been lying there for eight hours and missed dinner! Starved, they got dressed and went down in the elevator and through the deserted lobby and out to the street and started toward campus. His testicles and lower abdomen ached so much as he started walking that he told her he had a case of what he thought was called "blue balls." Her eyes grew large with wonder at this odd terminology. He wasn't certain what caused it, some kind of swelling, but he knew it was killing him and it was getting worse. At first she must have thought it was a ruse to persuade her to let him go back to the hotel for the night, but then when she saw he was limping along in such obvious agony, she took pity. If males did have their problems, she seemed pleased to be discovering what they were. They stopped at an all-night grocery with a warped wooden floor and she bought a bag of glazed doughnuts and he bought a White Owl cigar. By the time they came out again into the night air, his cords or tendons or scrotal ligaments or whatever-they-are were so tightened up that each step on the gritty pavement was excruciating. She tried to help him walk by draping his right arm around her neck as if he were a crippled Marine with a severe schrapnel wound. They rested on a cement slab in front of the Western Auto store and ate glazed doughnuts and licked their fingers and tried to size up their predicament. There was no way he was going to cover another two miles except on his hands and knees. So, she consented to his returning to the hotel as the only obvious solution. Happily, he staggered with her back to the Washington Duke, wincing all the way, one hand clinging to her soft Smith sweatshirt, the other trailing the stogie with its ember like a signal-light and its coarse masculine stench.

Moke pulls again into the parking lot, sets the emergency brake, and sits for a moment staring up at the recalcitrant Gothic rockpile, the majestic beehive of University buildings. Somehow they have come to represent the difficulty of his ever realizing the dreams of his adolescence. Stones of enormous weight dragged from some quarry in North Carolina in the New World and cemented together at unimaginable cost in 1931 in such a way as to resemble a 15th-century German fortress. Stones bought and paid for by a tobacco fortune that helped make the U.S. the lung cancer capital of the world. What possible connection did this farcical assemblage have to him, a person from Cincinnati, Ohio, who hardly smoked and whose girlfriend (*girl*friend!—wife) was going to marry someone else and whose *other* girlfriend (*girl*friend!) who was not even a U.S. citizen was probably at this instant fucking some half-baked lab assistant from Manitoba in the backseat of a rusting Edsel in some other country far to the north?

He locks the car and kicks leaves and heads toward these same buildings, up the steps and through an archway into the mighty citadel of learning. Friday night and already late enough for a frat party to be getting started at the Beta house. Couples amble down the flagstone walk in that direction, girls in white dresses, and the notes of a syrupy trumpet carry above the pines. Moke flees toward the Union, solemnly checks his mail, and wanders slowly back and forth along the cigarette-butted marble-floored hallway reading every title on every book in the row of darkened bookstore panes, carefully avoiding a confrontation with his own stone-sober hollow-eyed reflection looming in the glass like a ghostly companion.

Suddenly remembering the girl with the purple seed necklace in the library, he hurries out and across campus and into the cool, gray foyer of the library with its ribbed, vaulted ceiling like a burial chamber and slams through into the undergraduate reading room and goes straight to her couch. But the couch is empty and there is no sign of her—damn. He sinks to the couch himself and huddles into its upholstered embrace. If he only knew her name, he could call her up. He lurches up and out. No place to go but back to his room. He meanders along, weaving like a drunkard behind some couple strolling hand-in-hand toward the Beta house. The girl has shoulder-length honey-blond hair that shimmers like a dream of perfection in the mellow light from the lamppoles as they pass. "Your hand is larger than mine," she says to the boy, giving him an endearing look and a heartbreaking flutter of eyelashes. Moke leaps the chain link fence to the side and sprints away into the darkness, his heart pumping like a four-barrel carburetor.

By midnight he has downed most of a bottle of Beaujolais and re-read every letter Julie has ever sent, a mountain of perfumed paper and lipsticked envelopes, including her Colonial Hotel, Northampton, stationery, Washington Duke Hotel stationery, and just plain Smith College stationery. Every single god-damned one of them—except the one asking about Craig and the "Dear John"—are signed "All my love, All my life." Oh Julie, how could you? How could you say a thing like that to anyone and then take it back? He tries kissing some of the more interesting lipmark shapes on three or four of the envelopes, then spits into his wastebasket in disgust and runs down the hall to the bathroom and scrubs off his lips with a hot washrag. Finally he throws all the paper back into his footlocker (the one with *Lt. Wm. Galenaille, U.S. Marine Corps* on the lid) along with Julie's 8 x 10 graduation picture and Sonya's letter and picture, slams it shut, and bounces it out across the doorjamb and skids it down the corridor, where it crashes into the wall at the head of the stairwell. Hearing the ruckus, McNally peeks out of his door. "What in Hell's goin' on out here?"

"Nothing you'd care to find out about," Moke snarls, ignoring him.

Puzzled by this rebuff, McNally emerges in his houseslippers and robe to watch in utter amazement as Moke accelerates toward the trunk and gives it a kick that sends it blamming down the stairs. Other doors open up and down the hall, but Moke is already chasing down the steps. "Hey, Moke," McNally says, following him down. "What's goin on, good buddy? What are you so pissed about, huh? Man, I've never seen you so pissed in my life."

"Grab the end of that, will you?" Moke says, "and help me get it outside."

"Sure thing." McNally hefts the end and the two of them cart the trunk out across the quad. The trunk itself is heavier than its contents, but not so heavy as unwieldy.

"Where are we going with this?" McNally says, surprised at the distance they are covering.

"Right here should be good enough," Moke says, tipping the trunk to the ground and rolling it over, flopping the lid open.

"Why, in God's name, are you carrying all those letters in this big heavy trunk, man? You have really flipped out this time!"

"Have you got a match?" Moke says, slapping at his pockets. He finds his own and lights a corner of one envelope and lets it climb up the flap and feeds the flame to another.

"Man, this is too much like witchcraft out here for me," McNally says, eyeing the distant dorm-windows as if he is afraid he will be mistaken as a co-conspirator. In his flat-top, slippers, and robe he resembles a runaway mental patient. "This is about all I can take," he says. "You gonna be all right out here, Moke old buddy?"

"Yeah," Moke says, "I just want to burn these old letters is all." They both stare at the fire as flames grow around the paper, the edges curling.

"You'd better watch it—that picture's going to catch on fire!"

"I'm just going to burn all this old stuff. It's all right. Thanks, McNally."

" 'At's okay, Moke old buddy. Anytime, old buddy. Guess I'll go back now. So—see ya later."

"See you later." Moke does not look up from the small flaming heap but keeps adding new edges and occasionally fanning it with a wave of his hand since there is hardly any breeze. It is a long tiring process. The dew grows heavier. The stars pass in silent profusion, the crickets dose, and eventually even the liquid sound of the Beta trumpet is still.

He is standing in a daze of cloudy light from the library window with its shadows of ivy, his left leg nearly touching the armrest of the red couch, pretending to read the titles of the shelf of new novels. He does not see her out of the corner of his eye until she is only a few feet away and sinking now with her purse into the cushions at his very feet. She has no doubt just returned from the Ladies Room downstairs, has just brushed her hair so that it flows evenly down her back and shoulders, its auburn tones elegantly highlighted by the table lamp, has perhaps unbuttoned her Levis in the privacy of the stall, placed her perfect beautiful ass into the cozy indentation of the seat of the toilet and peed loudly into its sparkling porcelain throat with healthy unselfconscious abandon. Today she is wearing a wine-colored *red* turtleneck and a double-beaded dangle of *red* seeds, pulling the cloth close around her pert breasts—generous breasts but pleasingly and exaltantly pert. Her eyes, in the instant they pass over him, are a fierce and powerful blue, laying the room at her feet. Now in profile he sees the smooth skin of her cheek is shiny clean, her earlobes soft and thick, her lips full. Awed by her sudden magical appearance and her nearness, his mouth is suddenly dry. What can you *say* in a situation like this? If he only knew her name, he could call her up. It might be easier to break the ice over the telephone. Look before you leap—he who hesitates is lost. In a minute something would happen. . . .

What happens, completely unexpectedly, is that his very own red-seed girl stands up, stretches, collects her books and papers, clutches her purse, and leaves. What is this? Moke wonders, frowning awkwardly again at the row of novels. *Is this some message or maybe she has to be somewhere?* Maybe his lurking bothered her? Doubtful. Maybe she expects him to follow her and make conversation while loitering along the flagstones—of course! He hurries quickly through the reading room and out through the foyer, where there is no sign of her, and zips out the half-closing oaken doors, nearly colliding with a startled-looking Indian student, and rubbernecks it up and down the mall. Where the hell *is* she? He runs in the direction of the Union for forty paces and scans in the direction of the Chapel and back toward the Administration building—nothing. He turns back the other way and starts loping toward the Zoology-Chemistry-Medical-School-and-Hospital quad. Nobody in sight—he accelerates. Just as he is about to stop and pound on the nearest treetrunk in despair, he catches a flicker of red through the bushes by the Zoology building and his feet take wing. He zooms the 200 yards and around the corner past the same bushes, runs down a walk he has never noticed before, hurtles himself down a flight of some twenty stone steps in two giant feet-stinging leaps, and is just in time to see her raised thigh slide over a bicycle seat and the bicycle coast down an embankment and out toward the road to East Campus. Moke stops dead—mustn't let her see him chasing after her like a maniac. The bicycle and its occupant disappear behind a hedge. Seized by a sudden panic, he kicks after her again, coasting down the hill, around the hedge, and out into the road with its yellow curb and magnolia-tree and pine-landscaped perimeters, the pavement jarring his rubber-soled suede bucks and jolting his kneecaps, shirttail flapping and sweat breaking out on his face and across his back like Rafer Johnson's last lap in the Rome Olympics.

A big Oldsmobile passes and the driver pointedly ignores him as if this sweating, heaving struggle up the long slow incline through the thundering wake of exhaust is unseemly if not disgusting. She must have an English bike with gears, he thinks, to be gaining so much ground on him. It is a good two miles to East Campus. He jumps the curb and tries running in the thick soft sod of the grassy apron for a while but promptly trips, stumbles, and sprawls headlong, getting grass stain on his elbows, just as several more cars pass and their bored passengers stare at him in astonishment. One car even slows down momentarily until he picks himself up and resumes his pace. Damn! The red-seed girl is nowhere in sight.

He wanders around East Campus for three hours in a slow drizzle looking for the red-seed girl. She is not in the East Campus library, post office, deserted cafeteria or on any of the sidewalks, and there is no sign of her bicycle—all the bicycles look the same, black tires and water dripping from their spokes and handlebars. The graceful red and white Georgian buildings of East Campus and the uncanny bright green of the wet lawns seem a mirage or a trick performed with mirrors. He sinks finally onto a stone bench at the foot of the statue of Washington Duke and remembers a science fiction movie he saw once where a jet pilot accidentally breaks the time barrier and comes back to earth to find everyone gone—everything deserted, as it seems now. Rain pounds his scalp, the trees sway eerily, and he almost starts crying into his soggy sleeve, but luckily a cluster of black umbrellas appears by the Union and some nutty girl in bermudas tiptoes out and splashes in the mud-puddles, giggling like a hebephrenic. He realizes suddenly with a wave of trauma that the Medical College Admissions Test—the last one of the academic year—had been given that morning on West Campus at eight o'clock . . . and where was he? The computerized admission ticket, dated and paid for, is back in his room, still leaning against his study light. He cradles his head in his arms.

Incredibly, when he gets back, soaked to the bone, there is a letter in his mailbox.

Dear Moke,

I'm afraid I have some terrible news to report. Your Uncle Doc was killed in a bad accident last night in Cincinnati. As you know his driving was none too good and he may have been drinking but with his Parkinson's Disease getting worse and worse maybe it was the Lord's will who knows. That poor man deserved a better life— was there ever a more harmless and generous man than your Uncle Doc? I seriously doubt it. He never spoke a harsh word to man or beast except once in a blue moon if he had been drinking too much Seagram's. May God rest his soul.

We will be flying north for the funeral. Assume you will be too busy to attend at this time but will put some flowers in your name and deliver your condolences.

Dad has some other news to relate. Your father did such a good job for the Bible Ranch there is talk of selling the station. Isn't that something. If so, we may be moving back to Cincinnati. How would you like that?

Love,
Your Mother

Hi, Buddy!

I guess Mom told you about Doc. He was quite a man and we're all going to miss him. It doesn't seem fair that a man who begins life with such promise should have to end it the way he did. He was the first Eagle Scout in the state of Ohio. He was middleweight boxing champion at Miami University and a Commander in the Navy. He made us all proud of him, I'll tell you that.

191

Then when he got his M.D. instead of setting himself up in a wealthy suburb like he could have he started his Emergency Hospital in the West End of Cincinnati to help the colored people. A lot of us thought he was crazy at the time and tried to talk him out of it, but Doc went right ahead with it, as you know. My, how those people loved him! He helped bring them into this world and sewed them up when they knifed each other almost to death and cured their ailments—he knew the miracle of healing. I once saw him take a man whose finger had been cut off in some accident and Doc sewed it back on the man's hand as good as a new one. You may not know it but he was a legend to those poor niggers. They named their little jigaboo children after him. I bet there are ninety or a hundred little nigger children running around the West End of Cincinnati right this minute named C. F. Galenaille Washington and C. F. Galenaille Jackson. They would give him the shirt off their backs, and half the time that was all he ever did get. If they couldn't pay, he worked for nothing. He could have made a fortune doing almost anything else in the world, and they knew it and respected him for it. A lot of white people took a chance just walking around in that end of town. A bunch of young bloods cornered me one time down on Freeman Avenue on my way down to see Doc, but they let me go instantly as soon as they found out I was Doc's relation. They wouldn't let anyone touch a hair of Doc's head in that neighborhood or any of his relations, and he always parked his Cadillac right there on the street in plain sight and no one ever touched a single hub cap. They guarded it for him as if it was their own car.

It was a hellava thing for the city of Cincinnati to do to him to tear down his hospital after all those years of service to the community, but that's progress for you. I don't think he ever recovered from the shock of that—it was his whole life. After that it was all downhill for him. He hoped if he stayed alive long enough they might find some cure for his disease—he never lost his faith in medicine—but it wasn't to be. Bee might have saved him the trouble of divorcing the poor man and taking him for every nickel he was worth and the roof over his head—as now she will get everything anyway.

As Mom mentioned, I may be out of a job here shortly myself. There are some buyers interested in WTSF, and if they buy they will want to bring in their own personnel. It should mean a lot of money to the Bible Ranch for their rebuilding effort and nothing for me, even though I made the whole thing possible. Sometimes the Lord works in strange ways. Maybe He wants Mom and me to go back to Cincinnati where all our kin are, I don't know. It's awfully damned hot down here in the summers anyway and we do miss the change of seasons. Best of luck on your Medical School test, son; we're all rooting for you.

With love,
Dad

Magpie to Rubie-red. Magpie to Rubie-red. Over. We read you, Magpie. This is Rubie-red. We have an unidentified falling object at six o'clock, reading 34° 23' 14". Can you identify? Over. We read you, Rubie-red. This is M as in Magpie. Password: yellow marble. I am tracking your coordinates—Do you re-da-da-da-da-da-da-da-dow! Hello. Cachooooong! Magpie! Come in, Magpie. Blam! Blam! Calling M-as-in-Magpie. Calling Magpie. This is Rubie-red. Do you read us? Magpie? Magpie? Magpie? Come in.

Chapter Sixteen

Sha na na na
Sha na na na na
Ba-doom
Sha na na na
Sha na na na na
Ba-doom
Sha na na na
Sha na na na na
Ba-doom
Sha na na na
Sha na na na na
Dip dip dip dip dip dip dip dip
Boom boom boom boom boom boom boom boom
Get a job.

THAT MARCH MORNING —the sky is gray and sunless—Moke takes a cab to the Johns Hopkins Medical School a good two hours before his interview and eats his breakfast in the OK Diner across the street. There are no doctors in the diner, but three nurses are in a booth. One of the nurses has a pretty face and looks sad and tired. Moke watches the nurses until they go out. Then he pays and goes out himself and walks the streets until it is time for his interview. A number of doctors have erected small signs or shingles in windows or outside their offices in the area around the hospital: Bernard Schultz, M.D. Theodore Glassman, M.D. What would it really matter in the grand scheme of things if a Moke Galenaille, M.D., was added to this list? One more shingle. It seemed inconsequential.

Yesterday, in Washington, he has wandered, lonely and long-faced, from one national monument to the next, looking for some essential meaning or comfort in it all. He has never been to Washington before. "So this is Our Nation's Capital," he says to himself. "So this is how it really looks." He waits in a long line beside the enormous iron fence to file solemnly through the White House. The day is unseasonably warm; the cherry trees are not yet in bloom. He wanders up and down the Mall, stopping at the salmon-colored baroque monstrosity of the Smithsonian, browsing slowly through the history of aviation. He eats a hot dog, thick with mustard, under a maple tree, and watches the people go by. Flying in, they had tilted high above all of these curbs, traffic circles, and spacious lawns, out above the reflecting pools and obelisks, Arlington cemetery and the Capitol—seeing it all in miniature but on a grand scale, as if from the eye of God. What could any single life matter in such a beehive?

The skeleton of the tyrannosaurus rex and the fullscale recreation of the woolly mammoth at the National Museum of History—his last stop—astound him. Elijah Roark should be flown to Washington, D.C., immediately and forced to gaze upon the tyrannosaurus rex skeleton! How could those people deny the existence of such monstrous evidence of other epochs, other lives than our own narrow, circumscribed and petty human ones? At age seven, Moke's mother had taken a snapshot of him, tiny and swaggering, next to a brontosaurus skeleton at the Pittsburgh National History Museum. Viewers of the family album usually chuckled over it; but Moke was pleased with the picture—the skeleton made an impression upon him and he had wanted to remember it. What could be more hideous and more basic than a skeleton of something? It was like an X-ray of reality.

When he finds the room in the Medical School building where he had been told to report, there are a number of other applicants already seated before the door on leather seats, and he sits down himself and watches the passers-by and gradually sizes up his opponents. Two of them at the farthest end, who don't look particularly intelligent, are carrying on an animated conversation concerning labor unions, and Moke listens momentarily but grows bored at their pretensions and obvious nervousness and focuses his eyes instead on the glass doors which lead out of the building and across a grassy esplanade to another portion of the complex. A woman is approaching across the sidewalk, a svelte woman with a tight French twist in a hurry to get somewhere in her alligator pumps and a soft wool tailored dress swishing at her knees—all busi- ness and flying elbows, impressive as the devil. Most of the passers-by are men in white lab coats, doctors, some of them probably world-renowned specialists in their fields, Moke figures. After all, this is *the* place, he tells himself. *I am actually at Johns Hopkins Medical School.* Intermittently, these humble great men have their names mentioned over the paging intercom: "Dr. Gearhart," says an urgent feminine voice, "Dr. Gearhart!" The door to the room opens momentarily and a dignified man with very well-trained hair appears, smiles benignly in their direction, and asks if Mr. Jones would like to come in now. Mr. Jones gets up, shakes hands with the dignified man, and disappears behind the closing door.

A paunchy, unlikely-looking applicant sitting next to Moke says he is from Harvard.

"I would think that would be a definite asset," Moke says. "How many years have you gone there?"

"Oh, I've already graduated."

"Four years?"

"Yes, all four years." Moke notices the ODK pin on his maroon suit.

"I've only had two years so far."

"You must be trying for the new experimental program then, is that it? You combine *some* medical work with a liberal arts major?"

"I don't believe they accept anyone directly into the Medical School with only two years," Moke says. "I'd do it if they'd let me."

"Uh-huh. Yes." He turns away from Moke and looks at the door.

"My problem is I-I didn't . . . ," Moke begins.

"What's that?" The Harvard applicant swivels his neck around into the proper listening position but doesn't seem to be following with his eyes.

"My problem is I didn't take the Medical Admissions Test."

"Oh? How's that?"

"Well,"—Moke hears himself let out a rather frivolous chuckle—"I just didn't feel like taking it, you know. So when Dr. VanWeite called. . . . You know Dr. VanWeite?"

"Yes, he's the chairman of the Admissions Committee, the man who's been appearing at the door."

"Oh, *that's* Dr. VanWeite. I didn't know *he* was Dr. VanWeite. Somehow I didn't imagine him looking like that."

"Uh-huh. Uh-huh. That's who it is."

"Well, anyway, when Dr. VanWeite called, you know, I told him that I hadn't taken the test yet, and he said to come up for an interview anyway. He said that nobody had ever been admitted before without having taken the test, but if I'd like to come up for an interview, they'd be glad to hear what I had to say."

The Harvard applicant is shaking his head knowingly and scrutinizes Moke with an incisive glance. Then he begins studying the toes of his shoes.

"Very interesting."

Just then the door opens and Mr. Jones is dismissed. Moke can see several imposing men inside seated around a polished wooden table. The floor is a miracle of plush carpet, green as money, and the wall he can see is crimson with heavy gilt-lettered volumes. The same man, Dr. VanWeite—a man with deep lines in his face, attractively rugged-looking and grey-templed—enters the hallway from the room, again smiles his confident, dignified smile at the candidates, and calls another name. The applicant in the maroon suit immediately rises and after vigorously shaking the doctor's hand is ushered into the room, and the door shuts behind *him*.

Moke recalls the joke about the Harvard man: The Harvard man and the Duke man are in the Men's Room at adjacent urinals and after they have finished peeing, the Harvard man goes straight to the lavatory to wash his hands and the Duke man begins to comb his hair. The Harvard man sneers and says into the mirror: "At *Har*vard we learn it is more civilized to wash our *hands* after we *pee*!" The Duke man replies: "At Duke we learn not to *pee* on our *hands*!"

Moke doesn't know what he is going to tell the doctors when his turn comes to go into the room. He wants to be selected, of course, but he isn't certain he wants to attend. He is definitely not as certain he wants to attend as his fiery application-essay has probably led the doctors to believe. He will have to give the impression of being *that certain* if he is to stand a chance of being accepted. It will be a matter of lying.

197

When Moke's turn comes—he is next after the applicant in the maroon suit—he wonders if any contrast between himself and the others will be perceptible to the committee. Possibly he looks the part of the diligent, sober-minded medical student rather more so than the others? Or is this a delusion? Perhaps he will be the first student in the history of the University to be accepted to medical school without having taken the admissions test. Then he can attend or not attend according to what he finally decides later on. . . . He can write to Julie and say: "Guess what—you were wrong about me—I just got into Johns Hopkins Medical School!" And she would write back from her honeymoon spot in Acapulco and say: "Best of luck. I always knew you would make a terrific doc. Write me again when I'm sixty-three and need a first-rate gall bladder man . . . or maybe my tubes will need tying around 1999." Or she would send a wire from Las Vegas.

Western Union

IN LIGHT OF YOUR RECENT COUP AM HERE
FOR BROKEN ENGAGEMENT STOP PHYSICIST
WAS LOUSY IN BED ANYWAY STOP VERY
SMALL COCK STOP COULDN'T GET IT UP
HALF THE TIME STOP I NEED YOU STOP I
COULD TRANSFER TO GOUCHER STOP WE
COULD RENT A SMALL APARTMENT NEAR
HOSPITAL STOP FIVE YEARS IS NOT SO
LONG STOP

Stop—stop! He tries to make up his mind that he wants to be accepted.

There are three doctors in the room, including Dr. VanWeite. Moke is seated near the center of the long side of the heavy table and notices that the outside wall of the room, which is a large window, is blotted out by a phalanx of venetian-blind slats. The doctors wear faint heroic smiles and immediately appear to include him into their confidence.

> Give us some men
> who are stout-hearted men
> who will fight for the right they adore.

"Well, Mr. Galenaille, we might as well come right to the point in your case," says Dr. VanWeite, after introducing the others. "As I informed you over the telephone, no one has ever been admitted to Johns Hopkins Medical School without having completed the Medical Admissions Test. The test is considered an important factor in determining the extent of a student's knowledge in crucial areas, and because it is important to us, it has been listed on the application form as a *requirement* for admission to the College."

"I understand that," says Moke.

"We feel it is especially important to screen our two-year applicants with great care. This is a new and somewhat controversial program, as you know, and quite rigorous. We, of course, want to avoid drop-outs. We are looking for stamina, reliability, and stability—in a word, character—as well as academic accomplishment."

"I understand that, sir."

"Could you kindly explain to us then why you failed to take this test? Every other facet of your application is in order and speaks highly in your favor. Your recommendations in particular are outstanding."

Moke wants to answer the question fairly. Why didn't he take the test? Why didn't he? He begins to consider the problem in a soul-searching ad lib fashion.

"Well, I'm certain," he begins, "that when I originally made out my application for admission I was as enthusiastic as the application sounded. I was absolutely certain I wanted to come here for Medical School. I didn't want to wait two more years to do medical work."

"And you've changed your mind since the application?" asks the doctor in a white coat across the table. The doctor's square pectorals bulge with definition under the white coat, and a hard-plastic mechanical pencil is clipped to his tight pocket flap.

"No, not really. I've never decided I didn't want to come here. How shall I say? Well, whatever happens I've definitely decided to transfer from Duke."

"Have you applied to other schools besides this?" asks the doctor with the pectorals.

"Yes, I've applied to Antioch College and to the University of California at Berkeley."

"I see. And what would you study at these schools?"

"If I go to one of these schools, I would probably study literature or philosophy."

"Would you eventually go to medical school somewhere?"

"There's still more to the story really. I don't quite know how to put it."

"Why do you want to transfer?" asks the doctor to Moke's left. He is a jowly, bland, brown-suited man and looks somehow weaker than the others, administrative. Then Moke feels it coming on and knows it will have to be spoken about.

"Well, there's a certain . . . a certain girl who figures in here, I'm afraid," he says. The doctor in the brown suit lets a sign of embarrassment slip across his face at the way "girl" is enunciated, catching him unprepared.

"We were going to be married, she and I, when she finished and when I finished. She goes to school at Smith . . . " None of the doctors speak. "I suppose it was her—it was she—who-who wanted me to be a doctor in the first place." The doctor in the brown suit nods his head like a judge. "We've broken up recently—about the time of the admissions test it was, actually . . . ."

"These were the 'possibly extenuating circumstances' you mentioned over the phone?" says Dr. VanWeite.

"Yes."

"I see," says the doctor in the brown suit. "Well, these human considerations do figure into nearly everyone's choice of career, of course. We understand that perfectly well and the emotional factors that do impinge upon our students' lives, both inside and outside the classroom. It requires great discipline and a measure of self-control to follow a medical career. On that fact, all men agree."

"I think it's important to emphasize here, Mr. Galenaille," begins Dr. VanWeite, "that even if you are not admitted now to the medical school—and let's make it clear: because of the test your chances *are* slim (as I'm sure you already know)—this does not by any means suggest that you won't be admitted if you reapply later on." Moke nods his head.

"I know that you expect the students you admit to be capable and—and emotionally prepared—for the effort of it. All I want to say is, in spite of what's happened, I feel that I could work very

200

hard and—want to."

"The only reason we took the trouble to carry out this interview, Mr. Galenaille," says the doctor in the brown suit, "was because we were fairly certain from your recommendations that you are the kind of young man we want at Johns Hopkins, the kind who *will* work hard. And we have found you a person of unusual candor as well, I might add. We appreciate that." There is a general rumble of assent.

"The recommendations, you may be interested to know," says Dr. VanWeite, looking sympathetically at Moke, "are very high in your praises." His eloquent frown conveys at once charity, good wishes, and rejection. "In fact, they would have to be termed 'sensational.' You've obviously made a most favorable impression on some men who are very hard to please."

"Thank you, sir."

"Well, gentlemen, have we heard enough?" They smile and the doctors stand up and shake hands with Moke one by one.

"Don't be discouraged now, young man, if the application is turned down. Maybe you aren't ready just yet. But don't give up," says the doctor in the brown suit.

"I'm quite flattered and surprised that you were willing to invite me here for the interview," says Moke. "I didn't realize I was this close to possible acceptance. I only wish I had been able to take that test." The doctors have turned away. He is ushered back into the hallway.

After the interview Moke walks the streets for a while and then goes back to the OK Diner for lunch. He looks for the same nurses, but they are not there. The place is surprisingly deserted, as if atomic war had been declared and nobody has bothered to mention it to him. Any minute the flash will seal them in time like the citizens of Pompeii encased in lava and the plate glass window will implode with such an instantaneous splattering of shards he will be dead before he notices it . . . . Nothing happens. He imagines the tired pretty nurse in one of the rooms in the gigantic hospital building across the street holding a clear lucite oxygen mask up to someone's face. The person is dying of a heart attack, which she has seen many times before, his eyelids fluttering like the windows on a slot machine with a rehashed history of his life. She is wishing she were in Nassau.

Chapter Seventeen

My prayer is to lin-ger with you
At the end of the day
In a dream that's divine
My prayer is a rap-ture in blue
With the world far a-way
And your lips close to mine. . . .

On this trip home, there is no one to meet him at the airport. He catches a cab. Doc's Cadillac, which he has inherited and has come to claim, is parked in a back lot behind the service garage at the big Cincinnati Cadillac dealership. The sales manager, an elegant beefy fellow, escorts Moke through the showroom and a series of corridors, then out across a good acre of blacktop. With $500 worth of body work, new Good Year tires, and a front-end realignment, the car looks about the same as it had when Doc picked him up at the airport last summer, though that now seems like eons ago. Moke remembers how Doc had been sitting half up on the curb beside a fire hydrant when he and Sonya and Hazel had come struggling down the street with the women's luggage on their way to the Greater Cincinnati Airport bound for Florida.

Doc was so attached to that gold car, and the Cadillac was so much a part of his life that seeing it now, without its former owner, is painful, as Moke knew it would be. He stares at the chevron grille, and it is easy to imagine that his Uncle Doc might appear suddenly from some far corner of the lot and waddle toward them with his inimitable shambling gait. Moke takes the keys, gets in, and swings the big car around and out.

From there, he drives to Indian Park and cruises around the

Square and up and down Wooster and Homewood and Park Street, then out along Columbia Parkway above the familiar curve of river, and downtown to Eighth and Vine, Garfield Place, and, just once, slowly, past the Gayety. Then, without a qualm of any kind and with a sense of surety that he seems to have lacked for months, Moke guns the Cadillac up an exit ramp and drives straight for Montreal, Quebec, on those brand new tires—hundreds of miles of thundering concrete and pine-tasselled reaches, and the moon floating all night long above high, feathery clouds, poking through now and again with its broad, noncommital face.

He searches for Sonya's address half the day, lost and exhausted, and eventually he finds the tiny clapboard house in a working class suburb whose location corresponds to the correct street and number from her letter, but no one is at home. It is afternoon. He sits on the porch stoop for a while, listening to the bees in the shrubbery, then drives to McGill University, where he begins searching the halls and classrooms in the Biology Department. He runs into one girl who looks as if she might be a friend of Sonya's. He asks the girl if she knows someone named Sonya Velonis. She says she's heard of her—isn't she a dancer in one of the clubs? He goes back to the car and falls asleep.

It is evening. He starts visiting every go-go joint listed in the phone book. Finally, after hours, by nothing but raw luck, he opens a door and sees a girl who definitely resembles Sonya. She is on stage as he comes in, glowing with ultraviolet like a mirage, raked by the rotating shards of silver light from a mirrored globe above, and dancing her dance. He would know that dance anywhere, he thinks.

He sits down in the front row and orders a beer. The waitress brings it quickly, reaching into her black silk change purse and laying two quarters on the dark Formica. At this range, there is no doubt. He has found her.

When the lights change and Sonya moves toward him, her face a mask of blank professionalism, he has a moment of shuddering fear that she won't recognize him. The seconds seem to stretch out in a yawning void. But, of course, suddenly Sonya does see it is Moke, and her face lights up. She tosses her head and shakes her hair out in a wild kind of delirium. She doesn't miss a beat—this incredible girl—but she starts dancing her big climactic number just for him.